"Having excelled in academia [Dr. Shafer] now draws on his vast knowledge of literature to craft his own creative [novel]." (Dr. Nelson Price, Pastor Emeritus, Roswell Street Baptist Church, Marietta, Georgia)

"What a breath of fresh air *The Rose and the Serpent* gives with its compelling and refreshing Christian dimension . . . this Shakespeare-like clash . . . ! The novel is a masterpiece." (Dr. Mary Massoud, Ain Shams University, Cairo, Egypt)

"I cannot wait for the sequel. There   *radise Lost* which shows how the serpe   John Dugdale Bradley, Milton's Cottag   hire, England)

"[*The Rose and the Serpent*] is absorbing, especially so for those versed in the classics, in music and in the Christian faith." (Corbin Wyant, Retired Publisher, *Naples Daily News*)

"Ron Shafer has cleverly layered, as an artist paints, the present with the spindly, clawing hands of the past . . . . [Dr. Shafer] understands human nature; his ability to express it is compelling." (Jane Spanner, artist, Winford, England)

The Rose and the Serpent "maintains an accessibility for modern readers that is riveting, exhilarating and page-turning . . . . Harrowing action in an underground mushroom mine . . . holds us spellbound." (Sarah Horne, PhD candidate, Indiana University of Pennsylvania)

"In *The Rose and the Serpent*, the ancient adage of 'love conquers all' proves its truth . . . in the trials and triumphs of two brilliant young souls who cling to God and each other for survival against the insidious machinations of a malicious genius." (Dr. Coral Norwood, Humanities Professor, Lee University)

"An inspiring story of triumph over sin and suffering, *The Rose and the Serpent* is beautifully drawn against the backdrop of rustbelt America." (Andrew Laddusaw, Pastor, Living Water Church)

The Rose and the Serpent

— RON SHAFER —

WestBow
PRESS®
A DIVISION OF THOMAS NELSON
& ZONDERVAN

Copyright © 2017 Ron Shafer.

All rights reserved. No part of this book may be used or reproduced by any means,
graphic, electronic, or mechanical, including photocopying, recording, taping or
by any information storage retrieval system without the written permission of the
author except in the case of brief quotations embodied in critical articles and reviews.

This is a work of fiction. All of the characters, names, incidents,
places, organizations, and dialogue in this novel are either the
products of the author's imagination or are used fictitiously.

WestBow Press books may be ordered through booksellers or by contacting:

WestBow Press
A Division of Thomas Nelson & Zondervan
1663 Liberty Drive
Bloomington, IN 47403
www.westbowpress.com
1 (866) 928-1240

Because of the dynamic nature of the Internet, any web addresses or
links contained in this book may have changed since publication and
may no longer be valid. The views expressed in this work are solely those
of the author and do not necessarily reflect the views of the publisher,
and the publisher hereby disclaims any responsibility for them.

Scripture quotations marked NKJV are taken from the New King James Version.
Copyright © 1982 by Thomas Nelson, Inc. Used by permission. All rights reserved.

ISBN: 978-1-5127-9956-9 (sc)
ISBN: 978-1-5127-9958-3 (hc)
ISBN: 978-1-5127-9957-6 (e)

Library of Congress Control Number: 2017912526

Print information available on the last page.

WestBow Press rev. date: 9/21/2017

Acknowledgments

The idea for my novel, *The Rose and the Serpent*, was first conceived fifty years ago when I was a college student employed at the formerly-named Moonlight Mushrooms. I am grateful to those employees who gave me the chance to work in this fascinating underground world and, especially, to Roger Claypoole, President and CEO of Creekside Mushrooms, the expanded enterprise of later years. Mr. Claypoole's assistance in reading the manuscript, familiarizing me with the entire mine operation, and taking me on a tour of the facility was invaluable. I also acknowledge the help of Tyler Martilotti who gave me a tour of the original Winfield Mushroom Mine, where I was employed and which is the principal setting of *The Rose and the Serpent*.

The Center Hill Church of the Brethren and the surrounding village and countryside of which it is part are the settings for many of the novel's key scenes. This area is integral to both my entire life and the novel. I lack words to express my appreciation to the good folks of this community who have, across decades, inspired and encouraged me. It is my fervent hope that what I've offered in my nearly countless lectures and sermons in this church and in this saga of novels, of which *The Rose and the Serpent* is the first, expresses the heartfelt gratitude I feel and repays them for their consistent and blessed support. The help of the ministers, Dr. Wes Berkebile and Pastor Don Peters, is also much appreciated.

I extend similar gratitude to the congregation, Christians with a

Vision, which I've joyfully served as senior pastor for over a decade. Their prayer support and backing have been consistent, especially during the various cardiac sieges which have been my lot over the last decade. To Scott and Joanne Petras I owe a special note of thanks, for it is they who, after decades of work, finally spurred me to seek publication and assisted me with the technical aspects of this ambitious initiative. To Aaron Clouse I owe similar gratitude for introducing me to the region of the Allegheny River, especially "Jude and Cory's Trail," which is the setting for major scenes. The sign at the trailhead of this path remains the first tangible proof that the teeming world of my imagination would, one day, have its real-world corollary.

The university at which I taught for over four decades, Indiana University of Pennsylvania, is important as well for helping me find my fiction voice and crafting my art. The countless students and professors have been endlessly patient and encouraging as I've shared novel vignettes and storyline episodes. Former students, I give you *The Rose and the Serpent* at last. As Hamlet says, all things shall be brought to their destined end!

Backdrop to the entire venture, my family—especially my mother—has always been there to offer the love and support such a momentous enterprise requires. My mother spent her entire life, from the time she buried her husband (at age 45) and raised seven children, modeling Christ-like love, peace and wisdom. She remains the primary impetus behind the novels, for she demonstrated a faith and a fortitude that, for many of us, were indescribable, almost otherworldly. Mom, this novel is deservedly dedicated to you! Thanks for never giving up and always being there.

To Allegheny General Hospital, I owe a special debt of gratitude for the way they helped me navigate the cardiac shoals of the last three and a half decades. The electrophysiologists have, quite literally, saved my life on several occasions. To that staff—Dr. John Chenarides, Dr. Emerson Liu, Dr. Amit J. Thosani, Ms. Kathy Rouse, and Ms. Renee Sadowski—and to my cardiologist/GP, Dr. M. Prasad, I extend a hearty thank you. The same is true for the competent doctors and staff at the Armstrong County Memorial Hospital in Kittanning, PA. The care there, especially during cardiac crises, has been professional and life-saving.

To the various endorsers of *The Rose and the Serpent*—Dr. Nelson Price, Corbin Wyant, John Dugdale Bradley, Jane Spanner, Dr. Mary Massoud, Sarah Horne, Dr. Coral Norwood, and Andrew Laddusaw—I express my very deep appreciation both for the endorsements and suggestions for the novel itself.

To artist Jane Spanner of England, I am doubly grateful for her proofing various versions of the text and for her insightful suggestions concerning Cory as artist. Marian Samuelson deserves a special acknowledgment as well since she was my first-line proofreader and constant source of encouragement.

To photographer Cassandra Lorea (Cassie Clouse) I extend warm thanks for the front cover photography and design, and thanks as well to Hannah Shafer (Cory) and Ashton McGinnis (Jude) for the front cover photograph.

Roger Reitler deserves my thanks for his help with all the hotrod and auto body lingo and background info. Thanks, Roger—you're the best!

Thanks goes as well to Mary Jo Klingensmith and, especially, Robin Lash at D & S Business Services for the multiple photocopied versions of the novel and its various sequels. I much appreciate your timely and always reliable help.

I am grateful to WestBow Press for their professional help and guidance in seeing this debut novel through the various stages of the production process. Your assistance has been generous and assuring.

Finally—and most importantly—I thank God for sparing me and for diligently shepherding me through the 50 years of the creative process for this novel. Psalm 73:26 says it all: "My flesh and my heart fail; But God is the strength of my heart and my portion forever."

Ron Shafer, Kittanning, PA, September 2017

Chapter 1

Early May 1988

Pressing his fingers tightly against the photograph in his pocket, Jude Hepler languidly strolled toward the window at the rear of the classroom, his eyes on the floor. Near the window, he hoisted his gaze across the Oak Grove to the massive pillars of Fisher Auditorium. How like they were to those huge columns of Greek temples that he had seen during his travels in Europe. The glorious past flitted in his brain as he lifted his eyes to the building's architrave. How tempting to romp through those files of ancient Greek imagery in his mind!

In the middle of a discussion with two of his bright college students, Eric and Kathy, Jude struggled to stay focused on the discussion at hand. They had stopped by his classroom to bid an end-of-semester farewell and, taking advantage of the occasion, asked him about a final exam question concerning Robert Frost's poem "West-Running Brook." While Eric Slebodnik and Kathy Petras discussed their exam responses with each other, Jude walked to the window.

"To take a stab at answering my query," Eric continued, "we need to know what Frost means when he says the brook 'flows between us To separate us for a panic moment.'" He had raised his voice a bit and spoke in the direction of Jude to indicate that his remark was aimed at him. "Did the lovers panic because they were separated?" Eric arrived at his main point. "The awful consequences of separation—is that what Frost is talking about here? Is that his main point?"

Upon hearing these questions, Jude involuntarily flinched and looked away. A teaching associate in the Department of English at Indiana University of Pennsylvania for the last two years, he was typically enamored of such literary discussions, but today, within an hour of driving home to his grandmother's homestead in Armstrong County, he was unnerved by this question. His spirit of inquiry temporarily shattered, he softly ran his finger across the pocket photo and lamely—and uncharacteristically—threw the question back to the students. "What do you think the lines mean?"

As Eric and Kathy talked to each other, Jude turned his back to his students and took the photo out of his pocket. *Cory, how beautiful you are!* he reflected. *"The awful consequences of separation—is that what Frost is talking about here?" Eric, you have no idea how your question hits home!*

No wonder Jude had dealt with the panic of their tragic separation by running headlong into intense graduate studies. His breakup with Cory had been caused by a panic moment—that part was accurate—but instead of a brief separation, his moment had stretched into an agonizing five-year nightmare.

He looked in Kathy's direction to note the features of her face, so similar to Cory's—same long, wavy, blonde hair, perfect complexion, oval shape, high cheekbones. *They could be sisters!* When Kathy tilted her head in reflection, he saw Cory lift her head to watch the deer atop the ridge. When she adjusted her posture, Jude saw Cory shift her position at the sink in the farmhouse kitchen to look at the dogwood tree on the lower lawn. Contemplating the enigmatic lines in Frost's poem, Kathy slowly ran her hand through her hair—Cory's exact gesture when deep in thought.

After returning the photo to his pocket, Jude walked back to his desk and, feigning interest, opened up his anthology to Frost's poem. In an artificially enthusiastic voice, he said, "Don't you think the key to your question is contained in the earlier lines? 'We, in our impatience of the steps, Get back to the beginning of beginnings.'" Underestimating the impact of the line, because of its uncanny parallel to his own situation, Jude was further unnerved. The fake passion he tried to generate for the discussion died in a heartbeat. Out, out, brief candle.

Trying to remain calm, he spoke again. "Isn't that the lovers' only recourse, their only chance—getting back to the beginning? Getting back to the awful moment of panic when the separation occurred?" The words caught in his throat. "What other way to end the separation but to get back to the beginning—to revisit that tragic moment when the split occurred?" Shaken to the core, he spoke in a barely audible voice.

The poem perfectly described Jude's situation, so much so in fact that at times he wondered if he had placed the poem on the syllabus in order to resurrect the old feelings for Cory and, perhaps, somehow animate his paralyzed will. Like the lovers in Frost's poem, he too had to cross the strange west-running brook to start again. In the northeast United States, brooks and rivers run eastward to the ocean, but not the unique west-running brook.

He caressed the picture in his pocket and, seeing that the students remained in conversation, faced away and again pulled the photo from his pocket. *Can we start again?* He bent closer to the photo. *Can we get back to the beginning of beginnings? Cory, can you learn to love again? Can we make the river of our love flow eastward to the light? Make this river of death sparkle again with radiant, shimmering life?*

Just then one of the student workers in the English Department office knocked loudly on the open door, tilted his head into the room, and breathlessly spoke. "Mr. Hepler, forgive me for interrupting." Like a streaking sprinter in the five-hundred-meter dash, he gasped for air. "You have a phone call. The woman sounds really upset. That's why I ran the whole way to tell you." He paused again to catch his breath. "Do you want to take the call in your office? I can transfer it there. Sorry to be so blunt, but I'd hurry if I were you. She's an older woman and definitely agitated."

"Yes, thank you, I'll take it there. I'm on my way." He turned to Eric and Kathy. "Sorry, guys, but this call sounds important. Wonder who it could be? If you want to stop by my office in a few minutes, we can finish our conversation."

"Sorry, Mr. Hepler. I can't," Kathy said, walking toward the door. "I have to catch my ride home. Thanks for a great semester. Your class was wonderful!"

Jude quickly gathered up his papers and hurried down to his office, speaking to Eric on the way. "I meant what I said. I'd like to chat for a couple minutes before leaving campus. We were cut off at an awkward place."

"I'd like that a lot. I'll see you in a short while."

In his office, Jude picked up the phone. "Hello."

"Jude, is that you?"

"Hi, Grandma. I didn't expect it to be you. You never call me on campus. What's going on?"

"It's Cory." A pause while Jude's grandmother tried to gain self-control. "Are you coming home today?"

"Yes, that's been our plan right along. I'm leaving soon. Why do you ask?"

She desperately searched for words. "Please hurry."

"Okay, but why the urgency? You really sound distressed. Slow down, Grandma. What's going on with Cory?"

He could hear her heavy breathing. "I saw her dad at the mailbox yesterday. I don't have words to tell you how bad that man looks. But I can't get into that—that's not why I called." Jude's grandmother, struggling to stay calm, started again. "Pete's convinced that Cory's in trouble."

"In what way? Trouble? That's a strong word. What sort of trouble?"

"She's been seeing that awful Duke lately. Remember that huge man I've been telling you about who's been helping Cory and her brother with the farm work?"

"Yes, his name has come up in our conversations far too often."

"It isn't good, Jude. I hear bad things about him. The women in the church quilting group say he practically lives at The Inn. These women are not gossips. You know that. But they say he's—well—not a good man. Someone told Virginia that he's 'a low-life ruffian.' Those are the exact words. Imagine that! Beulah asked how Cory ever got tangled up with a guy like him." When they were talking about him, I wanted to hide under the quilt!"

As Grandma paused, Jude could imagine her wiping tear-moistened eyes. She spoke again, her voice raspy with emotion. "What's happened to our dear Cory?" Jude could hear the anger in her voice. "I'm not one to rush to judgment, but if the man really is a thug, how did our precious Cory ever get involved with the likes of him?"

Jude responded, though he had absolutely nothing to say. A speaking dead man. Headpiece full of straw. "I have no idea what's going on. But I am sure of one thing. I've heard nothing good about Duke Manningham. Ever." Jude paused, expecting his grandmother to carry on. "What else? There's something else going on." He hesitated, but she didn't speak. "Please get to the point. You called about something specific."

"That's where things stood last evening. I've been upset ever since I spoke with Pete at the mailbox, but I determined to wait till you got home today to talk about this. I just didn't want to bother you when you're so busy at the end of the semester."

"What made you change your mind? Why'd you call?"

"This. Right before I phoned you, I was embroidering on the porch. As I was sitting there minding my own business and finishing my hummingbird table scarf, I saw Duke go by in an old jalopy. Not the fancy car he usually drives. He flew by so fast that the tires threw up stones and scared the cows along the road. They went scurrying down the pasture. I tell you I've never seen them run like that!"

"The idiot. So he's an arrested adolescent. The whole world knows that. What's this have to do with Cory? Please tell me, Grandma."

"Here's what happened. I had walked out to the fence to look at the cows. They had run down to the lower meadow. My heart was still thumping from seeing them stampede. I guess I walked out there to make sure they were all right. Well, I was near the mailbox when here comes Duke speeding down the road again like a flash. He had driven over to Cory's farm and now was going back in the opposite direction. Only a few minutes had gone by. Just time for me to amble down the lane, you might say."

Exasperated and nearly shouting into the phone, Jude broke in. "The guy's a loser! Tell me how this deals with Cory! We can talk through the other details later, Grandma. I don't care about this."

"Yes, you do care. You care a lot." Grandma's voice was surprisingly firm. "As the car went by, I had a good look because I was standing at the end of our lane." Having arrived at the difficult part of her tale, she paused, took a deep breath, and blurted the words. "Cory was in the car with him!"

"Unbelievable!" A pause. Then a sigh.

"I tell you, Cory looked scared to death. As they whizzed by, I could hear her screaming at the top of her lungs, 'Slow down! Let me out!'"

Chapter 2

Unable to speak, Jude stared into space.

"Jude, are you there? Hello! Jude?"

"Yes, I'm here. Thanks, Grandma, for calling me. I'm just upset. Sad too." Another pause as he looked at the photo on his desk. "But I'm also mad. And disgusted. And discouraged. How could she do this to me? To herself? How could she do this to us?" He wiped a tear from his eye. "I'll be home in a bit. Just sit tight. I'm so sorry you had to endure that. Good-bye, Grandma." He slammed the phone on the cradle.

The picture front and center on his desk beckoned to him with a more intense urgency than usual. Always the picture. The ineffably beautiful Cory. How had it happened? How did he let it happen? Wasn't there some way he could have prevented that awful breakup five years ago, that terrible panic moment? They had vowed that they would never let anything come between them. He remembered a comment he made to Cory that last summer of their love as they walked along the Allegheny River at Reesedale. Jude had turned to Cory and said, "Our love is a river just like this massive Allegheny. We'll always keep it centered in the deep channel so that it will never run awry on the rocky shoals."

But like the lovers in Frost's poem, Jude and Cory stood by the lake near Slate Lick one day and bade farewell, ending their precious love. He simultaneously dreaded yet was inexorably drawn to that recent day when his class read Frost's poem, "West-Running Brook." He knew the reading of the poem would create an emotional space in his mind into which Cory would cozily take up residency. Over the last months, she wandered into most of the rooms of his mind and usually stayed. That was his consistent dilemma. The spirit of Cory was with him constantly but not her fleshly counterpart. She dwelt far away in Armstrong County. Very far away. On another planet.

Five years ago, Jude had fled from their shattered love by immersing himself in graduate work. He completed his course work and other PhD requirements in nearly record time, the quintessentially driven man in flight from crisis. His exemplary work as a teaching associate, which garnered the respect of students and colleagues, partially distracted him from the rubble of his failed love. But despite this meteoric rise in the academic world, he stumbled emotionally through the days, weeks, and months—a lost shell with a fake smile self-consciously pasted on his face.

In the years after the breakup, he repressed the deep ache with learning—always reading, always seeking, always distracting. But during the last few weeks of the semester, his incessant thoughts of Cory, the green fields of home, his grandparents' farm, and the prospect of a return to menial work in the mushroom mine had, even in this rigorous university setting, gnawed at him daily. His heart had gradually sloughed off its academic cloak. On the emotional plane, he was already cloistered in faraway summer fields. Allusions to lost love and even an occasional direct reference to Cory crept into his teaching as the end of the spring term approached and he cobbled together strength to reflect on their disastrous end.

As he sat this spring day in his office, he knew that the period of dallying in the safe shallows had come to an end and that it was time to work toward the river's torturous current. The lines near the end of Frost's poem paralleled his situation. "It is this backward motion toward the source, Against the stream, that most we see ourselves in." That was it. That was it exactly. He had to experience this backward motion to the source, even if it necessitated superhuman effort to fight upstream against that grueling current. Even if it meant confronting the hideous breakup again.

And always the overwhelming question remained. How had he drifted so far downstream from his beloved? Downstream into a strangely foreign sea on the other side of the globe. It was time, even at this late dreaded hour, to begin the backward motion. But how?

Especially now that Duke had been factored into this complex equation. Cory had wanted nothing to do with Jude before, and now to make matters infinitely worse, she had fallen into thuggery. Cory with a thug. He just couldn't believe it. Oh, what a falling off was there! Part of him wanted to rush out the door and streak for home, yet what would he do once there? Drive up and down the roads in search of Cory? Send out a rescue party? Plaster Cory's picture on milk cartons? Or the consummation devoutly to be wished—get into a fight-to-the-death brawl with monster man if he found him draped all over Cory at The Inn?

No, it couldn't be that way. He couldn't act on impulse. It was time for rational thought, time to engage the nobler impulses. Regaining composure, he decided it was best to stay put in his office, wait for Eric, and chat for a few moments before driving home. The diversion would settle him at least a bit.

He plopped into his desk chair to think. Once he had decided several weeks back to return to the mine and attempt reconciliation with her, he had thought of little else. But was reconciliation even possible? How splintered her heart had been in those days after their breakup! *Cory, my love, how have you survived the years of separation? Have you survived them? Did you kill off all the tender emotions we had for each other—that meandering river of love that lyrically rolled through hill and vale like a Provencal villanelle?*

He picked up the desk picture of Cory to examine its every detail. *Will you ever be able to forgive me for what happened? Have you worked past the pain when you rebuffed me so completely? Why did I not attempt reconciliation earlier? Surely, together, we could have worked our way through the torment, could have triumphed over the river's agonizing, backward motion. Frost, how true your words, how perfectly you encapsulate my feelings!*

Above all others, one worry had become his obsession, his constant companion in grief. Was reunion even possible since it would necessitate Cory's tearing down brick by brick the barricade about her heart, that fortress built to protect it against yet more slings and arrows of outrageous fortune? Did she have the emotional strength and attendant will for this colossal dismantling?

The underlying philosophic question needled at him hourly. Can a heart so badly damaged ever heal and laugh and love again? Her parting words had haunted him the entire five-year separation. Looking directly into his eyes with piercing intensity, she had said, emphasizing each word in turn, "I'll never open up my heart to love again."

Chapter 3

Was Cory's involvement with Duke an attempt to escape the prison walls of her own self-sabotaging nature? As he was contemplating this question, Jude heard a slight tap on his door, and his student Eric looked in.

"Hi, Mr. Hepler. Are you sure you want to continue our discussion? I'd completely understand if you need to leave."

"No, we can talk now."

"Are you sure? You look addled. Because of that phone call?"

"You're absolutely right. The call upset me a lot. No need to lie about that, but believe me, I welcome the diversion. Come on in and have a seat."

"Thank you."

Jude slipped over to the "student's" chair at the side of his desk and invited Eric to sit in his cushy, leather desk chair.

"Wow, I feel like a professor sitting in such a swanky padded chair!"

"It's nothing. This castoff belonged to one of the vice presidents. It's as close as I'll ever get to the bigwigs in Sutton Hall! I retrieved it from the trash bin. That's a true story by the way." Jude shifted his eyes from the old chair and looked at his intelligent student. "Okay, fire away, Eric. You had more to say about Frost's wonderful poem."

"It's a philosophic query about life more than a specific point about the poem." He thought for a moment about how to frame his words. The last thing he wanted to do was upset his favorite professor even more.

Seeing his hesitation, Jude spoke. "Don't hesitate. I assure you I'm fine. Ask away."

"Okay. I'll get right to the point. Is there hope for lovers like those in Frost's poem?" One of Jude's most intelligent students, Eric shifted his position in his chair and stroked his chin. "No, that's not what I want to say." He thought again. "Okay, here it is. I'll continue the river metaphor. Is it even possible to fight against a current that strong and get back upstream to the source? That's it. Do lovers get a second chance?"

Given Eric's penetrating astuteness, Jude feared this exact question but gambled that he wouldn't ask it. He was wrong. Dead wrong. Abstractedly, Jude looked out the window and fidgeted with his pencil. "I wish I knew," he said, his raw vulnerability painfully evident.

Depressed with his own weariness, Jude settled his eyes on a volume of Robert Browning's poetry on the bookshelf above Eric's head. A line from Browning's *Andrea del Sarto* came to mind: "I often am much wearier than you think. This evening more than usual." *How true, Robert Browning, how true! How very weary I am! Weary with all of it.* Jude was tempted to escape to the world of Browning's poetry—"My Last Duchess," "Soliloquy of the Spanish Cloister," "The Bishop Orders His Tomb at St. Praxid's Church." Any of the poems. Anything by the great Victorian poet. Anything. Any topic in the world but not Cory. He perused the books on the shelf but said nothing.

At last Eric, his chair pushed back from the desk against the bookcase, spoke. He frantically sought safe, middle ground. "I see you have a framed verse there on your desk. I can't read it from here except the first line in boldface, 'There is a river.' May I look at it?"

Jude handed the framed verse to Eric. "Please read it. Out loud."

"There is a river whose streams shall make glad the city of God. Psalm 46:4." Eric read it again to himself and then spoke. "I'm not exactly sure what it means, but I'm guessing it's pretty important to you, since you have it sitting right there on your desk directly beside the photo of that beautiful woman. Wow, she is one gorgeous goddess!" Eric looked down again at the plaque. "Can you tell me what the verse means?" As Eric looked up from the framed verse, he was surprised to see that Jude had a moist eye.

Jude spoke. "The psalm begins by saying that 'God is our refuge and strength, a very present help in trouble.' In the poem, David the psalmist contrasts the horrible instability of nature and its surging flood waters to a peaceful flowing river that symbolizes the future golden era when Jerusalem will become the center of worldwide peace. At least that's one interpretation."

Jude again paused, his voice starting to quiver. He waited for the wave of emotion to pass. "My girlfriend made this for me a few years ago, because this verse reminded her of our love." He hesitated on purpose to luxuriate in the memory. "Our love was like this peaceful river. You'll notice my verb tense. I said 'was.' It died a premature death." A large tear formed in Jude's eye, expanded its circumference, and spilled down his cheek.

"I'm sorry, Mr. Hepler. I didn't mean to upset you." Eric handed the framed verse to Jude.

Jude reached for his mug to take a sip of water. It was empty. "I always seem to have a dry throat anymore. Remember in class? I was always lifting an empty mug to my lips. Don't worry about the tear. I'm a big boy." Jude turned over the framed verse.

"Could you read it?" Eric asked.

"Yes, I'd be happy to." Jude read out loud.

> Around the hills and through the vales, the river
> winds and curls its jeweled journey to the sea.
> The river forges forward, finds a way, never stops.
> Our love is a river just like the massive Allegheny.
> Though it narrows to gurgling trickles around the
> mighty rocks, it never loses heart. It keeps the faith,

knowing a better day will come when its surging mass will triumphantly parade to the sea. Our love is that shimmering river of glistening gold. It will endure. It will not fail. We'll always keep it centered in the deep channel so that it will never run awry on the rocky shoals. I believe in the river of life as I believe in the river of our love and as I believe in you, Jude Hepler. This is our verse. Forever this will be my song. Always remember, Jude—there is a river! All my love ever, Cory

Holding the plaque, he said nothing for a moment. To give Jude a moment to himself, the embarrassed Eric turned around to peruse the shelf of books. He and Jude knew each other quite well. The literature course just completed was Eric's second one with Jude, and across those two semesters they had become friends and even had, along with a handful of other students, shared coffee numerous times at the Pizza House.

During these frequent conversations, they had covered a wide spectrum of topics, including lengthy discussions about Eric's long-distance love with his girlfriend, Denise, who was enrolled at Allegheny College in Meadville. Touching on heart-to-heart topics had become a matter of course for the two of them; thus, Eric was quite surprised to see his professor's emotional response. In a sense, they had been down this path before, but at those times the focus had been Eric's poignant separation, not Jude's. *What a role reversal!* Jude thought.

"Sorry, Mr. Hepler. I shouldn't have asked you to read it. That was dumb of me."

"Don't worry about it. It's just that I've been thinking a lot about Cory, 'the gorgeous goddess' as you call her." Jude reached for the photo. He held it in one hand, the framed verse in the other. "I'm going to live in Armstrong County this summer just to be near her and attempt to re-stoke the dying if not dead embers of our love. I'm not at all sure that they can be revitalized. But I do know one thing." He shifted his position in his chair and cupped his chin in his fingers. "Everything rides on my attempt. That's why I'm an emotional wreck. You wouldn't have known that, of course, if I hadn't told you!" He smiled, trying to put Eric at ease.

Eric looked at his professor for a moment and then resumed speaking. "I asked you a question about Frost's 'West-Running Brook' up in our classroom."

"It was an intelligent question."

"But it's not the one that's really on my mind."

"It isn't?"

"No. I came in the back door to the real question when I asked you to explain what Psalm 46:4 meant."

"Now you're scaring me, mystery man! Just what are you talking about?"

"Let me go back to the day we discussed Whitman's 'Crossing Brooklyn Ferry.' I thought I saw a tear in your eye when we talked about that brilliant poem. Your recitation was so moving to me that I can still hear you recite that line—'I too many and many a time cross'd the river of old.' Surely you were connecting with that poem at a very deep level. In fact, your recitation was so moving to me that for several days I found myself constantly saying that line, 'I too many and many a time crossed the river of old.' I still find myself quoting it!"

When Jude offered no response, Eric continued. "You were on such a roll that day. But then you're usually that way. The words just tumble out of you. Even among the other English professors, I've never met anyone half as verbal as you. At any rate, your commentary on Whitman was a poem in itself, a free verse poem as beautiful as 'Crossing Brooklyn Ferry.'"

"That's quite the compliment. Thank you very much, but you're embarrassing me."

"I'm completely serious about this. I find your speech mesmerizing. I often wonder if the students know the rare treat of sitting under what for me is spellbinding oratory."

"Now you're being ridiculous."

"Not really. In fact, I'm being totally serious. I've often wondered why your verbal skills are so advanced, so extraordinary. Any thoughts?"

"I'm totally serious when I say you're grossly exaggerating, Eric." Jude reflected for a moment. "Yet there is one fact that perhaps I shouldn't downplay. My mother was extremely verbal and taught me the value of wordsmithery. I still remember her recitations of poetry to me when I was a young child. She'd paused to comment on the absolutely perfect selection of diction in a poem, the right blend of euphonious words, the poet's adroit pairing of image with thought—well, you get my point."

"Yes, of course. Do any examples come to mind?"

"The way Shakespeare says in *A Midsummer Night's Dream* that 'the iron tongue of midnight hath told twelve.' I think I quoted that right. Here's the point. Why 'told' instead of 'struck'? Because bells toll and strike, but, in past tense, a tongue didn't strike; it told. See how the homophonous word 'told' suffices both meanings? That, my friend, is Shakespearean genius at work. Well, Mom gave me a real appreciation for articulate, precise speech. Of the sort which abound in Shakespeare's plays, I might add."

"Okay, that explains it. I can only marvel at what for me is a sensational gift."

Jude grew reflective for a moment and looked at the photo on his desk. "Cory used to say a similar thing." He drew his attention back to Eric. "But don't underestimate your own skills. I'd put you on a par with my most verbal graduate-level students."

"That is a huge compliment. Thank you very much. You give me the confidence to ask the question that's really on my mind."

"Ask away."

"Let me say this first. It isn't just the river as a body of water that intrigues you then but what it symbolizes—namely, your love for that stunning woman right there. Am I right about that?"

"Yes, you are. The river has come to symbolize so much to

me—Cory, the dream of our love together, the golden years of our youth, the single, frayed strand of our future—the whole gamut. I've been in a desert lately, and I just need to know if the river terminated back there in the past or continues into the future. That's the main reason I'm headed back to my grandma's home. Trapped in an absurdist drama of my own making, I can't find the exit."

"So why if you both loved each other so much did you separate? That's what I can't figure out."

"That's the key question and the one I don't have time to answer right now since I have to get home to Grandma. But I will say this. There were huge misunderstandings—things said, an unpleasant incident at the mine where we work, wrong conclusions. And much more. At the end of it all, Cory rebuffed me. Slammed the door in my face. Not tightly shut, I might add, and toward the end she had actually moved beyond anger. Still, she was done with me and went into hiding—a nocturnal animal living a subterranean existence."

Eric paused a moment before responding. "What is it about her that you miss the most? I ask that because I've been thinking a lot about what I miss the most now that I've been more or less separated from Denise since last September."

"I think about that a lot. Yes, I remember though it's five long years ago. It's terribly trite to say it, Eric, and you'll think those verbal skills you laud in me went right out the window."

"I doubt it!"

"Here it is. We were the most perfect soul mates you can imagine. Yes, we were young, but she knew my every thought, and she totally accepted me for what I am. What more does anyone want in his or her mate?"

"That is beautiful to hear." Eric caught Jude looking at his watch. "I know you have to leave, but may I say one more thing before we depart?"

"Please do."

"You know I'm a huge Beatles fan."

"You don't let me forget even though I'm more of an Elvis man myself!" Jude laughed—a kind of comic relief laugh but hollow and empty.

"I suppose you know that my saying "Hey, Jude" to you, which I periodically do, is an allusion to their song."

"Yes, I knew that much. Why do you mention it now?"

"Because the lyrics perfectly suit you and your current situation."

"You'd think I'd be familiar with my namesake song, but I'm not. Have at it."

"I'll just recite the opening lines: 'Hey, Jude, don't make it bad. Take a sad song and make it better. Remember to let her into your heart. Then you can start to make it better. Hey, Jude, don't be afraid. You were made to go out and get her.'"

Eric stood up to leave. "Well, that's my hope for you—that you can make this sad song better and that you can, as the song says, let her into your heart."

"Thanks, Eric. That means more to me than you know."

Eric shook hands with Jude and departed. Jude raised the photo to his lips with a trembling hand, kissed it, and placed it beside the verse on his desk. He leaned back in his chair and looked at them. *Was this Jude meant to go out and get this Cory? Do I, weary as I am, have the strength to fight the river's mighty current?*

Just then the phone rang again. Jude toyed with the thought of not answering. "It's probably a student wanting to know if I have the final exams corrected! They think professors have the results fifteen minutes after the exam!" He walked toward the door but on second thought decided to answer the phone. He remembered how upset Grandma had been. *What if?*

"Hello."

"Jude, is that you?"

"Hi, Grandma. What's up?" He could not hide his panic.

"I just got a call on the prayer chain from Pastor Gabe." The slightest pause. "Cory and Duke were in a car wreck!"

"What!" Jude slammed his office door and ran out of the building.

Chapter 4

Throwing caution to the wind, Jude Hepler raced westward on Rt. 422 toward his grandma's farm in Armstrong County. "Lord, please be with Cory. Don't let it be serious, I beseech you! Protect my darling love! Oh, God, let her be all right!"

Up to this point, Jude's plan for the summer had been easy to put in place. As in happy bygone years, he would live with his grandma, Rosetta Wakefield, work again in the mushroom mine, and help out with farm chores. The entire scheme had been concocted just to win Cory back, but would his attempt at reunion succeed? Would she even talk to him again? And what about this business with Duke? Was this meeting with Duke today a chance encounter or was there substance to the despicable rumor that she was involved in some sort of relationship? Cory with Duke? With Duke Manningham? If she was tangled up with him, what mad sequence of events had led to it? "Lord, soften her heart and make her receptive to my pleas." If prayers yellow with age, this one eerily crackled in lonely nights with saffron brittleness.

On passing his favorite panorama during his flight home, Jude reflected on his stopping here last autumn. He had spotted a farmer by the roadside on that October afternoon and impulsively pulled his car to the side of the road to ask permission to walk up the hill for an elevated view of the vista below.

The farmer gladly welcomed him. "I'm not surprised by your

request. You'd be surprised how many people want to walk up there. It's a lovely view. I actually accompanied a gentleman from Dayton last summer. If I didn't have to check the Angus in the lower meadow, I'd join you. Your car will be safe here by the barn. Take your time. This is God's country, and you're welcome to 'Pennsylvania, ah Pennsylvania'!"

Moments later, Jude had trudged up the knoll behind the farmer's home. The rolling hills of Western Pennsylvania are among the finest of America's scenic treasures. Undulating vales softly unfold their rolling, emerald domes—lush velvety verdure that sweep and glide to distant escarpments. Their pilgrimage complete, they bow in obeisance to the serene majesty of the horizon's Tiffany-blue temple sky.

Driving to Kittanning and finally far away from stacks of papers to correct, books to read, and classes to prepare afforded Jude a rare moment for soulful contemplation. How could a love as intense as theirs collapse in a maelstrom of misunderstanding and grief? Even now, five years later, Jude was at a loss to understand the events that had led to that sad farewell. How she had wept! Jude often felt that the image of their hands slowly separating, apart but still near, inverted Michelangelo's famous Sistine Chapel painting. The nearly touching hands of the famous center panel signaled coming life as God drew near to Adam and prepared to breathe life into his hopelessly inert form.

The image in his mind of their hands, also inches apart, signaled the opposite—death. The day they parted, Jude and Cory had held that posture for agonizing moments, their fingers inches apart, frozen in time, each afraid to draw away, sensing the heart-shriveling pain that lay ahead. Her hand was small, anemic, and trembling. Emotionally destroyed that day, Jude and Cory savagely contorted into ghastly shapes in the ensuing years.

He had seen her only a handful of times in the intervening years, and every time he remembered to look at her hands—not open, outstretched, and gleefully touching the world as they had during the days of their jubilant love but always tightly clenched, withdrawn, curled inward, rejecting everything the world had to offer.

And what about that hand now? Bandaged from the wreck, curled into a fetal ball, knotted into a fist that, given the chance, would blast him into next week?

An hour later, Jude slammed onto the dirt road that led to his grandma's and Cory's farms. He couldn't suppress his tenseness as he approached the section of the road where Cory's adjoining farm was visible across the fields. Despite his anxiety to know if there were updates on Cory's condition, he pulled to the side of the lane and stopped the car. He hadn't intended this impulsive move just as he hadn't intended the jaunt up over the field on Rt. 422 the previous October. Quietly he sat for a moment, then gathered his strength to get out of the car and slink up the knoll.

There, across the vale, lay Cory's farm—peaceful, ancient, enchanting, and unchanged. First the barn came into view and, immediately behind, the old farmhouse. He grew weak in the knees, and tears instantly blinded his eyes. Was Cory there behind those walls? Was she resting in her bedroom or had she been hospitalized? Would even a small part of her wounded heart be glad he had returned? "I'll never open up my heart to love again." How final and determined those parting words! Her teeth had even been clenched and her lips pursed to the bruised purple thinness of a frail, aged woman.

Back in the car, he sped down the lane and parked near the garage. Impatiently awaiting his arrival, Grandma sat on the porch in her Amish-made rocking chair as she so often did in the spring and summer months. Even at this distance, he could see the hummingbirds feeding mere inches above her head, so accustomed were they to this gentle woman.

Several years ago when Jude was living with his grandma, working at the mine and loving Cory, he had overheard Pastor Gabriel Wyant talking to some of the church friends, and Grandma's name had come up. A few of the women, commenting on the legendary inner peace that emanated from Rosetta Wakefield as sweetly as the scent of her freshly baked chocolate chip cookies, had asked Gabriel about her tranquility.

Jude could still paraphrase Gabriel's impromptu answer. "Few people in life manage to achieve a harmony between inner desires and external circumstances. Most cling too assiduously to unrealized hopes and unobtainable goals. When events and circumstances in life fall short of these mountain-high hopes, a creeping bitterness encases the heart in an ever-hardening shell. Rosetta has achieved an utterly rare harmony between the two. Let me put it this way. She has attained the ultimate goal the apostle Paul describes in his letter to the Philippians—being content in whatever state she finds herself. That, my friends, is utterly rare today."

Jude had been inwardly admonished by this conversation, which he regularly replayed in the intervening years, for he exemplified the exact opposite. Accepting little life had to offer, he rejected nearly all circumstances because, without Cory, they carried absolutely no significance. Little wonder Hamlet's line to Rosencrantz and Guildenstern, "I have of late ... lost all my mirth," perfectly encapsulated his mental state.

All this flashed through Jude's mind in a second as he streaked up the walk toward Grandma and her summer-fitted porch.

"Hi, Grandma. What's the latest on Cory? Do you have any other details?" The words fusilladed from his mouth.

"Yes, I have heard. Cory's all right. We don't need to be frightened after all. And so is Duke. But they had an awful scare. I can tell you that!"

"What happened? Do you have any more details?"

"Pastor Gabe told me that they were on their way to Beatty's Mill. Well, Duke was driving much too fast on the Slate Lick-Worthington Road and ran off the road. He was drinking again. The car rolled completely over but landed right side up. It's a good thing they had their seat belts on. That's the only thing that saved them."

"Where's Cory now? Do you know?"

"She's probably still at the ER. Or maybe she's gone home by now. They weren't keeping her. Pastor Gabe called a bit ago to give us the update. He saw her in the ER and said she's completely fine and not even bruised. But as he said, the bruising and soreness might appear later. Mind you, the car had only one dent in the back fender and scrape marks on the roof."

"I'd say she was one lucky woman."

"I prefer to say that our good God was looking out for her."

"Yes, especially that."

"I'm sure she's greatly shaken. I tell you the man was driving so fast he made the cows in the meadow stampede like a scared herd of buffalo! Did I tell you that? When I sat down on the porch, I remember thinking to myself, *That man is going to wreck someday. Little did I know it would be when Cory was in the car!*"

As Jude's grandmother spoke, he looked around. The flowerboxes and baskets, already planted in anticipation of Memorial Day, promised a good season. How often little Jude had sat on this porch with his grandpa and grandma. He could still see him there—his grandpa on the right, his grandma on the left, each in their Amish-built rocking chairs from Smicksburg.

Ever since he could remember, his grandma always had her surprisingly brown hair pulled back in a bun from her cheery, elongated face, which bore few wrinkles for one her age. As Jude sensed the warmth exuding from her gracious spirit, he understood anew why she was such a beloved person in the community. He marveled at her thin and well-preserved posture. She had been sipping a cup of tea to calm her as she awaited Jude's arrival.

He was so overwhelmed by this news of Cory's wreck and her involvement with Duke that speech temporarily eluded him. His eyes went to the plaque hanging under the porch light—"Home: Where each lives for the other and all live for God." Grandpa had chiseled that plaque the summer he was killed. Jude watched his aging fingers dexterously carve the rounded letters. Even as a young boy, he noted his grandpa's skill. Little did he know as he watched him labor at this plaque that he would be dead in a matter of days. *Grandpa, why did you have to die?*

Jude shifted his eyes from the plaque to his grandmother. Where to start? Grandma's health, his semester's teaching, the dissertation proposal that his grandma had asked about, or the one that was really on his mind—Cory? Should he call over to the Mohney farm to see how she was? Was she still attending church? How did she look? Had she ever mentioned him in recent months? Was she seeing Duke Manningham often or was today's encounter an isolated event?

Overwhelmed by the barrage of questions that battered his brain, he retreated from the militarized zone. "Grandma, you look so good, even better than at Easter. How are you these days? What a joy to see you!" He gave her another hug and kissed her on the cheek. He looked deeply into her eyes—a river of peace. Such calm. Could she see its antithesis in his eyes? Raging rapids? A west-running brook? Perhaps a desert? "I have of late lost all my mirth." Can the eyes disguise mirthlessness? What about his parched throat? Always dry. Did she know about that too?

"I'm over my pneumonia now. You can't keep a tough farm woman down! Don't worry about me. I'm here and ornery as ever—ha! I want to hear about you first. Tell me about your teaching. Did you start writing that dissertation yet?" She paused to look at him from head to foot. "How proud your grandpa would be if he knew you were getting your PhD. And at so young an age!"

"No, the actual writing comes later, but the proposal meeting went well, and my topic's been approved. My committee really likes it. I mean they like the subject of my dissertation and how I've structured my study. They've given me the green light, so that's in my favor. Now the real work begins!"

"Always at the books. You're just like your grandpa—always a book in his hands. That man's mind always churned with ideas." She paused almost as if she was seeing him in his study. "Especially in the latter years when he was writing his novel—always thinking, thinking. I swear every other word out of his mouth was George Washington!"

She stopped speaking and looked across the meadow almost as if Jeremiah was standing there looking at the Holstein cows in the pasture as he so often did. "I never saw a man who liked to learn as he did." She brought her gaze back to Jude. "You're the carbon copy of your grandpa! I've told you that before." She paused and again looked at him. "Now you're even starting to act and talk like him. The way you sit and some of your gestures."

For an instant, Jude saw Jeremiah Wakefield lying on the barn floor, the life hopelessly crushed out of him. Despite his best efforts at suppressing the details of the trauma that had instantly ended his childhood joy, Jude could still recollect some of the details of his death, even the books in his grandpa's pockets—a New Testament in one pocket and T. S. Eliot's *Four Quartets* in the other. Grandma was weeping so hard at the time of the accident that the coroner, seeing the awkwardness of handing the books to a woman whose face was buried in her hands, slipped them discreetly to Jude. Little Jude's hands were shaking so much that the books clumsily fell to the floor. *Breathe, Grandpa, breathe!*

Jude jerked his mind away from the barn. "How's everything at the church, Grandma? Pastor Gabe still doing okay?"

"He's fine. Same fireball as ever but in my judgment slowing down a bit. His knowledge of the Word is vast. Most of us think he has much of the New Testament memorized. That's another thing that reminds me of your grandpa. He moves us every time he preaches. Back in the winter, I told him to slow down. 'You're not getting any younger!' He immediately responded, 'They shall still bear fruit in old age. Psalm 92:14.' I remembered that verse because your grandpa used to quote it to me. Gabe asked about you a couple weeks back."

Pausing before continuing, Jude watched a flitting hummingbird and fingered a strand of loose webbing on his chair. "You know the real subject on my mind?"

"Of course I do. You've been looking over at her farm ever since you sat down. You don't have to run from it. Go ahead and ask."

Where to start? Jude had no idea. He gazed across the meadow in the way a person, far from the river's source, looks upstream.

Chapter 5

"All right, I'll ask. Don't keep me in suspense, Grandma. How is she? I mean how's she really doing these days? Is my beloved Cory all right? Is she still coming to church? Was she at Bible study on Wednesday evening?" Jude was sitting on the edge of his chair and leaning toward his grandmother as the questions cannoned from his mouth.

"Whoa. Slow down! You're asking so many questions I won't remember all of them!"

"Sorry, Grandma. Let's start with the big one."

"You want to know how she's doing. Is that correct?" Grandma paused before continuing, struggling to find the right words. She took another sip of tea and crossed her leg.

How stately she is despite her age, and always poised, Jude thought.

"I don't really know. We see her at church. She smiles and tries to be her normal self."

How to best describe the image of the forlorn woman in her mind? After a moment, Rosetta resumed. "The pained sadness in her eyes just doesn't go away. There's not a plastic surgeon on earth that can give those eyes a makeover. Eyes don't lie. That was something your grandpa always said." She watched Jude bow his head. "Sorry to be so direct, but I have to say it. I've never seen such a sad, depressed woman in my life."

Rosetta paused to give Jude time to respond, but he remained silent. "I was looking at your grandpa's Civil War books recently and came across the portrait of President Lincoln done by someone. Maybe Stephen Gardner. I'm not sure. How grandpa loved Lincoln! I'm sure you remember that. I can still picture you sitting on his lap by the hour as he'd leaf through his illustrated Civil War books. He always stroked your hair or had a hand on your shoulder as you turned the pages." She was looking dreamily into space. "Well, Cory's sad eyes are the closest thing I've ever seen to Lincoln's tragic face in the Gardner portrait."

Not knowing how to respond, Jude picked up a copy of the *Leader Times* newspaper that lay open to an article on the recent classic car show on Market Street in Kittanning.

Rosetta welcomed the diversion. "That's a picture of Duke Manningham there at the top of the page. I remembered that he had been featured in this article along with his car." Jude stole a look at the hulking form of the muscular man standing beside his prized hotrod. He was surprisingly handsome. And pure macho male. Looking away, Jude flung the paper aside.

Never one to run from difficult subjects, Rosetta knew it was time to return to the topic at hand. "Jude, I'm not trying to make this extra difficult for you, but I do need to be honest. I want to cry every time I see her. And that was before this wreck business today."

A tear came to Jude's eye as his grandma spoke. He tried to talk but the words caught in his throat. He stared across the meadow toward the Mohney farm. After a moment's silence, he resumed. "She didn't talk to me on Easter morning or even at the Christmas Eve service." A tear welled up in his eye as he thought again of those painful moments. "I can't say she exactly snubbed me, and she had the excuse of a swarm of people around me asking questions and saying hello. It may not have been deliberate, but I've always thought it was. Her walking away and not making the effort to see me haunted my sleep for weeks."

He lifted his eyes to the plaque above Rosetta. "Home: Where each lives for the other and all live for God." *The hearts of Jude Hepler and Cory Mohney,* he thought to himself, *which don't live for each other.*

Well, they used to but not anymore. He continued to stare at the plaque. *Grandpa's hands chiseled those letters. His fingers touched that very place!* He again looked at his grandma. "Do you think I have a chance?"

She remained silent for a surprisingly long time. "I don't know. You're so perfect for each other. Drats to that Abe Badoane. I think a lot of this somehow goes back to him. I know I lack the facts, but I have to put stock in my female intuition. Never want to sell that short in us farm women!"

Rosetta's response surprised him. "Really, Grandma? Do you honestly think that? I know smiley Abe may not be an angel, but he always seemed like a pretty decent guy to me. I used to love talking to him in the lunchroom at the mine." Jude waited for a response, but his grandma remained silent. "Am I right that Grandpa liked him a lot?"

"Your grandpa was impressed by Abe's intelligence. He often said he was the brightest man he'd ever met. Still, I can't help but think there's a lot people don't know."

"I can vouch for Abe's intelligence. We used to talk about famous writers during lunch at the mine. No matter the writers I'd mention, Abe would be familiar with them. I used to try to stump him. I'd bring up obscure authors nobody knows about. He'd get them all. We probably bored other people to death with our discussion about writers and famous works of literature."

The conversation continued just as it had by the hour in past years. There was always much to talk about and to learn from this dear woman who had come to mean so much to Jude. The goodness of her character could be seen in the way she forgave Jude. She didn't hold him a bit responsible for the death of her loving husband. It had been an accident. "You shouldn't blame yourself. You're not to blame. God's will be done." That had always been her response from the time he was a young boy.

If Jude could only forgive himself half as much as she had! That had become his never-ending dilemma. He tried to move forward into the future when his head was looking backward, his finger glued to the replay button. The backward motion toward the source. *I have of late lost all my mirth.*

Chapter 6

A short while later, Jude made his way upstairs to "his" room, a copy of the *Leader Times* newspaper in hand. Here he had stayed during summers from the time he was a young boy until his sad departure at the end of his college career. The joy of graduating from college at twenty-one was offset that spring by his breakup with Cory. Now in his midtwenties, Jude was back in his beloved bedroom.

Every detail of this room brought forth a rush of memories—the IUP pennant Cory had tacked to the wall and the IUP pillow on his bed; the Steelers mug on his desk that Cory had bought as a memento when they attended the Steelers/Browns game; the Smith history of Armstrong County she had placed on the shelf—right there with her own hands; the carved wood bear she had bought for him in Cook Forest; the Maid of the Mist mug from their trip to Niagara Falls; and countless other reminders of a failed love.

Down in the kitchen, his grandma turned up the radio. Arranging materials on his desk, Jude could easily hear the DJ.

"Robbie-O has a surprise for all you good folks out there in WTYM radio land. We can't play all the fifties and sixties love tunes you requested. There were too many this round, but on-the-ball Ginny has spliced together excerpts from a montage of your faves and raves. So here goes. I give you a handful of snippets—just brief excerpts, radio fans—of the great love songs from the golden years. Let your radio blast and sit yourself down. This trip to the past will ease every frown. We kick off with the Everly Brothers' 'Walk Right Back.'"

With the song playing in the distance, Jude hummed along as he arranged a box of books on the shelves.

> I want you to tell me why you walked out on me
> I'm so lonesome every day
> I want you to know that since you walked out on me
> Nothing seems to be same old way

He dawdled more than usual as he positioned the volumes with exaggerated neatness, either fearing the poster board of photos on the wall or savoring them for last—he wasn't sure which. But eventually he stole a glance in that direction. Soon he could wait no longer and walked toward the wall to look at the photos—some of the early years when Jude and Cory were mere acquaintances, a second group in the middle when they were good friends, and then finally the priceless photos of the later years when they lived for love. He slowly stooped to look at one of the photos, all the while singing to the Everly Brothers tune.

> Think about the love that burns within my heart for you
> The good times we had before you went away—oh, please
> Walk right back to me this minute
> Bring your love to me, don't send it
> I'm so lonesome every day

Jude stared at the picture of the two of them on the hay wagon, legs dangling as they leaned against the bales of hay and awaited departure on the hayride. This had always been one of their favorite photos. How in love they had been that summer! He studied each detail. Wind-blown hair wisped across her forehead, the cheek-to-cheek pose, the easy laughter, hands clasped in knuckle-white tightness, eyes gleaming with joy, and the setting sun bronzing their faces the hue of a Greek statue. And that smile on her face! How radiant, how alive she had been in the later months of their love before she died of an incinerated heart.

The golden fifties medley continued as the Everly Brothers tune melded into Roy Orbison's "In Dreams."

> I close my eyes, Then I drift away
> Into the magic night. I softly say
> A silent prayer like dreamers do.
> Then I fall asleep to dream my dreams of you

Jude shifted eyes to a photo of the two of them churning apple butter together in the old copper kettle that grandpa had used on the old Oak Ridge homestead above New Bethlehem decades ago. Grandpa said the kettle dated back to the late nineteenth century. Jude detached the photo to look at this favorite photograph more closely. He sang to the picture as he did so.

> In dreams I walk with you.
> In dreams I talk to you.
> In dreams you're mine. All the time
> We're together in dreams, in dreams

As Cory stirred the paddle with both hands, steam rose from the bubbling apples. She was smiling in response to a wisecrack Jude had just said. He stood behind her, arm around her shoulder. Careful about her work, she stirred vigorously so that the apple butter didn't stick to the bottom of the kettle. Her head was pointed downward to the kettle, but just for that split second, she turned toward the camera. In love with life as well as Cory, Jude flashed that big smile, upper and lower teeth fully visible.

The Orbison tune blended into Elvis Presley's "Don't Ask Me Why" as Jude slowly moved his eyes to photos when they were swinging on the knotted Tarzan rope along the Allegheny River near Reesedale. In one photo, they swung together, arms around each other, the large branch of the oak tree drooping with their weight. The sun, filtering through the trees, danced in their hair and gilded the tips of eyelashes and noses. Jude hugged Cory's side so tightly that her rib cage protruded.

> I'll go on loving you
> Don't ask me why
> Don't know what else to do
> Don't ask me why
> How sad my heart would be
> If you should go

In another photo at the Tarzan vine, Cory and Jude were caught mid-drop—legs bent backward at the knees, one set of arms tightly hugging each other, Cory's bathing suit, pushed upward by Jude's arm, revealing her fullness, outer arms lifted upward in triumph, and her hair flying wildly overhead. Jude could hear their laughter as "Don't Ask Me Why" eased into Elvis' "I'm Yours." Again, Jude sang along.

> My love I offer you now
> My heart and all it can give
> For just as long as I live I'm yours
> No other arms but yours dear will do
> My lips will always be true
> My eyes can only see you, I'm yours

In another favorite photo, they were riding horseback, the rising sun silhouetting them with its backlit golden hue. The morning mist rose like Arabesque incense from the Allegheny River. The brilliant morning sun, radiant as fiery gold, etched Cory's back and head into a diaphanously soft, pencil-thin line against the mauve brown of the early dawn. Their hands embraced as love cascaded from Jude with a force equal to that of the dawning sun whose light stampeded across a galaxy and, feeling compelled to dazzle with a grand finale, spangled amber ore through dappled woodland trees, glistening like gossamer gold.

Brushing a tear from his eye, Jude walked back to his desk and slumped in the chair. Thinking of his grandma's comment that Duke Manningham had helped with a considerable amount of farm work, he picked up the newspaper article and looked at the picture of the ruggedly handsome Duke. Duke Manningham. Macho man. The ultimate male. The Hulkster hunk. The fifties medley morphed to Pat Boone's "Remember You're Mine."

If you go dancin'
And he holds you tight
And lips are tempted on a summer's night
Your heart beats faster
When the stars start to shine
Just remember, darlin',
Remember you're mine

Looking at the picture of Duke standing beside his '57 Chevy, Jude angrily flung the newspaper into the trash can.

He stomped to the window and opened it as he so often did on summer days long ago to allow the smell of fresh-cut hay to drift into the room. During those rare instances when they weren't together all those years ago, he often came to the window to see if by chance Cory was singing in the fields or the orchard that adjoined the two farms. She often sang there in the months after her mother's tragic death. Along with younger brother, Joey, Cory had been forced to assume adult responsibilities, since her father could no longer work owing to a job-related shoulder injury and the terrible depression he suffered from his wife's death. Even tending to day-to-day chores lay beyond Pete Mohney's ability. It was no secret that Cory held the family together by a tattered thread.

Jude began to hum "Whispering Hope." How had Cory gotten the nerve to sing that hymn at her mother's funeral? Nobody had the answer to that question, but fortunately it had been recorded. Jude played it often during the recently completed spring term.

So far so good. He had broken the ice with his grandma, unpacked his belongings, endured the sweet agony of looking at the photo collage, and now slowly gathered up the nerve to walk down the hall to his grandpa's study. Ambling down the hallway, the end of the Buddy Holly tune, "True Love Ways," drifted up the stairs.

> Sometimes we'll sigh,
> Sometimes we'll cry
> And we'll know why
> Just you and I
> Know true love ways.

Quietly, lest he be heard by his grandma, he whispered, "'Sometime we'll cry.' Sometimes? Are you kidding? How about relentless oceans of tears? Tears every day? Shakespeare, you had it right in *Julius Caesar*: 'If you have tears, prepare to shed them now.' This is going to be tough." Like a prisoner headed for the gallows, he walked toward his grandpa's study.

he remembering ... ... continued

Chapter 7

The fifties and sixties music montage continued. Remembering
that Connie Frances' "Among My Souvenirs" was one of Jude's
favorites, Grandma Rosetta turned up the volume even more. Its
strains were easily heard as Jude entered his grandpa's study.

> There's nothing left for me of days that used to be
> They're just a memory among my souvenirs
> Some letters tied in blue a photograph or two
> I see a rose from you among my souvenirs

Still exuding its rarefied and ancient enchantment, the room had
always been hallowed ground for Jude. His eyes went first to a shelf on
the outside wall, crammed with books, a couple Bibles, and some local
artifacts—a chunk of limestone quarried at the mushroom mine in
the nineteenth century, Delaware Indian arrowheads and projectiles,
mini-balls from the Civil War, iron rings from the Bonner Cemetery
at the Center Hill Church to which the horses were tied in the old
days, china from the Wick China factory in Kittanning, and so on.

Jude looked around at the contents of the familiar room: the old
desk and worn leather chair; the walking stick in the corner that a
friend had given him from the woods near Walden Pond in Concord,
Massachusetts; the Civil War-era chest that Jude's great-grandpa had
made; and on the coffee table his grandpa's favorite tea mug depicting

famous English writers. Little had changed from those days when Jude stayed at the farm as a little boy.

Pictures lined the walls, windowsill, and tables. On a stand near the door was a photo of his grandpa holding Jude on his lap, another of them milking the cows, and a special favorite—the photo of his grandpa posing with Jude at the front of the Center Hill Church as Jude held the Bible that the church had presented to the high school graduates. Each of the men had a hand on the sacred book. Another photo depicted Jude and his grandpa standing by the barn door, but Jude quickly looked past this one.

The Connie Frances tune continued to play:

> A few more tokens rest within my treasure chest
> And though they do their best to give me consolation,
> I count them all apart and, as the teardrops start,
> I find a broken heart among my souvenirs

One spot in his grandpa's room he hesitated to examine. Was he mustering the nerve to look there or savoring this consecrated moment for last as he had the photo collage in his bedroom? He wasn't sure, but at last he sat in his grandpa's desk chair, fingered the cracked and aged leather of the arms, and slowly lifted his eyes to the shelf of revered books that sat on his grandpa's desk: his personal Bible, worn with age and use; histories of Armstrong County and Pennsylvania; a biography of William Penn; Bible commentaries by J. Vernon McGee and John MacArthur; a book of anecdotes that his grandpa had written—*Growing up in Western Pennsylvania: Voices from the Farm*; biographies of the apostle Paul, Washington, and Lincoln; a copy of d'Tocqueville's *Democracy in America*, its pages crumbling from use; a volume of Shakespeare's plays; a prized first-edition of Lew Wallace's *Ben Hur*, that beloved gift from an earlier pastor; and beside it the empty space where the manuscript of the novel once stood.

The novel. The gaping hole. Where was the precious manuscript now? As Jude fingered the empty space, his eyes filled with tears. Nobody, not even his grandma, knew how many decades Jeremiah Wakefield had feverishly labored on *Kittanning*, the novel he always called "his life's work." When Jude had asked his grandma for details about the missing manuscript, she said little, but one day she mentioned to Jude that she thought it strange that a book titled *Kittanning* should speak so much about America's founding fathers, especially Washington. "What do the founders have to do with our county seat?" "You'll see. You'll see." That was all Jeremiah would ever say.

Jude imagined the manuscript buried in some obscure place. If only he could find it to redeem himself. If only Jude could remember what his grandpa had said about its whereabouts with his dying breath! As his fingers caressed the empty space, the picture of his grandpa lying on the barn floor, agonizing for breath to say where the novel was hidden, flashed in his mind with the blinding force of the noonday sun. After the fall from the hayloft, his grandpa had lain stone still for several moments—little Jude thought he was dead—and then gathered enough strength for his final whispered syllables. Jeremiah had slowly opened one eye—the other was swollen shut from the injury to the side of his face—raised his head slowly, looked piercingly at Jude, and then paused from exertion before uttering those few tragic words. And the rest was silence. He was gone forever. Jude shut his eyes in an attempt to halt the gushing torrent of memories.

But the river of memory, now surging forcefully, wasn't about to be stopped. Jude was once again in the barn, and for that microsecond before he could halt the flashback, he heard his grandpa's anguished cry, watched the body flail through space, and heard the awful thud when he hit the barn floor. The passion with which the dying man spoke haunted Jude to this day. As he lay there dying, his grandpa knew that his life's work depended on Jude's locating the novel. He had whispered those final words with an awful intensity, gasping each syllable separately, painstakingly, with gurgled breath.

He had done his part. Little Jude was his dying hope for the novel's discovery, but even to this day, try as he might, Jude couldn't remember those precious words! *What did Grandpa say? Why can't I remember those few syllables that contain the key to the novel's whereabouts?* Deep down, he knew that he had repressed the horror of his grandpa's death but not the image of the falling, thrashing body.

Jude arose from the chair and turned away. As he prepared to exit the room, he cast a look backward. A hole on a bookshelf, a woman with a hole in her heart, a hole in the ground containing a manuscript, a hole in the cemetery where his grandpa was buried, a hole in his destiny, and the biggest one of all—the one in his heart. Where did one begin? Was it possible, given this quota of defeats, to start again? He felt utterly helpless. *"I'll never open up my heart to love again." "I have of late lost all my mirth."*

As he walked outside, a Wordsworth poem came to mind: "It Is a Beauteous Evening Calm and Free." *It might be beautiful,* he thought, *but it surely isn't free. Or at least I'm not free to enjoy its beauty.*

He aimlessly ambled down the lane toward the orchard and looked away as he neared the barn, its door slightly ajar. He closed the barn door without looking inside, resumed his walk, and then paused. How long would he run from the memory? Was he going to allow it to haunt him forever? He had returned to the farm for the summer in part to confront his various fears and to terminate their control over him. He walked back to the barn, clutched the handle, and paused. *Should I or shouldn't I? Why not later? There will be time for such a word as this.*

No—it must be now! Slowly he opened the door. He paused at the door and picked up a blade of grass, which he put in his mouth. The stalling tactics complete, he took a deep breath and went inside. The moment for healing was right, but was he?

Chapter 8

The smell of the freshly mowed hay bales permeated the air as he entered the barn. He took in the sights, moving his eyes like a camera—the tractor and farm machinery at the far end, bags of grain piled high, the old wagon in the far corner, harnesses and saddles on the back wall, hay bales not yet placed in the loft, dusty cobwebs hanging from the beams, old rakes and shovels standing in the front corner, burlap bags draped over the grain bins, and a rusty Route 66 sign affixed to one of the barn beams.

He had played the delay game long enough and finally looked up at the loft. Grandpa had stood up there—on the top rung of a high ladder in the upper loft, which extended clear to the barn ceiling. So much higher than Jude remembered. "I forgot it was so high. What a distance to fall!"

One summer morn, a young boy got up from a large mound of hay, into which he had fallen, though from a great height, and walked away without a scratch. The hay mow—it had been right there. But a few feet away an old man had the life crushed out of him when he landed on the hard barn floor. *Right here. This very spot*, Jude thought as he walked a few paces toward the loft. *Is there a dent in the floor here? Caused by his body? His head—that beautiful head with its full shock of white hair?*

He walked to the upright vertical beam to which were nailed the ladder steps. How often he, his grandpa, and countless others had climbed these steps to the loft above. He put his foot on the lower step, paused to remember, and looked up the ladder. What a long way it was to the top! He looked around for the three-step stool. Surely it still wasn't there as it had been all those years before. It had been the real culprit. Jude scanned the barn's interior, paused when he saw something in the far back corner, and hastily walked in that direction.

There it was—the stool! He walked to the corner and tightly clasped the sides of it. His fingernails dug into the wood. Blinding Jude's eyes, giant tears fell onto the stool steps.

With bowed head outside the barn, he resumed his walk in the direction of the upper ridge above the two farms that, as a teen, he had named Vinlindeer. Why, Cory had once asked, did he select that name for the hill? Because he had come up with that name in a poem, "Let Me Sing," which he had written as a young teen to commemorate his aunt. To this day, the ridge bore the name Vinlindeer for both of them.

Would Cory be in the fields? Maybe the orchard? What would he say if he saw her? Would she talk or run like a frightened gazelle? The opening exchange was so very important, and he lived in fear of making another failed beginning. Wasn't it Eliot who said something like that in the *Four Quartets*? Something about every new beginning being a different kind of failure? There had been enough failure. *No more of that, please!*

His pace was measured, but he was impelled to walk over there for the new beginning, the swim against the current, the backward motion toward the source. Though a start of some sort was necessary, he walked in dread. What if she saw him and rebuffed him again? *"I'll never open up my heart to love again." "We, in our impatience of the steps, Get back to the beginning of beginnings." Frost, I wish you were alive to tell me how to get back to the beginning.*

He thought of Eliot's famous lines from "East Coker": "Trying to learn to use words, and every attempt Is a wholly new start, and a different kind of failure." *How depressing*, he thought. But that was it. Every attempt at a new beginning was a different kind of failure. *Eliot, how do I prevent another failure? How to do it? Just how to get to the source?*

He walked the hill and gained the summit of the ridge that overlooked the vale below. Jude bowed his head to listen, to take in the grandeur. Birds chirped, a distant tractor plowed a faraway field, the breeze rustled in the trees, an occasional cow mooed or a lamb bleated, a distant jet took off from the Pittsburgh airport, but no Cory and not one sign of life at the Mohney farm.

Cory, my Cory. Was she lying down after the wreck? Were there any post-crash symptoms? Bruising? Possible concussion? For a long time, he sat by a fence post, took in the scene below, and agonized over the way to approach her.

He sat up, strolled aimlessly along the pasture fence, and looked down at Cory's farmhouse. Was that someone in the window? Possibly Cory? The curtain in an upstairs bedroom appeared to be pulled back. Or was it the breeze blowing it? At this distance, he couldn't be sure but was warmed at the thought that it might possibly be Cory.

As he slowly shuffled down the hill, he surveyed the grand panorama of the stretching fields below and thought of Tennyson's lines from "Tears, Idle Tears." In the poem, the poet looks on "the happy autumn-fields" and reflects on "the days that are no more." The sights and the memories of their love together, the happy autumn fields, the days that are no more—all of it flicked through his mind as fast as the pictures on his grandpa's View-Master that he played with by the hour when a little boy.

Ambling aimlessly along, he suddenly stopped in his tracks. What was that sound? He listened intently and heard Cory's soft voice wafting through the silvery evening air. That angelic voice! Jude sped down the hill to a spot where he had a good view of the orchard, crouched breathlessly behind an apple tree, and listened. She was in the orchard singing one of her favorite hymns, "Just a Closer Walk with Thee"! Jude wept as she sang.

When my feeble life is over
Time for me will be no more
Guide me gently, safely over
To Thy kingdom shore, to Thy shore.

From this lower elevation, especially when the breeze blew in his direction, he heard her distinctly. Tears flooded his cheeks as the enchanting strains swept over him like a harpist's silken fingers. *When my feeble life is over. There's a line that perfectly suits our situation. Singing of life's end when barely past her youth. What a rich commentary!*

Her voice was more full-bodied and richer than he remembered. The thought that she might have followed through on her dream of taking professional voice lessons darted through his mind.

Indecision came over him as he studied his next move. *Should I move toward her or not?* He decided on an intermediate step. When she was strolling away from him toward her farm, he ran down the hill and crouched behind a row of hedges a couple hundred yards closer to her. From here, when she turned again in his direction, he had a perfect view of her. *Is she looking at me?* he almost yelled out loud.

Even at this distance he could see the sadness in her eyes. Were they red from weeping? He couldn't be certain, but the drooping shoulders, bowed head, and the shuffling, short steps indicated a profound sadness. Cory's citation of the line from *Macbeth*, which she had recently quoted to Pastor Gabriel when exiting the church, accurately described her: "I begin to be a-weary of the sun." *When my feeble life is over, time for me will be no more.*

When the song ended, Cory paused, leaned against a tree, and was silent. Was she praying, thinking, or just escaping the sadness of her home? Then a thought struck Jude. Maybe that had been Cory at the window, and maybe she had seen Jude up there on the ridge! Might she have come to the orchard to see him? Was her presence here intentional, a kind of peace offering, a beginning? Cory knew that "Just a Closer Walk" was one of Jude's favorites.

She then began to sing "Whispering Hope" with the energy and feeling of the early years. Jude was suddenly in the church at Mrs. Mohney's funeral. He could see Cory's mother lying in her casket at the front of the church, Cory walking away from the pulpit and standing behind the casket as she sang this very song.

The scene was indelibly printed on Jude's mind—the spray of English red roses on top of the casket, Cory's dress quivering as she nervously sung, her hand shakily sliding back and forth on the casket, the stifled sobs through the congregation. How nervous she had been as she tried to control her hurricane of emotions.

Why was she singing these two particular songs, both Jude favorites? Was it her gift to Jude? Her movement down the river toward him? "It is the backward motion to the source, against the stream, that most we see ourselves in."

Cory walked to the brow of the hill, and right before descending stopped, turned around, and cast an eye toward the Wakefield farm. Was this also a signal to Jude, a more deliberate one? Had she indeed seen him up there on Vinlindeer? Jude arose from his crouched position behind the hedge and waved just as she was turning away. She didn't respond. Had she seen him? Was this a snub? She entered the house, and the door shut behind her. That ended it.

So near and yet so far.

With a volume of poetry in his hands, he drove a short time later toward Beatty's Mill on Buffalo Creek to think through the momentous events of this first day back in Armstrong County. Often Jude and Cory canoed on this lazy country stream. This evening the memory of doing so tugged at him irresistibly. Moments later he arrived at the creek, pulled the car to the side of the dirt road, and meandered down the hill to where a few old canoes and kayaks lay along the bank.

In the early years when he first visited his grandparents' farm, they would often bring him here to swim. It was quite the swimming hole in that earlier day. It wasn't used for swimming now, though area campers kept kayaks and canoes here for public use. Jude and others occasionally availed themselves of their charitable nature.

Owing to the spring drought and the light snowfall during the winter months, the stream and its tributaries were exceptionally low, making canoeing a great deal more difficult than Jude anticipated. He scraped bottom on the stones several times and eventually entered a narrow part of the stream where the undergrowth had vined completely over the creek. He entered this thicket of brambles and briars as he paddled the canoe into a shallow bed of water. Eventually the canoe ran aground.

He remembered a sermon when Pastor Gabe had cited one of David's psalms. "My soul thirsts for You God. My flesh longs for you in a dry and thirsty land where there is no water." *That's it—where there is no water. Why am I always thirsty?* As it was a very hot summer evening, Jude longed for a cold drink. *Instead of living moisture, I have only dust and ashes in me,* he thought to himself. He wiped his drenched brow as he looked at the pitifully shallow stream. A dry and thirsty land.

Feeling the dryness in his mouth, a momentary image of a spouting water fountain, sparkling in the sunlight and shooting a massive water jet skyward, flashed in his mind. It was a sight that had strangely come to him one night in his sleep and occurred intermittently over the years. Once when he spoke of this dream to Pastor Gabe, the minister said God specializes in turning defeat to victory and deserts to rivers and then quoted Psalm 107:35—"[God] turns a wilderness into pools of water, and dry land into watersprings." He went on to say, "Maybe that spurting water fountain will play an important role in your life one day. Dreams, you know, shouldn't be downplayed." While Jude had remained silent, he wanted to sarcastically respond, "Yeah, right! As if you'd find a fountain in my desert!"

The spurting fountain at the center of an expanse of water and his grandpa's fall in a barn, his two recurring dreams—one bathed in watery, joyful light, the other etched in barren, macabre gray.

He wiped the sweat from his brow, pulled the canoe out of the shallow water, and carried it through the thicket to its original place, where he dropped it with a thud. *If there's a river, this isn't it. Not this dry and thirsty land.*

On his way to his grandma's house, he felt depression settling over him like the thick morning fog in the pasture meadow. In his room that evening, he went directly to bed without looking out the window in the direction of Cory's farm—the first time that had ever happened. He covered his hands with his face and thought of Dante's line in *The Inferno*. The line had made such an impression on him that he even memorized the thirteenth-century Italian: "Che io non avrei creduto che morte tanta ne avesse disfatta": "I had not thought death had undone so many."

Well, it's sure undone me!

Chapter 9

In 1896, a quarrying operation commenced to mine the rich limestone deposits in Butler and Armstrong Counties in Western Pennsylvania. By the time the Buffalo Stone Mine had completed the quarrying enterprise some thirty years later in 1926, a maze of underground corridors and huge cathedral-size rooms had been carved out, "an underground city beneath the lush rolling hills," as the locals called it. The labyrinth of quiet stillness totaled some 150 pitch-black miles. At its height, the limestone quarrying operation produced six hundred tons of limestone per day and approximately 900,000 tons a year. The place was alive with two hundred scurrying employees and the raucous noise of the loud equipment. Once the miners departed a few decades later, the newly fashioned underground world was enshrouded in deathlike sleep.

By 1937, the ingenious idea of growing mushrooms in these underground chambers, where the temperatures hovered consistently in the midfifties, had been conceived. By the next year, a unique system for growing mushrooms had commenced in Western Pennsylvania. The original scientists and entrepreneurs found that the right blend of straw, hay, corn fodder, water, nitrogen, and race track manure produced richly fertilized compost that was perfect for creating optimum mushroom growth. The compost filled some eight hundred trays per day.

After the compost attained its proper level of alkalinity and acidity, the trays were placed in the pasteurization rooms where they were heated to nearly 140 degrees for two to three days to purge the rich soil of all contaminants. The length of time from filling to spawning was nine days. Once the trays spawned, they were taken to their quiet abode deep in the recesses of the mine. The 1,400- to 1,500-pound trays were stacked one upon another, a total of four high, with twelve inches of space between them to allow room for the pickers to reach in and harvest the crop. Of the total 44,000 trays in the mushroom mine operation, approximately half were used in the harvest cycle at any given time. Jude and Cory had learned that, while modern improvements and technologies streamlined the production over the intervening years, most of the original operational procedures remained intact.

Scientists had also learned that great caution was required to create the mushroom spores and prepare them for planting. In the plant world, the mushroom is unique in that it produces no flower, fruit, or even seed. The spores, microscopic organisms in the gills of the mushroom, prolifically germinate until some one million of them are produced. As these spores grow, they become mycelium, broken pieces of which are placed on sterilized wheat.

When two mycelia fuse together, a spawn is created, which is then placed in the trays of compost to assure that the right moisture level is maintained during germination. Eventually nodules pop up in the soil, which mature into full-grown mushrooms in several days. The elapsed time from spore to full-grown mushroom runs from two to four months. At the end of the growing period, the trays are dumped and sterilized for subsequent use.

By the time this operation had hit its full stride years later, some 1,300 employees were producing a record fifty-four million pounds of mushrooms annually. The operation was proudly hailed as one of the unique manufacturing operations in the nation and, at its height, the world's largest mushroom growing plant. In those early years—the happy years before their love ended—Jude and Cory were proud to be part of such a successful operation.

The mushroom mine had started the practice of hiring college students sometime in the 1960s, according to the best information Jude could obtain. The students proved to be reliable and hardworking employees who provided valuable help during the popular summer months when many of the regular workers took their family vacations. For that work opportunity, Jude had been very grateful. It gave him a chance to live with his grandma and to make amends in some indirect way to her. He brought up this point so often that one could easily tell that his grandpa's death remained an obsession for him. Working at the mushroom farm in those early years also enabled him to save money and defray ever-increasing college expenses and, best of all, fall in love with Cory. No wonder the past glowed in his mind with the golden radiance of a misty summer rainbow.

Ever since his graduation from high school, Jude had spent summers in the mine. As a result, he came to know many of the employees and had established himself as a dependable and trustworthy worker. Most summers he worked in the mechanics' shop in the evenings servicing the equipment, but on occasion he was assigned as a driver to the daytime picking crews. This was his favorite job since it enabled him to explore the labyrinth of underground tunnels and learn the various routes through the maze of corridors, including the routes to the packhouse, the hub to which the freshly picked mushrooms were taken.

During these treks through the mine, he marveled at the ingenuity of those limestone miners of yesteryear who had struggled so laboriously to quarry all those thousands of tons of metallurgical limestone. Jude and Cory often wondered how it had been used—in Pittsburgh steel mills, construction projects, or possibly cement?

Meticulously careful miners, the original limestone workers had chipped the limestone in the spacious rooms into relatively straight walls. Even ceilings were impressively smooth-faced. The final effect, thus, was a world of large underground rooms that were interconnected by a maze of tunnels and intersticed corridors.

When Jude drove through the mine during his high school years and looked at the ancient walls of limestone, he used to think of the line from Keats's "Ode to a Grecian Urn"—"thou still unravished bride of quietness." These ancient walls, quiet and enduring as Keats's ancient Greek urn, would outlast the mortals who daily labored within them. They too sang their limestone song of truth and beauty—a truth that ever endured in this silent world, and a beauty rugged in its stark simplicity.

On the morning of his first day in the mine, Jude had been put on miscellaneous detail, having been instructed to run various errands and take care of odd jobs that had accumulated in recent months. Part of this necessitated his making several journeys into the mine to deliver supplies to the lunchrooms and lavatories, carry messages to crew bosses, and replenish the stock of picking baskets for the pickers. Everywhere he went, in corridor and growing room alike, Jude discreetly looked for Cory, but he never saw her.

Grandma had told Jude earlier that she was still on a picking crew—a difficult job that involved backbreaking work in the cold day after day. Some of her work associates made her work additionally difficult for her. Most were decent and fine people, the great majority in fact, and they were noted as hardworking, responsible citizens in the community and proud parents and grandparents.

But as in all workplaces, some of the employees were rough and crude. Profanity among this handful was abundant, the vulgar jokes constant, backstabbing and gossip a way of life, and the tales of immoral escapades and dissolute behavior the frequent topic of conversations. Cory was nevertheless grateful for this source of income, which she desperately needed during the long months when her father was unemployed. Whether she liked it or not was a moot point. She needed the work if the family was to survive.

Nevertheless, the work here was a long way from her life's dream, which she had entertained since a young girl—going to college to major in art and English. Her love of art and literature and her dream of pursuing them were completely frustrated as she slaved in the mine year after year. Work associates knew of these dreams, and thus Cory was an unlikely associate in this unique underground farm.

As a high school senior, she had visited Indiana University of Pennsylvania, fell in love with the campus and programs, and longed to pursue her education there. She was fortunate during this high school visit to sit in on two literature classes and revel—and even occasionally participate in—discussions of Shakespeare, Emily Dickinson, and other great writers. She could just imagine sitting in the classes and discussing literature or working in the various art labs. The few enchanting walks she had taken with Jude across the university's Oak Grove had been the stuff of dreams for years. How far from that enchanting dream was the tedious work in the dark underground world!

Her frustration grew by the day, and ever since her breakup with Jude, she found it nearly intolerable to stay in the mine. Memories cascaded from every niche and wall in the mine, happy memories of the rapturous years. Truth to be told, she found it hard to stay not just here but anywhere. A young girl in her early twenties, she looked at the world through weary eyes. Grandma reported to Jude shortly before his return home that the pastor had heard her quoting Shakespeare's *Antony and Cleopatra* as she exited the church one Sunday morning. "The bright day is done, and we are for the dark." Looking at him through lusterless eyes, she cited the line in a lifeless monotone. In case the pastor missed it, she said a second time, "The bright day is done. We are for the dark."

The pastor shot back at Cory a Shakespeare quotation that balanced this despairing view. "But remember the Bard's line from *Macbeth*: 'Angels are bright still, though the brightest fell.'" Pastor Gabriel was rather pleased with himself that he had come up with this quotation so spontaneously.

Looking back over her shoulder as she descended the porch steps, Cory quipped, "What good is angelic brightness if it doesn't shine in this dark world?" Then before crossing the highway she had turned at the bottom of the church steps, frontally faced Pastor Gabriel, and quoted the famous lines from Milton's *Paradise Lost*: "The mind is its own place, and in itself Can make a heaven of hell, a hell of heaven."

Twenty-three years old, burnt out, and despairing of life. "I haven't seen her smile in months," Pastor Gabriel Wyant had later said to Jude's grandma.

After lunch break on this first day back at work, Jude was plugging in the electric cart to the wall outlet, immediately outside one of the lunchrooms. He crouched down behind the cart and necessarily took precaution as he, for the first time, plugged in the powerful 220-volt cable in a darkened area. The high voltage required care, especially when handled in the dim light. While leaning over, he heard the lunchroom door open and watched a few women exit. He instinctively looked over his shoulder. No Cory. And then another group. No Cory. She was likely in one of the other two lunchrooms.

Jude was about to stand and enter the lunchroom himself when, to his utter amazement, Cory walked out and stood there before his eyes. By herself, she had not yet donned her miner's helmet as most of the women had. The line from an Elvis song darted through his mind—"My wish came true to my surprise When you stood there before my eyes."

Her one cheek appeared pinkish red in the dim light. A bruise from the wreck? Long, full tresses of her blond hair draped about her face. "Statuesque Grecian beauty," Jude gasped to himself. He froze in place. Her walk was aimless and slow. Pastor Gabe was right. Completely lifeless. No expression on her face, a blank look of "emotional death"—as Jude later wrote in his journal upon seeing her, right there in front of him for the first time. Her eyes, fixed straight ahead, peered into a black universe of nothingness. "The bright day is done. We are for the dark."

Tears immediately flooded Jude's eyes. So his grandma's assessment was exactly right. He wanted to run and embrace her and get on his knees to apologize on the spot, but he could not make a scene. Not here. Not just yet. There were too many people around. Earlier he had feared rejection and agonized over making a wrong first move. All of his fear and pride immediately died when he saw her face. He had never been so entirely humbled in his life, and he would do absolutely anything to rekindle the love, even prostrate himself here in front of all.

She took a step or two and paused for no apparent reason. Was she deep in thought or had she sensed something that made her stop? The despondent Cory carried the weight of the world on her shoulders. He saw firsthand the ravages that had been caused by their broken love. The issue now was timing. Other workers were exiting the lunchroom, and he could not subject her to what would inevitably be a difficult beginning in this place. Would Duke be the next one to come out the door? The thought paralyzed him. His only recourse was to helplessly watch in agony.

And crouch rock still.

Chapter 10

ory Mohney tied a scarf around her head to tuck in her hair, placed her miner's helmet on her head, and wearily trudged on. The very act of putting one foot in front of the other was a feat for her. Crouched there in chilly fifty-six-degree temps, Jude brushed the back of his hand across his forehead. He was sweating profusely, the blood completely drained from his ashen face.

The rest of the afternoon was a torment for Jude. He prayed for an opportunity to see Cory alone, fall to his knees, beg for forgiveness on the spot, and prove that, more than anything, he wanted to reconcile with her. *I love you, Cory. I love you, Cory. I love you, Cory*—he kept saying to himself all day.

On trips through the mine corridors, he crept by numerous picking crews and searched each diligently, but no Cory. Foiled through the day, he had hoped to see her in the parking lot after work that afternoon. Still, no Cory. Dejected and lonely, he climbed into his car at the end of his first workday and drove home to his grandma's. This was not the beginning he desperately wanted and had prayed about for years. "We, in our impatience of the steps, Get back to the beginning of beginnings." But how to get there, how to begin? Hey, Jude—*how* to make it better?

At the dinner table that evening, he bared his heart. "Grandma, I saw Cory today. She's a walking dead woman. I've been depressed ever since."

"I knew you'd be shaken. That's the look we see in church every Sunday, even though the worship services snap her out of her shell at least some. She sings like an angel during worship, and Pastor Gabe's sermons rouse her a little. So we don't see that awful death-in-life look all the time."

Rosetta paused as she contemplated the profound sadness of this young woman, wondering how much she should tell Jude. Just how much could he handle in these first days back on the farm? She settled the decision in her mind after a moment's reflection and resumed speaking. "I met her at the mailbox a couple weeks back. I made small talk and asked about Mr. Mohney. I was barely able to disguise my shock at her appearance. Jude, she looked terrible. What has happened to our beautiful Cory? I almost called you to tell you, but I knew you'd be worried sick, and I also knew there wasn't a blessed thing you could do."

Further shaken by these comments, Jude felt like picking up the phone immediately and calling her or, better yet, dashing over there to the farm. Was that the beginning of beginnings?

"Do you think she'd talk to me, Grandma?"

"I think she would. At least in time. She loves you deeply." That Cory at one time loved him was true. This part of his grandma's assessment was correct. But what about now? Jude had never told his grandmother how completely she had rebuffed him at the time of their breakup. Would Cory have the strength and will to tear down those carefully fortified psychic walls? Through this strategy, she had deftly managed self-preservation, and while this evidenced a kind of courageous nobility, it had simultaneously sealed her off from any and all emotional connection to life, especially connection with Jude.

"I just wish I knew how to proceed." He remembered the last time they spoke back in the fall. He had come to see his grandma at Thanksgiving and bumped into Cory at a social event at the church fellowship hall. In his too-bouncy, too-self-assured way, he had waltzed up to Cory, smiling broadly, and said, "So how are you doing?" She said nothing and didn't even look at him.

Then after a pause, she looked full in his face and quoted Milton's *Samson Agonistes*—"O dark, dark, dark amid the blaze of noon"—and then walked away. Jude was so shaken he dropped his punch glass on the floor. There had been an instant hush in the hall as all eyes fixed on him.

Rosetta interrupted his thought. "It's been especially difficult for her of late. Her dad's depression has worsened, and Joey's in spring training for football season. You know what an athlete he is. Well, this means that even more of the chores fall back on Cory this time of year. You see, Joey doesn't get home from practice until late in the evening." She watched as the despondent Jude hung his head. "Don't be discouraged. Love eventually melts even the coldest of hearts. If it's of God—and I think it is—love will make a way."

Joey Mohney, two years younger than Cory, was routinely called "a prince of a guy" by area folks. He was hardworking, muscular, and determined. His girlfriend, Laura Hileman, had, over the months, become a real help to Cory. Several years younger than Cory, she was beautiful and like her in so many ways. Cory often told Laura that she had been exactly where Laura currently was several years ago: full of life, in love with a perfect guy, surrounded by a loving family, and aspiring for high but not unobtainable things.

But then the bottom dropped out for Cory: her mother died, her lover departed, her father plummeted into depression, and she found herself buried in the coffin of the mine. Dark, dark, dark amid the blaze of noon.

One evening in the spring, shortly before Jude returned, Laura was helping Joey and Cory in the orchard. In a quiet moment when Laura and Cory were alone and had a chance to speak, Laura asked Cory how she was doing. Cory looked particularly stressed of late. Laura later recounted Cory's response to Jude's grandma, which she passed on to Jude. "I can't circumvent the past. I can't move on. Can't move on." Cory had paused and then said to Laura, "Did you ever read *The Great Gatsby*? I know you and Joey aren't heavy readers." Laura shook her head. "I didn't think so. Well, Fitzgerald perfectly describes me in the novel's famous last line—'So we beat on, boats against the current, borne back ceaselessly into the past.' That's me, kid, that's me. You're still in Eden. I'm living on the east side of the garden after the fall and going farther and farther downstream every day. Ceaselessly, relentlessly, into the past."

Again, Jude snapped himself back to his conversation with his grandma. "You're always so wise, Grandma, but in this case, I just can't see how you can be right. I'm referring to your point about things working out and love finding a way. Sorry to be so negative, but that is one despairing woman I saw today. If we're to get back together again, it will be God and only God who shows us the way. We used to liken our river of love to the mighty Allegheny, but now we've become a washed-ashore eddy cut off from the mainstream and swirling in meaningless, muddy circles."

Rosetta looked at Jude, who was completely perplexed by his situation. What to say to him? What would her deceased husband, that wise man Jeremiah, say to Jude right now? *Oh, Jeremiah, I miss you so.* Looking across the meadow, she spoke again. "I can't tell you what to do. All I can do is pray, and you know I do that daily. I've never seen two people so much in love. I was so shocked when you told me all those years ago that you were splitting up. I cried for days. It just seemed so impossible."

"Thanks for talking to me, Grandma." He gave her a big hug and a peck on the cheek and headed up to his room. He reflexively went to the window to listen. The fields were quiet, the orchard empty. Where was Cory? Helping her dad, getting dinner, washing the evening dishes, sitting alone in her room, weeping on her bed, massaging a bruised cheek, writing in her journal? Was she still writing poetry on occasion? What about her painting? Had that died too? That along with her voice was her great passion.

The torment of not knowing and of not seeing her was agonizing to him. He walked to the phone and was ready to call when the haunting refrain played again in his head: *I'll never open up my heart to love again.*" He froze in his tracks and tried to write a poem, but the words came slowly.

Finally, he choked forth a few words on a page. He called it "Love's Song":

> Burning holocaust,
> Smoking debris,
> Sick, unquiet times,
> Death-strewn trek,
> Where's youth's fiery dream?

He wrote a few more despairing lines, and then, steeled by his grandma's thought that love would find a way, he destroyed those and scrawled a more hopeful verse paragraph:

> Dancing together on dream's mist
> Entwined in ivory dawn,
> Enraptured couplings spawn sweet love
> On velvet wings never gone—
> Love's ashes jubilantly birthed,
> Love's hope eternally bright,
> Love's kiss supernally blessed.

Jude fell on the bed, slammed his fist into the mattress, and whispered to his pillow, "Death has certainly undone my Cory!"

Chapter 11

The next day in the mine, Jude was again assigned to run errands. Early in the morning, his supervisor sent him to the facilities manager's office where high-level officials were meeting to discuss which section of the mine should be developed for future expansion. Numbers of outlying rooms were available but had not yet been adapted for plant use. A pattern of brisk sales in recent months necessitated a thorough investigation of these undeveloped areas that were particularly suitable. A distant mainline corridor was selected because of the size of the quarried rooms and their proximity to the packhouse. Once the decision was made, Jude had been summoned to the manager's office to hand-carry a written note to the foreman of the bolting crew, those employees assigned to prepare the mine, especially the roof, for future use.

These visits to the various managers' offices were quite rare for Jude. In his earlier years of employment, he had only a few coveted glimpses of the offices. These enjoyable side trips exposed him to the humble humanity of the managers. They wore blue jeans and common clothing like the workers, avoided the use of titles and managerial affectations, kept an open door at all times, and dispensed with typical CEO privileges. Yet they exuded a quiet power as they oversaw 1,300 employees and an operation that produced over one million pounds in weight of mushrooms per week. Needless to say, the once humble farm had become big business over the years, and the managers dealt daily with heavy responsibility.

Jude found this particular visit to the office of the physical plant manager especially interesting. On the entire back wall of his office was a huge blowup of the mine, which depicted the miles and miles of underground caverns and corridors. As Jude perused the map, he tried to locate the various locales in the mine—lunchrooms, the underground lake, the various growing rooms, and so on. These places were not labeled on the map, so one had to scrutinize the similar-looking corridors quite closely to identify specific locales.

A large aerial-view blowup of the countryside in Armstrong and Butler Counties filled the adjoining wall. Jude tried to imagine its superimposition on top of the mine blueprint. He knew the terrain of the county well and had often tried to determine, as he drove along its country lanes and fields, what section of the mine lay directly underneath him at such and such point. When fishing at Buffalo Creek, he often wondered, *Am I now above one of the mushroom farm growing rooms? Or am I over a main corridor in the mine?* When in the mine, conversely, he often found himself doing the exact opposite. No matter where he was in the underground corridors, he would often look up and wonder, *What's directly above me at this spot? Am I beneath the church, our two farms, the bridge over Buffalo Creek, the old mining town, the locals' favorite pub, or the high hill at Winfield?*

When he commented to the manager about this imagined positioning of the aerial photograph atop the mine blueprint, the manager kindly retorted, "Yes, I catch myself doing the same thing. It's sort of a game, isn't it? I was especially fascinated to learn for instance that the Center Hill Church of the Brethren—I live near there—is close to this section here." He was pointing to the area that had just been selected for expansion.

The manager leaned back in his chair and invited Jude to sit down for a minute. Jude was all too happy to chat with this man about the operation that over the years had come to interest him so much.

The new section slated for expansion was the particular topic of the moment. The manager pointed to the large blueprint of the mine network on his desk, oriented Jude to the location, and with his pen indicated the designated section.

The information excited Jude, since this was a spot that lay just beyond a place that he and Cory used to visit during lunch breaks. He remembered turning off their miners' lamps to experience the thick, eerie blackness. Because no overhead lights had been installed, the employees' hat lamps were the only source of illumination in this area. "It's like the inky blackness that the ancient Egyptians endured when God had cursed pharaoh with one of the ten plagues. This is total darkness!"

"I've selected you to carry this message," the manager concluded, "because you're so verbal and expressive. It's fitting that someone like you should convey this message."

"Thank you, sir. I'll be on my way. Have a pleasant day!"

Jude placed the handwritten note in his shirt pocket and drove to the bolting crew foreman. It was the first time in weeks that he felt the heaviness in his heart lift just a bit. In the past, Cory and Jude used to imagine the time in the future when this very section of the mine would be developed, and now the hope was nearing reality. Once fitted for use, Cory and Jude would be able to explore it. But would that really happen? Would Cory be by his side? Reconciliation seemed so impossible.

Arriving at the location of the bolting crew, Jude delivered the manager's decision. The foreman opened the envelope with piqued interest since those few lines determined the bolters' next work site for many coming weeks and, in some instances, months. Nearby bolters, pausing in their work, fixed their attention on the crew boss. Those in the immediate vicinity came directly to him, keen to learn their next labor locale. The foreman in this instance looked at Jude with a wrinkled brow. The surrounding men immediately reacted, noting the foreman's negative body language.

"What's the matter," Jude inquired, "if I may be so bold to ask?"

"I know this section of the mine too well. It has been the site of serious cave-ins in bygone years. Ever heard of the 1963 disaster? Several men were killed in those very rooms." He turned to the men near him. "You guys aren't going to like this news." The nearby men overheard the comment and spread the news through the crew like a whizzing howitzer cannonball.

Jude bade good-bye, his spirits somewhat deflated. Maybe the idea of exploring these rooms with Cory wasn't such a good one after all. Returning to his crew boss to update him about his progress with the morning errands, Jude drove somewhat more rapidly than usual, preoccupied as he was about the news he had just conveyed. Humming "Just a Closer Walk with Thee" as he hurriedly sped by a picking crew, he forgot to scout the pickers to see if Cory might be among them. Later, he would come to know which pickers were on which crews and would know in a second if Cory were present, but that came later. For now, he was forced to look individually at each worker on each crew.

As he was nonchalantly passing the pickers, he peripherally noted one of the workers picking alone behind the others. She was partially blocked by an imposing man who was talking to her and screening her from view. Was that Cory? He slammed the brake, and the cart skidded to a stop. He backed up, took another look, and there she was—Cory in all her sad beauty looking directly at him. Jude got off the cart and started to run toward her. He knew the words would tumble forth in a gushing torrent. He was home for the summer. Staying with his grandma. "Were you hurt? I mean in the wreck. Can we talk? Right away? How are you?" Words, words, a torrent of words.

He had taken several steps from the cart when the six-foot, five-inch man beside her turned full body toward Jude, legs spread, arms folded, biceps bulging. Was this brute of a man Duke Manningham? "His shoulders were so broad I thought he had on football pads," Jude later wrote in his journal, "but with his helmet on, he didn't look exactly like the man in the *Leader Times* picture." The man scowled at Jude in anger, his head haughtily tilted backward. He resembled a quarrelsome man Jude had met years before in the mine. Offering a tentative half wave, Jude instantly knew that this was not the time to make his initial contact with Cory even though she had seen him. He turned back toward the cart, stumbled as he awkwardly mounted it, and drove off.

The embarrassing incident made him even more indecisive about how to proceed, yet seeing Cory with this borderline lowlife instantly filled him with deep anger and self-disgust. How clearly Jude saw the consequences of the foolish and impetuous separation of their youths. He pounded the wheel in anger as he drove away.

No sooner did Jude depart than the tongues started wagging. The news of his arrival at the mine flashed through mine corridors and lunchrooms. The pickers had heard that Jude was back for the summer. The older pickers recalled their love with tender warmth, and some even knew Jude personally. The new pickers were quickly brought on board and were alerted to the brewing trouble—the inevitable showdown between Duke and Jude.

The gossip among Cory's work associates kicked in with special intensity. "Was that the man you were talking about?" asked one of the young pickers.

"Yes!" an older woman replied. "That's Jude, and did you see how Cory craned her neck to look at him?"

"Did you see Duke's face?" whispered another. They were huddled together, their heads well under the trays, which afforded the perfect opportunity for gossip. They had mastered the art years ago.

"If looks could kill!"

"Jude was always a prince of guy, but so out of place here."

"I bet princess still loves him."

"The professor better watch himself."

"Do you think Cory has any feelings for Duke? You eat with her sometimes, Pam. Did she ever say anything?"

"Not a word. But if you want my opinion, Jude is a prince

compared to maniac macho man. You can tell just to look at him. The guy's a class act. What's he doing here? They say he's very intelligent."

The women turned their faces toward Cory. She was looking in their direction, sensing no doubt that they were talking about her. Walking away from Cory, Duke shot a cold look in their direction but was helpless to stop their gossip. Did he note Cory's flushed face and racing pulse or the involuntary gesture of her hand clasping her breast? Thank goodness for the protection of darkness!

"One of the girls quipped with a smirk, "Guess who's not happy! Good for you, Duke. Ha! Ha! Ha!"

That afternoon, right before quitting time, Jude had been summoned to help one of the crew drivers who was tending to a malfunctioning wheel on his personnel carrier. The pickers were transported throughout the mine by these carriers, a train of several cars linked together and pulled by a powerful engine called a mule. Because the wheels on one of the cars had been grinding and smoking, the men surmised that the bearings were dry and required grease.

As the two men were bent over to examine the wheel, Cory's crew passed by this personnel carrier on their way to the exit. Because of the narrowness of the corridor at this particular point, Duke had to slow his carrier to a crawl to pass the parked one. Seated on the side next to the stopped carrier, Cory saw a man crouched close to the ground in the distance. As he favored Jude's profile, she was immediately attentive.

Nearing the man, she knew in an instant that it was indeed Jude. How handsome he was, but how out of place he appeared. The intellectual, accustomed to grappling with libraries and the ranging world of culture and learning, was now domiciled in a little world where white mushrooms were picked in a dark, underground maze. She felt pride as the women who knew of their past love looked at her with admiration and envy. They knew she was fortunate to have been loved by such a man, even luckier to possibly renew it. How quickly Cory's negative emotions—the anger, the injustice, the frustration— dissipated! Deep in her heart, she knew she was madly in love with him and always would be.

As the car in which she rode approached Jude, it came to a virtual stop. Because the two engines with their large, projecting side mirrors were passing up ahead, Duke was forced to squeeze his train through a narrow pass with only inches to spare at the sides. Cory was directly above the crouching Jude!

Chapter 12

ory held her breath in excitement when some of the women seated next to her started yelling. "Hey, professor! Your lover's here!"

"Duke, you getting a good look at this little romantic scene?"

The loud sounds of the noisy engines that reverberated in the tight corridor made speech difficult, but it didn't stop the girls from nudging Cory and making snide comments. "What a hunk!" Cory's face was sunburn red, and her heart sledge-hammered her ribs.

As the women exited the personnel carrier a short while later, the talk continued.

"Hey, Cory, you sure did get a good look! I think you burnt a hole right through the back of Jude's helmet!"

"No wonder you're hot to trot for him! What a catch he'd make!"

"Duke's a loser compared to Jude Hepler. Hey, Cory, tell Duke to take a hike!"

"Yeah, right off the planet! Ha! Ha!"

Cory smiled involuntarily. If only Jude had looked up when she was right there hovering over him, mere inches away. She longed to see him, to talk through the hurt and pain, and get back together, but given the circumstances and the complicated history, especially the recent involvement with Duke, reconciliation seemed impossible. After all, she reasoned, if Duke knew Cory was interested in Jude, he'd become the aggressive alpha male who would inflict violence on either Cory, Jude, or both.

If only she had known Jude was coming back, she would have summoned the strength to repel Duke's incessant overtures. She had withstood his advances across months, but his help with the farm work and frequent nagging gradually wore her down. Though feeling no emotional connection with him, her resolve weakened as the months went by. Surely a date or two, as a way of expressing gratitude for his good help with the mountains of never-ending farm work, wasn't inappropriate. What harm was there in a couple fast dates? She would be civil and warm, reciprocate his kindness, and then withstand all future advances, her obligation sufficed, her freedom regained.

That had been the plan. She continued to have no real interest in him, but, strangely, before Jude's arrival at the mine, she felt increasingly affirmed by Duke's barrage of kind gestures. Because Jude's rejection had hurt her deeply, Duke's interest was a comforting balm massaged into the wound of the earlier jilting. Normally, she would have had the good sense and strength to reject it, but owing to her acute vulnerability during the long winter months—that never-ending barren stretch of dark, arctic days—she had caved in. The relationship with Duke commenced, and one prison house was exchanged for another. Her only recourse? Helplessly waving at Jude through the bars.

At the end of the workday a short while later, the miners stowed their picking baskets and tools, turned in their helmets for battery recharging, donned their light spring jackets, and headed for the punch clock to check out. Clustered everywhere in pockets, women excitedly gossiped about the recent development.

"Jude Hepler's working at the mushroom mine this summer!"

"We saw them this afternoon!"

"Duke's fit to be tied. He was cursing like a wild man at the packhouse."

Tongues wagged, necks craned, and fingers pointed.

What the women did not notice was the brooding presence of a man in the background. Hidden from view in the adjoining lounge, he feasted on every syllable. In case anyone randomly looked in his direction, he feigned interest in a magazine article on photography that he pretended to read. This was a good ruse since he read incessantly about photography and recent developments in the world of imaging, but in this instance, his attention was riveted to the gossip. With each passing syllable about Jude and Cory, Abe Badoane's face contorted into a scowl, which he turned away from the crowd. Knuckles whitened, he held the magazine in his hand. Moments later, he pasted a wide smile on his face, made his way for his time card, and punched out at the clock.

Nearly six feet tall, Abe Badoane functioned in the dual role of personnel carrier driver and head foreman of the crew drivers. In his midfifties, he bore himself with a quiet dignity, an erect posture, and studied bearing. Each action and each word were calculated for their effect on others. His mind always worked with feverish intensity, making his fellow workers comment, "He even looks intelligent!" His elongated face was pronounced because of his jutting jaws and flat chin. In profile, it appeared that a slightly bent line ran directly from his lower lip to his throat with a mere bump at its center for the chin. His steely eyes, even more noticeable than his square jaw and chinless profile, unnerved people for the way they pierced into others. At times the eyes looked softly outward, even kindly, but when put on the defensive, they were laser beams that burned into adversaries.

Abe Badoane sported two scars at the side of his forehead between the temple and his right eye. One short and the other longer, the scars intersected almost at the precise center, creating a slanted cross. Shortly after Abe had started working at the mushroom mine, one of the younger employees joked with Abe about his taking the biblical precept of carrying your daily cross very seriously. "You carry your cross with you all the time—ha!" Abe grabbed the man by the sweatshirt and threw him into the limestone wall with such force that people feared a concussion even though the man wore his helmet. Abe screamed at the man through clenched teeth. "Don't you ever say that again!" Recounting the event to his wife later, Bud said, "The guy was so close to me that I smelled strawberries on his breath!" No one ever referred to the scars again.

Abe laid down the photography magazine he pretended to read and prepared to exit the building, the long workday completed. "See you tomorrow, Abe. There you are smiling again. Happiest guy I know," a nearby employee commented.

Outside in the parking lot, Jude waited for his eyes to adjust to the glaring light and then scanned the various cars to see if he might see Cory. As he prepared to lower himself into his car, his eye caught her across the lot. She too was entering a car with a few other carpoolers. He waved and started over, but the driver of her car, unaware of this eye contact and Cory's desire to speak, put the car in gear, forcing her to hurriedly take her seat. But had that been a faint smile Jude saw on her lips? He was encouraged and vowed to see her that evening.

As Jude drove away a moment later, he saw Duke and Abe whispering near Duke's car. Abe was talking to Duke behind a cupped hand, and Duke, listening intently, glared at Jude. Abe warmly waved good-bye to Jude.

Standing beside Duke's new car, Abe Badoane took the opportunity to shift his attention to it—a hot rod 1957 Chevy that was the pride of Duke's life. In mint condition, Duke lavished attention on it the way most parents did their newborn infant. Everybody in the mine knew it was his baby. Passing by, Jude paid particular attention to the image of the two men talking. Something didn't seem right.

That evening during dinner, Jude, at his grandma's request, summarized the highlights of his day. In between eating his meatloaf, mashed potatoes, carrots, and coleslaw, Jude commented about the slow beginning to his reconciliation with Cory. "We just can't get a chance to be together. It's driving me crazy!"

Spreading some apple butter on her homemade bread, his grandma stoically responded, "Love never allows failure to be final. Be patient."

Was she right? A woman of great wisdom, she was highly respected for her spiritual depth. But in this instance, was she correct?

As a result, the professor was beloved by the Grove City College
... ...

Chapter 13

fter helping his grandma with a few chores in the early
evening—adjusting the height of the porch swing, replacing
a lightbulb on one of the ten-foot ceiling lights, and mowing the grass
around the farmhouse—Jude headed toward Vinlindeer, the ridge
with the commanding view of the valley below and, front and center,
Cory's farm.

He found a spot near a fencepost, leaned back, and commenced
reading *Hamlet*. Professor Charles Claypoole, who had become one of
Jude's close friends over the years, was a professor of English literature
at Grove City College, where he taught courses in both American
and British literature, though Shakespeare and Milton were his
distinct favorites. One of Charles' good friends from the University
of Pittsburgh was directing a summer production of *Hamlet* and had
asked Professor Claypoole to be his assistant director. As a result,
Chuck, as he was known in the community, was reading and thinking
anew about Shakespeare's masterpiece and had asked Jude for some
insights. Hence, Jude had commenced rereading the great tragedy
shortly after his return to Armstrong County.

Charles had also been one of Jeremiah Wakefield's best friends.
Well-read, the professor was conversant on an endless number of
topics and possessed as sweet a spirit as anyone Jude knew. With his
formidable knowledge base, he had the uncanny ability to remember
sheer volumes of data and effortlessly connect, synthesize, and

integrate it in a manner that amazed students and colleagues alike. As a result, the professor was beloved by the Grove City College community where he had developed a fine reputation for excellent teaching. With his broad forehead, white mustache and goatee, and black-rimmed glasses, he bore the appearance of the quintessential professor. He stood six feet, two and a half inches tall—"same exact height as George Washington," he quipped to his students.

Jude saw in him a father figure, mentor, and good friend. Their discussions on poetry, religion, and life in general were often as illuminating as those Jude had with his students and colleagues at the university. What Jude did not realize, however, was that in recent years a gnawing skepticism ate away at Professor Claypoole. A practicing Christian and highly moral man, he nevertheless harbored doubts about his faith, which his years in academia had intensified. The questions of the ages nibbled at his beliefs. How does a loving God allow—or should he say "ordain"—cataclysmic devastation and natural disasters? If humankind is truly predestined, how do humans have an operable and autonomous free will? Were the moral teachings of the ancients in Israel applicable for distantly removed and technologically advanced cultures?

In a real sense, Professor Claypoole with his highly polished exterior—"a rock-solid foundation of a guy," as a colleague quipped— was another Jude. Both men skillfully masked an inner universe in their hearts, which featured more than a few black holes. Pastor Gabriel accused Professor Charles of spending "too much time in the world." The pastor, a twinkle in his eye, had said to him on more than one occasion, "Beware lest anyone cheat you through philosophy and empty deceit, according to the tradition of men, according to the basic principles of the world and not according to Christ." The pastor amplified the apostle Paul's word of caution to the Colossians: "Be careful, Charles. We are to be in the world but not of it."

"You, Gabe," Charles retorted, "exemplify the truth of the proverb you quoted in last week's sermon. 'The lips of knowledge are a precious jewel.' I dare say, your lips are forever issuing precious jewels. And I know in this case, you're exactly right! I remember the verse but not the citation."

"Proverbs 20:15."

Jude remembered very well his parting conversation with Charles even though it had occurred several years earlier. Their discussion had come around to the most enigmatic figure in the entire mushroom mine—Abe Badoane. This broad-shoulder man with wavy hair parted in the middle of his head fascinated Jude and most others. Abe's feats of intelligent problem solving spellbound the workers in the mine. The report among the employees was that Abe possessed a photographic mind, and while Jude was not able to corroborate this perception, he had seen enough in the past to believe it.

In time, Jude eventually articulated a difference between the two intelligent men. Charles was possibly more well-read than Abe Badoane, but in the area of recall, Abe was every bit his match. As to the matter of sheer intelligence—raw cognitive ability—the edge, Jude surmised, was probably Abe's. Jude recoiled from using the word "brilliant," since it was used too loosely in the modern era, but Abe Badoane, in his book, was one individual who deserved the high accolade. No doubt about it, Abe's superb intelligence easily deserved the epithet brilliant.

Jude intended to speak to Chuck Claypoole about Abe. *Why is he so intensely mysterious? Even more, why is such an intelligent man satisfied with menial labor when he could easily be the CEO of a major corporation in Pittsburgh?* Mysterious Abe Badoane engendered mixed feelings in people. To many he was the very essence of warmth and kindness, but in Jude's opinion, highly incongruous elements melded together in this complicated man. Jude witnessed the fun, the lightheartedness, and the witty surface banter, but he also sensed an indefinable, sinister undercurrent. It bothered him. Jude had only returned to the mine for a short time before he more fully understood why Abe was called the "mine mystery man," that illuminating phrase he used in his journal. Reading *Hamlet* again, Jude saw in Abe similarities to the arch villain of Shakespeare's masterpiece, Claudius.

Seeing Abe speak with Duke after work awakened the old fascination and reminded Jude to resume the conversation he had in the distant past with Charles about Abe Badoane. Details were fuzzy, but Jude remembered Chuck's saying something about the situation surrounding his appointment as professor of English at Grove City College. Jude's return to the mine prompted the recollection of certain details—something about Chuck and another candidate being the two finalists for this teaching position. Although the other candidate had been the frontrunner, the job had been given to Chuck. Jude remembered Chuck's saying that as he bounded out of the English Department building at the completion of his job interview, he saw a man sitting in a car in front of his. The man, slouched in his seat with his face hidden by a lowered hat, pounded the dashboard and cursed loudly. Charles had described the incident in such graphic detail that Jude, years later, recalled the picture of the distraught man hammering away at the dash.

That was as far as Chuck had proceeded in the story when, for whatever reason, one of them had been called away. Why had the professor started into this narrative? Who was the slouched man in the car? Was it none other than mysterious Abe Badoane? Jude had dismissed the whole incident years ago, but seeing Abe again reminded him of the unfinished story. He hoped to complete the delayed conversation soon.

On the hill that evening, Jude read, meditated, and gazed in the direction of Cory's farm. Would she come out tonight? He had been on the verge of stopping over after dinner and had even started down the lane when a thought struck him. If Duke was as possessive and jealous as others said he was, then he would be asking Cory if Jude had made any moves to reestablish contact. Jude couldn't remove from his mind the image of the lowering man who had squared off to face him, fists clenched and muscles bulging. He could imagine Duke's barbs to Cory: "Did you see your old hot lover? Did you get a good look at him today when the two personnel carriers were inches away?" Duke's diatribe could be potentially vicious and place Cory in real jeopardy. To keep from putting her in a compromised situation, Jude was forced to wait for her to make the first move. But no Cory appeared in the meadow or the orchard. How agonizing to wait and do nothing!

That evening, as he read a couple acts in Shakespeare's *Hamlet*, he came across a passage that reminded him of the time when Cory rebuffed him. Jude had sent her flowers and poetry as had Hamlet to his girlfriend, Ophelia, in Shakespeare's play, but all had been returned after the collapse of their love.

Ophelia's response to her father early in *Hamlet*—"I shall obey, my lord," indicating her intent of rebuffing Hamlet—haunted Jude, since it reminded him yet again of Cory's despairing refrain, "I'll never open up my heart to love again." Jude slammed the book shut, brushed off the hay from his shorts, and walked to the orchard where he waited for some time. No Cory.

Just when he could stand it no longer and was ready to move— either toward Cory's farm or back to his grandma's, he didn't know which—Cory came out of her house. The distance was too great to be sure, but she appeared to cast her eyes to the ridge and then to the orchard in his direction. Did she see him?

He started toward Cory, who took a few hesitant steps in his direction. Jude's heart quickened. She continued toward him, instantly stopped for a moment, and suddenly darted toward the house. As she approached the door, she turned and waved deliberately. Of that there could be no doubt. The gesture filled Jude's heart with both consternation and joy. She seemed to want to talk, but why, after walking toward him, had she retreated? Was this intentional rejection? Why did she change her mind? Had something or someone called her back to the house? More mental turmoil was Jude's lot that evening.

It lasted all the next day. He had been assigned to the compost yard and spent the entire day out of doors turning the ricks of compost. Jude learned from his worker friends that one rick of compost in the yard was composed of some four to six trailer loads of race track manure, which was mixed with thirty to forty-five tons of mixed hay, twenty tons of crushed corncobs, 16,000 pounds of gypsum, 50,000 pounds of chicken manure, and a few other ingredients. It was the job of Jude's crew to turn the compost—four turnings in a nine-day period. Two of these large ricks filled on average eight hundred trays.

Staying physically fit was a major challenge for most graduate students, so the opportunity to perform physical work in the ricks was the equivalent of a good workout for Jude. Plus, it gave him a break from the excessive mental expenditure of intellectual energy that had been his lot for years. How novel to give the mind a rest even in the odoriferous compost ricks!

But such an assignment at this particular time frayed Jude's nerves. Away from the mine, he would likely not see Cory. And he didn't. The day was exasperatingly long for Jude. Nor did he see her in the parking lot after work. Her crew had finished early and, as a reward, had departed a half hour before the others.

That evening in his bedroom, he looked across the vale in the direction of Cory's home. So near and yet so far. He drank yet another glass of water and wearily fell into bed.

Chapter 14

On Wednesday evening, Jude and his grandma walked with a quiet reverence into the old Center Hill Church of the Brethren for the evening Bible study. Dating from the early 1800s, the church evoked an array of hallowed emotions in Jude. When presenting a talk to commemorate the anniversary of this old southwestern Pennsylvania building some years ago, he had done considerable research on the original structures that stood here, the early believers, their agrarian way of life, and the rich historical context.

"Did you know that Thomas Jefferson was president when the early believers started worshipping on this hill? Were you aware that when Jefferson and the founders contemplated the Louisiana Purchase, our forebears contemplated the purchase of this land for the church site? Let me put it this way: Jefferson negotiated the Louisiana Purchase to grow a nation. Our ancestors negotiated the Center Hill purchase to grow a church."

When Jude saw the excited reaction of his audience, he continued. "Did you know that the men buried out there in the front corner of the cemetery had seen extensive action in the Civil War and fought in many of its major battles—Chickamauga, Kennesaw Mountain, Stone's River, Chattanooga, and others?" His research and delivery were warmly received by these country folks who welcomed the scholar into their midst. No one had ever placed the church in such a rich historical context.

As Jude entered the building on this Wednesday evening, he thought of how unique this community was compared to the university life where he lived and worked. He knew people frequently romanticized rural life and had done so throughout the ages. Literary descriptions and images of the bucolic life where one rusticated in the wilds of nature far from the madding crowd were common. Jude was not about to fall prey to such reductive assessments of the hard life of the farmer in the modern era, yet he was also highly aware of the uniqueness of the Center Hill community. Ancient traditions and even quaint customs that had survived the onslaught of modernity were more completely evidenced here than in most other small towns and rural areas.

The tradition of door-to-door Christmas caroling, for instance, had died many years earlier even in country churches, but the practice was very real even to this day at Center Hill. The community breakfasts, quilting bees, summer festivals, communal apple butter churnings, soup and salad dinners, church workdays, and the annual Fourth of July church picnic—all welcome by church and area people—were still going strong. The good country folks supported these activities in large numbers and looked to each other for community. Their values, Jude surmised, had been forged in communal tradition, not the ephemeral fads of a culture in moral free fall. Like many visitors and nonmembers, Jude felt, upon entering the church, that he had stepped into a time warp, since much of the past survived the encroachment of the modern era that had so completely disseminated the American culture of yesteryear.

These reflections, along with the innumerable memories of his happy days with Cory in this very building, galloped through his mind as he entered the ancient vestibule. Walking into the sanctuary, he hurriedly canvassed the crowd to see if Cory was present. There she was, seated in the third row on the right side. Filled with anxiety about the seat his grandma would choose, he nevertheless held back and allowed her to lead.

She chose the third pew on the left side. Jude sat next to the aisle.

He smiled and waved cordially to people who well remembered him and were happy to see him back at Center Hill again. Cory looked at him and flashed a faint smile. At least he thought it was a smile. Truth to be told, he wasn't sure, seeing more with his heart than his eyes. He took his pulse as he sat down. *I knew it would be elevated.* He nodded to the minister and smiled.

Pastor Gabriel Wyant and he were good friends from long ago, and though they had little recent contact, the deep bond between them was evident. As Jude noted in his journal, "Gabe and Chuck are my intellectual kindred spirits in Armstrong County!" The reality was that Jude, having lost his own father when he was a young child, saw surrogate father figures in these two men.

Standing five foot nine, the pastor was shorter than Charles. His thinning brown hair was parted on the right side. He wore no facial hair, and the crow feet lines at his eyes were deeply defined, the result, people said, of a perpetually joyous look on his face. His skin was smooth and nearly wrinkle-free, especially his forehead, though of late his color was less vibrant than in bygone years. Some of the more discerning people in the church worried about him. "I'm telling you the dear man is overworked." "He needs to slow down!" But possessing an old-school work ethic, he was not about to lessen the pace. When anyone commented on his exhausted appearance, he would inevitably quote Holy Writ. "The night is coming when no man works. We must work while it is yet day."

On one occasion at the Fellowship Hall when Zane spoke of his insane busyness, the pastor had pulled out his pocket calendar and read from one of the many quotations and snippets of scrap paper he invariably tucked between its pages. "Life's journey is not to arrive at the grave safely in a well-preserved body, but rather to skid in sideways, totally used up and worn out, shouting, 'What a ride!'" He added with a twinkle in his eye, "There's a definite truth to that!"

A skilled expositor of scripture, Gabriel Wyant was an astute man of God who had happily chosen this humble country pastorate. His worldview, knowledge of scripture, verse-by-verse preaching, and shepherd's heart made him a favorite with these country folks. He had been pastor for some fifteen years already, during which time his flock's love and respect for him deepened.

Concentrating on the Bible study was difficult for Jude this particular evening, but Jude forced himself as much as possible to listen attentively. Gabriel's text was Galatians 6:9—"Let us not be weary in well doing, for in due season we will reap if we faint not." He had chosen to expound on the virtues of adversity and, probably for the professor and Jude's sakes, cited in passing Shakespeare's line from *As You Like It*, "Sweet are the uses of adversity." Jude smiled when he caught the pastor's wink first at Charles and then him—a kind of private joke among the three of them. Warming to his subject, the pastor cited in passing three biblical characters who prevailed through and greatly benefited from adversity—Job, the apostle Paul, and the apostle John on the isle of Patmos.

Fascinated by the relevance of the study to their situation, Jude couldn't resist a quick look at Cory. He was greatly heartened to see that she was also looking at him, this time with a full smile. More than one person sitting behind Jude and Cory witnessed the quick exchange of smiles, nudged each other, and nodded approvingly in their direction. Many of the people in the church knew that their love was forged in heaven and that they had tragically separated.

The Bible study over, Jude greeted the pastor warmly and then exchanged pleasantries with a few of the nearby parishioners. He turned to his grandma when she nudged him on the arm. "A couple of the women on the Witness Commission are going to meet briefly with the pastor. Something's come up. We'll need a half hour or so. You can use this time to renew acquaintances, or maybe you could find a friend and take a walk." Jude couldn't help but note the twinkle in her eyes.

He whispered to her, "Grandma, you are such a matchmaker!"

Cory was waiting on the porch when he exited the church. Had she tarried on purpose, hoping to see him? Jude wondered about that, as he did his grandma's impromptu "meeting." Because people had gone to their cars by the time Jude met Cory on the porch, she was standing by herself and looking toward the Bonner Cemetery. Jude was grateful that the first difficult exchange wouldn't be complicated by an audience.

He stepped onto the porch and paused briefly before speaking, feeling that the entire reconciliation hung on this initial conversation. What a heavy freight this small train of words was destined to carry! He fortified his will. "Hi, Cory. I've wanted to talk to you ever since I arrived at Grandma's last weekend."

He carefully looked at her face. Was that a bruise on the cheek or shading from the setting sun? "Thank you. That's kind of you." Her face bore no emotion whatsoever.

"Can we walk for a while up in the cemetery, or do you have to get home to your dad right away?"

"No, I can walk. Joey and his girlfriend, Laura, stayed home with Dad this evening so I could come to Bible study." Joey Mohney and his girlfriend, Laura Hileman, were together as much as Jude and Cory had been in the past.

"How are you feeling? Grandma told me about your car wreck."

"I'm fine. It was scary. I certainly admit that, but apart from a sore back, I'm all right." She paused for a moment and then said, "Thank you for asking." Again, no emotion.

They paused beside the side of the church and looked toward the cemetery before starting their walk up the knoll. The choir members had already assembled at the front of the church and were singing the refrain of "More Like the Master" in anticipation of their special song for Sunday's worship service. Even in that nervous moment, Jude caught the ironic relevance of the lines to his current situation.

Take Thou my heart, I would be Thine alone;
Take Thou my heart and make it all Thine own;

"Take Thou my heart"—the exact words he wanted to say to God about his spiritual heart and, infinitely more to the point, to Cory about his emotional heart. *Take thou my heart. Will she?*

The rich scent blowing across the hill from the newly cut hay fields and the twittering of the summer birds added to the magic of the balmy May evening. Jude noted these and other details in his journal: "the neatly mown lawn of the cemetery, the sweet scent of the lilac blossoms (reminding me of Whitman's 'When Lilacs Last in the Dooryard Bloomed'), the sweep of the wind through the hay on the nearby knoll, and the rose-shaped cumulus cloud." Starting up the lane, Jude unconsciously placed his hand on the small of Cory's back. An onlooker would have surmised that they were the lovers of old.

As they ambled up the cemetery lane in silence, Jude nervously bit his lip and kicked a pebble on the path. "I don't know where to begin, Cory."

"How about the beginning?" Her coldly logical response, though gentle, unnerved him even more.

"Which one? There are so many." He sought a common ground between them. Literary quotations had always done the trick in the past. What about now? "Remember the opening lines of Dante's *Inferno*, which we used to read on summer evenings? 'Midway through life's journey I found myself in a dark road, the right road lost.' No other words describe so accurately my feelings at this instant. I'm on the wrong road, Cory, and I'm lost and frightened in a dark wood."

She stopped walking and looked at him in disbelief. "How can you say that? On the verge of getting your PhD, not much past your midtwenties, you look like you're perking right along to me. What makes you say so emphatically that you're on the wrong road?"

"Because you're not on it."

"Whose fault is that?"

Touché, he thought.

Chapter 15

It was another hit, a very palpable hit and one that he partly deserved. Yet no anger was present in her tone, nor did she seem to intend the comment as a barb. Her direct, matter-of-fact question nevertheless penetrated like acid to Jude's very nerve center. There had never been any verbal dancing with Cory, no flitting around the edges of topics, since full disclosure and total honesty of communication had always been the hallmark of their love.

Taken aback, he started to do what he often did when tense or tentative during a difficult conversation. He temporarily detoured into the recesses of his encyclopedic mind and started dredging up facts and data, trivia and background information, anything that bore varying degrees of relevance to the topic at hand. This is what he had wanted to do in his IUP office when he longed to dwell on the poet Robert Browning to escape an unnerving conversation with Eric.

Through this mechanism, which facilitated self-preservation in tight places, he had learned to circumnavigate touchy topics, thereby dodging the scary side of his being through well-honed deflection. He knew just a little about his dark side and was frightened to learn more. Depending on his audience and the social context, these periodic escapades into the universe of his mind—for the most part they amounted to a recitation of fascinating facts—were typically interesting, sometimes even amazing. He had become so skilled at dodging bullets that people often didn't realize that he was clandestinely sidestepping unpleasantries.

Cory had placed her hand on one of the older tombstones, a small spire leaning with age that marked the graves of four of the earlier pioneers in this region. He did not want to begin this difficult first conversation by immediately tackling the answer to her most delicate question, "Whose fault is that?" because it involved, front and center, the tricky matter of fault attribution. That way lies madness!

It was time to pursue the well-worn deflection path. "Cory, can you beat that?" He pointed to the writing on the grave monument on which Cory's hand rested. "This David Bowser was born in 1795! Can you believe it? That's the year the great English poet John Keats was born. What a long time ago that was! Washington was president of the thirteen colonies at that time, and the Constitution was a fledgling eight-year-old document with its ink barely dried."

Jude walked to the other side of the monument and stooped down to examine the engraved letters. He nervously talked on. "Look at this other side of the monument. Here's another David Bowser. He must have been a relative in the same family. This David died on September 27, 1860, aged seventy-two years. That means he was born in 1788, the year most of the thirteen colonies ratified the new Constitution. That was the year the election started, which eventually made Washington president in 1789."

The information, gushing out of him like a torrent, offered a convenient getaway from the moment. But it was only a temporary dallying back and forth along the edge of the precipitous chasm in front of him—responding to Cory's question. Jude wished that he had already crossed it, but there was no nearby bridge.

"Jude," Cory broke in, "I appreciate your reminding me of such interesting history." She looked directly at him. "But there's a white elephant standing between us. Your recitation of facts is a mere avoidance strategy. Your diversion is nakedly transparent to me." She stopped speaking and looked at him. "You're forgetting that I know your capacity for deflection during troubling conversations. I know you inside and out." She paused for a while, and Jude, sensing more was coming and wishing he had a cool glass of water, remained silent. "We only ever spoke the truth, and that's what we must do now." She bent down and picked up a blade of grass. "As we both know, only the truth shall set us free."

How pregnant sometimes her replies are, he thought. Her forte had always been direct and utterly truthful speech. Apparently, it still was, even more so. He had commented about this in the past and never forgot her response. "We are to speak the truth in love." Admonished as he was, he couldn't help but marvel at the depth of her insight and her sheer love of emotional honesty. It was time to track back to the comment that had derailed him, time to get back to the source, that feared beginning of beginnings—"Whose fault is that?"

"I take responsibility for the breakup, Cory … at least for my considerable part of it. I always have. You know that. We've only ever been honest with each other." He watched her carefully to note her response.

Tears formed in her eyes, and she looked away. He saw her brush her cheek. "Five years is a long time, Jude." Again, she paused, gathering strength to push the thought to its terminus. "I cried myself to sleep for months. Did you know that?" Memories of the pain of separation and the anguish of loneliness swarmed in her brain—hours of sitting alone on Vinlindeer, piles of wet tissues on the kitchen table, daily treks to an empty mailbox, days of waiting by a silent phone.

She was frustrated at not being able to articulate the hurt and make him understand what she had endured during the quiet years. "Do you know what it's like to lie in a lonely bed and ache for love, ache all over to love and to be loved and to show love the way God intended? I used to hold the pillow tightly and fantasize that it was you. I wanted you so much. My pillow was wet with tears." She stopped speaking for a moment and looked away. "It got so bad I couldn't stand to go to bed at night."

Tears filled Jude's eyes as he saw anew the pain their separation had caused them. "I'm not at all surprised that you cried yourself to sleep. I did too. But I suppose I'm the weaker person. I had the opportunity to run from the pain—rather, I created the opportunity to run—and did, by immersing myself in graduate work. You stayed and bore the unending horror like a Civil War infantryman on Little Round Top at Gettysburg. I played the role of the happy postwar gallant. I need to emphasize the theatrical metaphor—I played the part." He paused to take in the exquisite beauty of her sunlit face. "Actually, I've become the consummate actor since we parted."

"May I offer my opinion?" She looked at him directly, but her eyes were somehow more mellow. "You weren't just immersing yourself in education these past years. You engaged yourself in rainbow-riding across the loftiest mountain peaks of your rarefied dreams. And me? I was stuck. And still am, I should add. My theme song for years has been Robert Browning's line from 'Andrea del Sarto': 'A common grayness silvers everything, All in a twilight, you and I alike.'"

The recitation of the poem softened her and made her think back on those happy days. After a moment, she turned to him again, her face warmer, her voice gentle, her eyes dreamy. "Remember how we read Browning by the hour? Well, that line perfectly describes my life—then and now. Everything has been gray, lifeless, and sterile, and it still is. That's a confession, Jude—a right-from-the-center-of-the-heart confession." The thought hardened her face again. "That's me, Jude. My name is Common Gray." She thought for a moment of her metaphorical name. "My middle initial is E for empty. Or maybe ebony. Yes, that will work—Miss Common Ebony Gray."

This initial conversation with Jude was extremely difficult for Cory. On the one hand, her prayers were answered and her dream, at least a part of it, had come true—she was with Jude again. He was here in the flesh! How that made her heart rejoice!

But simultaneously she registered an equally strong competing emotion—the bitterness that was slowly transforming to cynicism. How could a good God have allowed all the heartache? Why was He so slow to intervene, and how could He allow Jude to emerge from the breakup unscathed, seemingly stronger than ever? Where was justice in that? The voices pounding away in her head, she forced herself to listen to Jude.

For his part, Jude was profoundly discouraged. *Why am I trying?* he thought to himself. *Her heart's so hard that she'll never allow me near again.* He watched her as she walked a few paces in the cemetery. How beautiful she was. Even in this difficult moment he couldn't help but notice that perfectly curvaceous shape. He thought again of the future he had imagined with her: marriage with its heated couplings, frolicking wild nights. He watched her walk across a grave. *There's the perfect emblem if there ever was one. Instead of the gasping, uncontrollable thrashings, and primeval groans of the marital bed, we have the stinking bones of a rotting carcass. Yes, she walks on a grave instead of sports in a bed. Talk about a relevant symbol!*

It was time to stop the cynical reverie. Jude sighed aloud and spoke again. "Everything doesn't have to remain lifeless and sterile. You can be freed. We can be freed from this deathlike world that haunts us like a Poe horror story. Things don't have to stay the way they are." He felt he was getting nowhere but talked on against the current. "Whoever said this despairing reality is the one we have to settle for?"

"How, Mr. Houdini Escape Artist? How can I escape my death-world trance?"

"Cory, please don't be angry. I've lived and breathed and obsessed over this moment, this very conversation for months—the way to have it, what to say, and how to say it. Please help me."

She looked stricken. "Yes, I believe you, Jude. I'm sorry. I intended no unkindness. We had once promised to set aside sarcasm forever. But my life has shriveled to nothing. I don't know what to make of my diminished life—shrunken dreams, shrunken hopes, and, of late, a shrunken soul. I scare myself. I don't know this person I've become."

"You sound like Robert Frost in 'The Oven Bird.'"

The citation piqued her interest. "I don't know that poem. Remind me."

"As the contemplative bird reflects on the end of his happy

summer season and the coming winter of lonely death, Frost says, 'The question that he [the bird] frames in all but words Is what to make of a diminished thing.'"

"That's it, Jude. Exactly. What does one make of a drastically diminished thing? Like a diminished life with its embarrassingly teensy dreams and hopes?" She looked pityingly at Jude, loving him madly, wanting to embrace him passionately, and hating him for her wrecked life, for the lost and wasted years.

He cast his eyes to the domed hill adjacent to the cemetery. In the distant past, a village farmer had told Jude that an old stone marker had been found at the top of this perfectly rounded knoll on which were written the words, "Centre Hill." Jude had asked him at the time about the spelling. Yes, the marker, according to the farmer's recollection, featured the old English spelling—"centre" instead of "center." The farmer had opined that this gently domed hill, visible from all directions and standing magisterially alone, was the hill for which the community, Center Hill, bears this name.

What a unique name for a village, Jude used to think. *If the community is named that, then there must be a hill somewhere at the middle—the center hill. Surely the name means something.* The farmer's comment piqued his interest, but on their various walks across the rounded knoll, Jude and Cory had never found the ancient stone marker. Was it a myth or had the actual stone been buried decades or even centuries ago amid these luxuriant rolling hills and undulating vales where farming had been the livelihood for centuries? Maybe talk of the center hill would divert attention from Cory's diminished life.

"Remember how we used to walk on the center hill?" Jude asked.

"Yes, I do." Her voice was tender, controlled.

"I don't think we ever determined if the ancient marker really exists."

"It does. I know it does."

"How can you be so sure?"

"Old Mary saw it once when she was a little girl."

"Are you serious?"

"Absolutely. Complete with the English spelling for 'centre.'"

"That's amazing. I never knew that had been verified."

The diversion complete, Jude again tried to formulate his thoughts. What to make of a diminished thing? How to proceed? *Midway through life's journey I found myself in a dark wood, the right road lost. I'll never open up my heart to love again.*

Why not plunge into the heart of the matter? Resolved in his spirit, he knew it was time to get back to the beginning of beginnings, time for the backward motion to the source. Words at last issued from his mouth. "Do you think in time you'll be able to forgive me?"

Cory made no reply.

Chapter 16

Turning away, Cory rested her hand on another grave monument, lifted eyes to the horizon as if to find solace there, and spoke after a moment. "That's not even an issue, Jude Hepler. I forgive you totally, even before you ask. Surely you know that. Can't you read it in these eyes, see it in these trembling hands, and hear it in this pounding heart?" She made a half step toward him as though to embrace him but then drew back.

The gesture made him think of the line in Herbert's "Love III": "Love bade me welcome but my soul drew back." *She has so often drawn back,* he mused. *Even from the time we were kids. Always drawing back. Pushing me away. Going underground. Cory, how death has undone you!*

Her forthright words and her second-guessed movement complicated his reply. "I wanted to think so but couldn't be certain. You made it very clear that you'd never open your heart to love again. Do you have any idea how that statement caused me suffering for all these years?"

"I said that when I was a walking wound, totally abandoned. I was crawling off the battlefield"—she paused midsentence and looked directly into his eyes—"and trying to survive a nearly lethal shot to the heart." She withdrew her hand from Jude's and walked a few steps away from him. After a moment, she again faced him and spoke. "You say my statement caused you suffering? Do you have any idea how I've suffered?"

Every word she spoke was true. Jude was again astounded at her ability to speak forthrightly and to do so without a hint of anger or resentment. Those negative emotions had long ago been incinerated, since her life had been, in recent years, one sustained baptism by fire. Forgiveness, apparently, was not the issue. Neither was malice or resentment. The real issue was regaining the will to go on and, that done, clearing the air of all past misunderstanding.

But where to start? The fragility of their renewed acquaintance was painfully obvious to both. Even with their great love for each other, they knew another misstep, like that of the past, was a distinct possibility. The razor-thin ledge at the top of the canyon between them was difficult for even the best of mountain climbers. For novices with damaged emotions, smashed dreams, and shredded hearts, it was a tightrope walk across Niagara Falls.

"It's true, Cory. We've both been gashed badly by the events of the past."

Cory stopped walking and lifted her eyes to the clouds overhead. "Funny you should use the word 'gash.'"

"Why's that funny?"

"Because Pastor Gabe said the same thing in a recent sermon. In fact, he used the same word—gash."

Jude was relieved to hear this since it meant they could talk about a safe topic that would get them away from the precipice. "Do you remember what he said?"

"Yes, I do, but I prefer not to speak of it now if you don't mind. I prefer to drink in the delectable beauty of the present moment." She looked at him warmly. "I'm standing here with you. At least our bodies are side by side even if our emotions aren't." She laughed a bit, and Jude found enormous comfort in that.

By this time, they had ambled to the Civil War-era graves at the front part of the cemetery.

"Do you know, Cory, what the very worst part of the separation has been for me?"

"What?"

"Christmas."

She reflected for a moment. "I suppose so. Christmas is a tough holiday for the hurting, but what made it particularly difficult for you?"

"Every year I couldn't wait for the holidays to receive your Christmas card. Each card gave me hope that in time reconciliation might be possible. I couldn't wait. I'd always rush to the end of your handwritten note to see if you signed it, 'Love, Cory.' Those cards sustained me through many cold and lonely months. Even though we weren't seeing each other, you still signed your card with love. That was a glimpse into your true heart. That was the reality. The silence, the misunderstandings, the cold looks—well, those were just little pebbles on a yellow brick road."

He stopped speaking just to savor the moment. How beautiful she was! "When you stopped sending cards the last two years, I knew it was over for good. That's what killed me. I hated to see Christmas coming those last years because as I celebrated His life, I remembered our death. How does one live without hope?"

"The question of the ages. You sound like Solomon. 'By sorrow of the heart the spirit is broken.' Or something close to that."

"I prayed your love would be strong enough to forgive me and to start all over again. When I knew that the communication avenue between us had been shut off completely, I used to contemplate ways that I could speak to you again to let you know my heart. I agonized about the way I could show you my love."

Jude looked at her. The setting sun glistened in her blond hair like a fiery glow. He thought of Robert Burns—"O my love's like a red, red rose." He just wanted to look at her and not speak, but a question was in the air. He paused and looked across the summer fields. The sound of distant gas drilling on a neighboring farm was borne over the fields by the evening breeze. He looked in that direction not to locate the source of the sound but to muster strength for the biggest question of all. Finally, he worked up his nerve. "Do you want to start over again, Cory? Do you want to assure me that nothing's changed?"

She paused before she answered, took a few paces toward one of the grave markers, and turned to Jude to speak again. "I saw a recent TV special on those beautiful bald eagles in Alaska—huge creatures with eight-foot wingspans. The Alaskan eagles are bigger than the ones here in Pennsylvania."

Jude broke in excitedly, "I saw the same program." He wondered what this reference to eagles had to do with his question. Was she too playing the deflection game, or, even worse, was she running away from a negative answer she didn't have the courage to articulate?

"Then I won't need to describe it to you. But remember when it showed the two eagles, the male and the female, during their mating ritual?" Jude nodded. "I was so touched when I watched the heart-stopping way in which they prove their love or whatever it is they do during the mating ritual. For weeks I thought of the way the eagles lock talons and, together, start into their free fall from such a dizzying height—rolling and tumbling, spinning and turning in their death-defying declaration of love. I almost stopped breathing when I watched their entwined, spinning bodies get so close to the ground and, feet away, release their grip and swoop upward in that majestic, inverted heart pattern. I couldn't get that image out of my mind for weeks. So close to death and saved at last." She looked in his eyes. "And together forever."

"Same with me. But remember how the larger of the birds fell even farther than its mate and swooped even more dangerously close to the ground? I always imagined that larger eagle to be the male who swooped farther, dared more, and risked all. Sometimes I close my mind and watch them fall, wondering if that larger eagle will make it. What a flirtation with disaster! Does an eagle ever misjudge that hair-breadth space, roll too deeply, and not make it?"

Cory looked at him. How eagle-like Jude was to her—majestic, proud, regal. She quizzically asked, "Did you watch the whole program?"

"All but the very end."

"That explains the one detail I think you're misunderstanding."

"What's that?"

"You think the larger eagle is the male, and hence you picture yourself as the eagle who risks more by falling farther. Am I right?"

"Exactly."

"You miss a crucial point. The larger eagle is the female. She's the one that keeps falling, even after her companion swerves in the nick of time and rises to heights of majestic glory."

Jude didn't know how to respond to this comment. What was Cory's intent in saying this? They had been doing so well, and it looked as though reconciliation, in time, may happen. But what did she mean by this added detail of clarification? He spoke. "I see. So the female is the larger, more daring of the birds."

Another pause as they wandered amid the tombstones. He stopped and faced her directly. "Did the female eagle survive the fall? Do female eagles make it? Do they want to make it—I mean, to go on and, together, climb to that high atmosphere where, alone, they romp and roll and sing and soar? In other words, to love again?" He spoke with passion since the analogy had opened the door to this most important question.

Cory again paused before answering and framed her words carefully. "The eagle survived. But not all survivors are eagles."

Chapter 17

"Just what does that mean?" He tightly clasped her upper arms in his strong hands. "Sorry, Cory. I didn't mean to raise my voice, but so much is at stake here. Let me ask it again. Can you love me again, and do you want to start over?"

"More than anything in the world, Judah Hepler. You know I've always loved you. I worship the ground you walk on. If I weren't a Christian, I'd say that you are the god of my idolatry."

"Then you'd be quoting *Romeo and Juliet*! That line's from Shakespeare's play." He drew her close to him. "Remember how we cited lines from the Bard's plays by the hour? I think you had half of Shakespeare's plays memorized. Well, it seemed to me that when things got rough between us—I'm referring to the end right before we broke up—that you weren't hearing me. It seemed as though you didn't want to work through our differences. It got to the point that I was afraid to start over again or get in touch with you. You'd never let me talk about it. Remember, you did hang up on me a couple times and wouldn't return my phone calls. I cried over those repeated rebuffs for months. Talk about a death trudge through Siberia!"

"It was too painful to think about, all of it, especially the awful lunchroom incident at the very end. The phone calls, at least most of them, came right after it when I was livid and not thinking rationally." She looked helplessly at Jude. "Put yourself in my shoes. There I was in the lunchroom in the mine with all the gossipy women, when Tina

Reynolds ceremonially walks in like the queen of Sheba and pulls out some photos as though she's presenting magnificent Solomon with a gift of priceless frankincense. Right in the middle of the table she threw the eight-by-ten photos of you and Meg. Jude, I was shocked and enraged out of my mind! I couldn't think and couldn't hear myself above the cacophony of these mocking women. Their savagery still rings in my ears. 'They're sure having the time of their lives!' 'Jude's enjoying himself to the max!' 'What a stud!' 'Hey, Cory, I'd dump your true love, Jude, in a heartbeat. Yeah, you can sure tell he's crazy in love with you!' 'Who has his phone number? I'd like to have him show me such a good time! Ha! Ha.'

"Jude, I was mortified." Cory was speaking rapidly, her face flushed with anger as she relived the horror. She withdrew from Jude and faced the setting sun.

He couldn't prevent the tone of impatience in his voice. "We've been down that road before, Cory. You knew those were doctored photos. That was not me." He turned and also faced the setting sun. "But the damage to our reputations was incalculable. I know it greatly added to your pain." He put his arm around her shoulder. "I still can't believe we never found who pulled that awful prank."

"Yes, but a lot of water had gone under the bridge by the time I learned for certain that the photos weren't of you. By then I couldn't breathe life into my own dead emotions. I believed you, but try telling that to the others who gloat in my face even to this day. It was your face in the photo. You even admitted it. The mole on your shoulder blade, in their book, offered the final proof. I'll never forget that day in the parking lot when the guys pinned your arms while another pulled up your shirt. There was the mole on your shoulder blade big as day. They called you Mole behind your back for months. You were gone, steeped in books at IUP. I was stuck here listening to their endless taunts. 'Wonder who marvelous Mole's mooching today?' Imagine my embarrassment. I still cringe every time I think of it."

"If we could only find who made the photos. Someone's very clever."

"I'd say very evil."

"Yes, especially that." Walking in silence for a moment, Jude hesitated to mention one more aspect of the doctored photo, but his desire for closure got the better of him. "Do you think the business with the photo was the main reason we split up?"

Walking in the cemetery a few more steps, Cory remained silent. Soon, backlit by the setting sun, she answered his question. "It didn't help. But I have to be honest and say it wasn't the main reason. The bigger problem was my old fear."

"What do you mean?"

"My fear of a deep relationship. Every time we'd draw close, I'd do something to sabotage the relationship. Think of that. Think of the times I ran from you. I think I was afraid of the road ahead. Hiding was the safer path."

"You never said that before. I guess that explains a lot—the unanswered phone calls and letters, the cold shoulder at church functions."

"I didn't mean to hurt you. I honestly didn't. I was just so confused in those years and didn't know how to handle love. It scared me. You scared me. Pretty sick stuff, isn't it?"

"I could have done better at winning you over and convincing you that our love was safe and beautiful. But I really did try. Surely you know that!"

By this time, at the top of the cemetery, they stopped walking and looked across the fields toward the McKelvey homestead. Cory resumed speaking. "Look at the deep blue color of the sky above the homestead. Does that shade of blue remind you of a painting we used to talk about?"

"Not particularly."

"That sky is exactly like Vincent Van Gogh's *Gardening Patches on Montmartre in Winter*. Remember that beautiful blue sky in his painting?"

"Yes, I do now that you mention it. You have that painting in the book on the Impressionist painters I gave you as a Christmas present, right?"

"Yes."

Away from the church and road, Jude stopped talking, moved closer to Cory, and put his arms around her. She edged toward him hesitantly. "I love you, Cory. You mean everything to me." He drew her tightly to him. Cory's giant teardrops fell on his shirt collar.

"I love you too, Jude. I always have, and I always will. You're the love of my life. I have waited for this moment. I've dreamed about it for years." She squeezed her body tightly to his.

"May it never end. May nothing ever come between us again." Jude kissed her. Not the passionate kiss of bygone years, but their lips met for that joyous instant.

Cory cuddled her head onto Jude's shoulder. Bathing herself in the beauty of the moment, she said nothing and reached over to Jude's shirt to straighten the collar. "What are we going to do about Duke? Maybe you haven't heard of his violent rage. Just how do we get out of this mess? How do I get out of this mess? Duke's the strongest guy I've ever seen. His feats of strength on the farm are unbelievable. His biceps bulge like Superman's."

What to do about Duke? That was the question. "Cory," he said, treading cautiously owing to the toxicity of the question, "how did you ever get tangled up with him?"

Jude was greatly relieved when she showed no signs of displeasure and answered immediately. "He started coming around and offered much-needed help on the farm. My poor dad broke into a smile every time he showed his face. Duke plowed and harrowed the fields himself and worked with Joey by the hour to do the work Dad could no longer do. He wouldn't take a cent and genuinely enjoyed helping Dad. I felt in his debt. After his endless badgering, I decided to go out with him a time or two as a way of saying thanks. I intended to be kind and civil and then end it right there. The idea seemed perfectly workable. I had no way of knowing that he was borderline alcoholic, nor did I know about his savage temper. He masks this away from the workers most of the time." She brushed the hair away from the side of her face. "I didn't know he'd become a parasite. He just doesn't take no for an answer. Dad thinks he walks on water because of all he's done at the farm."

Words came out of her like a torrent as she reflected on the past months. She continued. "I can't get the courage to tell Dad the truth about Duke. I just don't know what to do. I'm afraid of what he'd do if I walked away, and I'm totally scared to death of what he'd do to you. I told you, the guy's built like Samson."

Her description touched a nerve in Jude. "Cory, has he abused you in any way whatsoever? Please tell me."

Cory looked away and didn't speak.

Chapter 18

Cory looked across the fields at the old McKelvey farmhouse. How many happy memories they shared on that farm—basketball games under the summer spotlight, pickup football games in the side lawn, wiener roasts in the adjoining field under the moon, hayrides that had started there by the old barn. Life was so simple and beautiful then. How often Mr. McKelvey had cut Joey's and her dad's hair there in the front room of that ancient farmhouse.

"He hasn't hit me," Cory finally responded. "But his verbal abuse has become more frequent of late." She curled her lip in anger. "He feeds on my own self-deprecatory nature."

"What in the world does that mean? You sound like a psychologist!"

"I think you know. I have such personal disgust and self-loathing at times for letting us split up—I mean you and me—and for what I've become in life that I sometimes think I use him to inflict on me the punishment I deserve. I'm such a failure, Jude." She looked at him through pitiful eyes. "What do I have to show for my life? You have moved on, are somebody on campus, and have a life in front of you. You'd need a railway boxcar to hold your dreams. Mine would fit in a thimble, and my accomplishments would get lost on a pinhead." She paused as tears filled her eyes. "Do you know how much that hurts, especially for one who had been pegged for big success when in high school? You have seen my high school yearbook. There are as many pictures of me in that yearbook as any other person. Here's a question for you, Professor. Where's the great Corinna Adelena Mohney today?"

"Cory, do you know how sick that is? I mean the bit about how you sabotage yourself out of a need to inflict punishment on yourself. Come on, Cory. You know grace makes possible total forgiveness. That includes forgiveness for ourselves when we really mess up. As both of us did in mangling this love, which is the best and most beautiful thing the two of us have ever experienced."

"Yes, I know it's sick, but self-laceration doesn't turn off like a light switch. I'm my own worst scourge." Cory felt comfortable enough to plummet to the depths. "Here's what happened. Duke's compassion filled the gap at a time when I was emotionally vulnerable. Silence on your end ate away at my heart like leprosy and, in the end, destroyed the final vestiges of my self-confidence." She drew closer to him and again fidgeted with his collar. "Jude, let me be perfectly honest with you. I intend no abuse here, nor am I trying to put more nails in my own coffin. I love you too much for that."

She stopped again as she summoned strength to speak the difficult truth. The setting sun filtered through the clouds on the distant horizon, amber speckles of gold that fairy-dusted her blond hair. "You need to know the whole truth. Those long, empty days even destroyed my will to live. There I said it. The worst part's over. It can only get better from here." She closed her eyes and faced the sun. "Maybe."

"Cory, forgive me. I ask again, will you ever be able to forgive me?"

"I already did. I told you that. I forgave you when I first saw you at the mine. I forgive you with every prayer. But your sweet words don't fill the crater in my heart. They don't rewire the emotional circuitry in my brain. They don't expunge the pain of my five-year suicide note. See my point? And here's the real death knell. Our forgiving each other doesn't remove Duke Manningham from our lives."

"But I need to hear that sweet music of forgiveness again and again." They took a few more steps walking hand in hand. Each enjoyed the lovely quiet of the evening and the magic of being side by side. The tenseness gone, hope had once again been reborn. Deep in thought, Jude commenced speaking. "Why can't you just stop seeing Duke? Just tell him you're no longer interested. People move on all the time. Why can't you? In our day, many relationships are short term, and in the mine more than a few are one-night stands. We both know that to be true. So why can't it happen in your case?"

On and on they talked in the growing dusk. When they came down the cemetery road a short while later, they noted that the flowers annually planted around grave headstones for the coming Memorial Day weekend were already blooming. They held hands, looked at each other, and smiled. Tears, this time of joy, filled their eyes.

Pastor Gabriel Wyant and Professor Charles Claypoole were exiting the church as the couple came down the cemetery lane. Having completed their conversation about Charles' serving as assistant director for the upcoming production of *Hamlet* in Pittsburgh, they stood on the back porch of the church facing the cemetery. When they heard voices, they looked up and saw the two lovers at the top of the knoll. Gabriel and Charles slyly winked at each other, elated to see this precious sight for which both had prayed for many long months.

Charles spoke quietly to Gabriel as Cory and Jude came into sight. "Here comes our own Hamlet! He reminds me of Shakespeare's protagonist more than any man I've ever met. And he's every bit as articulate. I don't think there's a professor in our department as communicative as Jude Hepler." Looking again at the strolling couple, Charles spoke again. "When have you ever seen a happier sight? I have to admit I never thought they'd ever get back together. I know. You'll say that's the skeptic coming out in me."

"You're right—he's our Center Hill Hamlet!" The men waved in the lovers' direction. "Hi, Cory and Jude!" Gabriel shouted up the hill. As the lovers walked down the road, he turned to Charles and quietly spoke. "Oh ye, of little faith. I always believed God would answer our prayer for their reunion. My point to Jude and Cory is that they don't need to repeat or relive that past horror. They can grow beyond it. I read that very point in my devotional this morning. In fact, it made such an impression on me that I wrote it down." Pastor Gabe took out a folded a scrap of paper from his pocket New Testament. "Here it is. It's a quotation by Maya Angelou." He turned sideways so that the sun illuminated the note. "'History, despite its wrenching pain, cannot be unlived, but if faced with courage, need not be lived again.' That's good, Charles, very good. That's my point to Cory and Jude. They can't unlive the past, but they need not drag its horror into the future."

"Hello!" Jude and Cory replied in near perfect unison as they neared the bottom of the knoll.

"They're absolutely beaming," the preacher whispered. "I haven't seen joy like that on Cory's face for years! I give you Jairus' daughter raised from the dead. Hallelujah!"

"Yes, what a beautiful sight! I didn't think joy like that was possible. Well, good-bye, Gabriel. I imagine you're calling it quits for the day?" Charles massaged his breast as they spoke.

"Not quite yet. Old Mary's been ailing of late, so I thought I'd stroll down the hill to see her. She's typically on her porch swing on summer evenings. She likes to watch her hummingbirds feed."

"Tell her I said hello and that I'll drop by to see her soon. She promised to tell me the entire rose vision someday. I need to hear all those wonderful details sometime. It's an amazing story that's been with her most of her life. She's been quiet about it for years, but it's come into her mind of late. She wants to talk about it."

As they waved good-bye, they saw Jude and Cory walk down the tombstone-lined cemetery lane, cross Old Freeport Road, and enter the parking lot, Jude's arm tightly clasped around Cory. The pastor nudged Charles in the arm. "I say again, have you ever seen a more joyful sight?"

That evening, Jude and Cory walked alone on Vinlindeer above their farms underneath the moon. Such was the nature of their love for each other that in a single conversation they had swept away most of the hurt, the differences, the fears, and the confusion of the five silent years. They loved each other with a passion even greater than that of the past. The deep hurt enabled them to see the rarity of their beautiful love. People in a fallen world dream of such love, frantically search for it, but find it infrequently. Jude and Cory had walked through a minefield and lived to talk about it. Safe in each other's arms on the other side, they clutched each other tightly as they looked back in horror.

Jude spoke. "That's a smoking and mangled ruin that nearly annihilated us forever!"

Chapter 19

Earlier in his career, Charles Claypoole had opportunities to move to a big state university but settled for the quaint and academically prestigious Grove City College in Western Pennsylvania. Because of its successful, nationally renowned tangles with the federal government, all of which the college had won, he had sought it as his first choice. He was elated to have been appointed professor of literature there, and his having been named a recipient of a lifetime distinguished chair was the highest academic commendation of his illustrious career.

A deep thinker by nature, he became intrigued with Jude Hepler from the time little Jude first started visiting his grandpa and grandma's farm as a young boy. He knew the young lad had been traumatized by his grandpa's death, but because no one would talk about it, Charles had difficulty, both then and now, piecing together the tragic events in young Jude's life. Rosetta Wakefield had sealed her lips, and Jude too had apparently been sworn to some sort of secrecy.

In itself, that didn't matter so much, but what did matter was the effect of the tragedy on Jude. The report in the village was that the young boy had been present the day of the accident and had been seriously affected by it. The whole incident, nevertheless, had been locked up in the community's historic chronicles. To them the past was dead; they had mourned it extensively, and there was little one could do but move on. These were hardworking farmers, and prodigal wallowing in counterproductive emotions was a luxury that life's struggles didn't afford and faith didn't allow.

But the professor could not let it rest. There were too many unanswered questions and too many ongoing reminders of the tragedy. So this evening, after seeing Jude and Cory reunited in love at the church, the professor upon entering his study took an old folder from his desk and glanced over various documents—notes, scraps of paper, photocopies, and sketches. The common denominator of all of them? Jude Hepler and his grandpa Jeremiah Wakefield. The real breakthrough—the signal event that had ignited his heightened interest in Jude—was his fortuitous conversation a few years earlier with Dr. William Wilburn, one of Jude's professors at IUP. It had occurred near the end of Jude's sophomore year when Charles bumped into Dr. Wilburn at a Ray Charles concert in Fisher Auditorium on the IUP campus.

The conversation began with a simple hello, but when the two professors learned that they shared the same interest in the bright and variously talented Jude Hepler, a friendship started more or less on the spot. Before the evening was over, Charles Claypoole, accompanying Dr. Wilburn to his office, had been invited to peruse Jude's end-of-semester writing portfolio. Since there was nothing private about the file—members of the class and friends routinely read each other's material and responded to it—Dr. Wilburn experienced no ethical qualms in sharing Jude's essays and scraps of poetry. He even invited Charles to take them so that he could peruse the writing samples more carefully.

Moments later, Charles was seated in Stapleton Library looking with rapt attention through Jude's notebook, papers, essays, and even sketches in the margins of his notebooks. What a treasure trove it was! He felt like an intruder, but still he knew the mission was justified, given his honest intent to get to the bottom of Jude's pain. He availed himself of the professor's offer to "photocopy as much as you want. After all, we're doing this for Jude's good."

On his way out of the library an hour later, Charles met Professor Wilburn again. Charles spoke first. "I can't thank you enough for sharing this information. I return it to you with deepest gratitude."

"You're more than welcome. As I said earlier, Jude has intrigued me from the first day he sat in my composition class. My interest was considerably piqued when I got to know him more fully in a later English majors course on the Romantic poets. I've never seen anyone read more intensely and identify with the great poets so completely as Jude Hepler. When we were reading Keats's great odes, the students witnessed this deep connection—Jude's unique way of seeing into the heart of things. One of them even quipped, 'I think you're John Keats reincarnated, and your comments during class discussions are every bit as poetic!'"

"Did you realize that some of the pieces, like a couple of the poems, the marginal cartoon doodles, and the essay about mushroom growing in Western Pennsylvania, are decidedly autobiographical?"

"No, I didn't," Dr. Wilburn responded. "How can you be so certain?"

"Because Jude actually worked in the mushroom mine. Because the sketch of a man falling in the barn artistically renders an event he actually witnessed as a young boy. Because the Lara of the poems is modeled on the love of his life—Cory Mohney."

"Really?" Dr. Wilburn's heart skipped a beat. "I had no idea he was drawing on real events so completely, though I suspected that he, like most writers, was invoking past events to some degree. That surely offers important insights into the poems and even more the man. Did you have a chance to glance at the scraps of poems?"

"Yes, I did."

"The one about the lovers canoeing on the stream?"

"I know the exact place he describes in the poem. I've been there many times and have actually fished for trout in that very stream. It's a place called Beatty's Mill."

"Well, I'll be! I wish you'd stay in touch, Professor Claypoole."

"Please call me Chuck."

"Good. And I'm Bill. Let me know if I can be of further help. You have a monumental task in front of you. Good day then."

The men shook hands and parted. Professor Wilburn turned to walk into the library, but a thought struck him, and he quickly turned as Charles Claypoole descended the steps.

"Chuck," he called.

Professor Claypoole turned around at the bottom of the stairs.

"I have one more question," Dr. Wilburn began. "Jude always struggled when it came time to write the creative material. He'd fly through the expository essays and rhetorical modes—persuasion, argumentation, comparison/contrast, and the like. But he always held back on the creative writing assignments. He completed them with difficulty, even reluctance, as if he resisted creative writing. Those couple poems were the most I could get out of him. That always baffled me because those assignments are usually the students' favorites. I'd question him about it, but he'd always clam up. Are you aware of this reticence or have any insights into its cause?"

"I actually did know of it."

"Does he still have it?"

"As far as I know. I don't have the reason, but I'd bet money it relates to his grandpa's death. You see he too was a writer. I have no idea how all these pieces connect. Maybe the two of us together can solve the problem!"

"I didn't know a thing about the grandfather's death." Dr. Wilburn paused and looked across the Oak Grove. "What a fascinating young man!"

"I completely agree. Good evening." The men departed.

Chapter 20

In his study that evening, Charles once again pored over the contents of the "Jude folder"—notes from his conversation with Dr. Wilburn several years ago, a photocopy of Jude's writing portfolio with its sketches of a man standing on a high pile of hay bales at the top of a barn loft, another of a man in a midflight fall, his arms gesticulating wildly as he hurtles through space. A fragment of a couple poems—one entitled "Ode to Corinna"—but none of them finished. The Jude mystery. What did it all mean? And how did this material fill in the gaps about this mysterious young man?

Jude was in many ways an open book under the penetrating gaze of the professor, but some of the key events in his past remained impenetrably sealed in a coffin of lead. Of what import were they, and did they offer any insight into this on-and-off love relationship between Jude and Cory? He vowed again to get to the bottom of the mystery. All locks have keys—he indulged the cliché—and surely this one did too.

That was one village mystery and for the time being perhaps the most significant, but in Charles' opinion there were several others, including the whereabouts of Jude's grandpa's novel. What had become of this monumental novel that had consumed years of Jeremiah's life? Why did Jeremiah feel the need to bury this manuscript, which he had been writing across years? When speaking to Jeremiah in the final weeks of his life, Charles detected a kind of irrationality. Unlike himself,

Jeremiah was a person of great faith who worried about virtually nothing through his long life. But near the end, he had developed pronounced and unprecedented fears. Had Jeremiah slipped into dementia in the final months of his life and his burying the novel its sad manifestation? How could one possibly begin to solve these mysteries?

Charles Claypoole fanned out Jude's papers on his desk and turned to another official-looking document in his file—the contract for the lost novel that the publisher had sent him. After signing and notarizing the document, Jeremiah had been instructed to return it, upon receipt of which the advance would be issued immediately. To think Jeremiah had already found a publisher for the buried manuscript! The document filled Charles with great sadness. He remembered that Jeremiah was completing his reading of the manuscript and was all set to mail it. Why had he buried it instead?

The next paper in the file was a copy of the signed contract he had with his publisher concerning another book, *Growing up in Western Pennsylvania: Voices from the Farm*. The professor looked to his bookshelf, and there was the book. This one had been published, and while it merely recorded a series of short stories and anecdotes that related to rural village life in bygone years, the superb writing style was evident, especially in the latter chapters. This early book was Jeremiah's prologue, "written to find my voice and to better prepare myself for the coming magnum opus," as Jeremiah related to Charles.

Another paper in the file was a copy of a letter Jeremiah had written to Abe Badoane. Only half the torn letter was present in the folder. Jeremiah commenced the letter with introductory greetings and then proceeded to the lines that so deeply stirred Charles: "You, Abe, are the better writer. You're the one whose book should have been published. I hope and pray that you will live to write it. Don't be discouraged. Past failures matter little. What matters is the future, which invitingly beckons to you. Even multiple failures do not a great life wreck. 'A righteous man may fall seven times *and rise again*' (Proverbs 24:16). Or as David the psalmist says, 'Though he fall, he shall not be utterly cast down. For the Lord upholds him with His hand' (37:24). Rise again, Abe, rise again to live, to dream, and to love! Though you have fallen, you are not utterly cast down. Rise, Abe, rise! He *will* uphold you. Warmly, Jeremiah." Those lines embodied Jeremiah Wakefield's spirit—humble, other-centered, contrite, and compassionate.

After examining the contents of this mystery file, Charles picked up the phone to call Pastor Gabriel. "Hello, Gabriel. You weren't in bed, were you? Sorry for calling so late."

"Not a problem, Charles. When have I not had time to talk to you? No, I wasn't in bed."

"You're too kind, Gabriel. My seeing Jude and Cory of late has awakened the old mysteries we've spoken of in the past. I know Jude has a genuinely warm and caring nature, but he also has a secretive, inaccessible side." Charles toyed with the telephone cord. "Why have we never been able to penetrate it? That's what's on my mind and my reason for calling." A pause while Pastor Gabriel responded. "Yes, but it's not the only reason. Another problem perplexes me every bit as much. Whatever happened to Jeremiah's novel? Do you think we'll ever be able to find it? I'm wondering if you've unearthed any pieces of the missing puzzle over recent months. I just can't believe we've never been able to locate this important work."

"No, I hate to admit it, but I've gotten nowhere either. You do amaze me, my skeptical professor friend. You're normally too pessimistic to think such a good turn of events could result after so many barren years." He paused for a moment as he mulled over recent events. "Plus, there are other related factors that make this village's Gordian knot even more difficult. I've been thinking anew of why Jude doesn't write. A person of his communicative prowess would make an excellent wordsmith. I can't make any headway as to why Jude doesn't forge ahead with his personal writing. You've said that his professors readily testify to that, as do his past writing efforts, yet he won't write anything other than the scholarly essays that, according to his own testimony, bore him to tears. When I used to bring this matter up to him years ago, he flippantly responded, yet I know he was dying to write. Has he tried any creative writing in the years while he was away?"

"I can't believe you're bringing up the topic of his professors. Had I ever told you about my conversation with Dr. Wilburn in IUP's English Department? Jude had been enrolled in a couple of his classes during his undergraduate years. Dr. Wilburn said he always saw Jude as holding back, always tentative, almost afraid to write. Dr. Wilburn even allowed me to look through Jude's writing portfolio. But even that doesn't solve the overwhelming question—the source of his fear, if indeed it is a fear. Do you think it connects to his grandpa's death? I've often thought it may, but how can we prove it? More to the point, what good would it do if we did prove it?"

"These are difficult questions to answer. And this added consideration complicates it even more. I refer to Cory. Do any of them relate to her?"

"I have no idea, nor have we recovered those missing details of what happened that dreadful day in the barn when Jeremiah died. Surely that was the defining moment in little Jude's life. He witnessed it all and has suffered through it alone these many years. From what I understand, he can't even talk to Rosetta about it. The past is a cancerous growth to her. So Jude has no recourse but to let the cancer eat away at his soul."

"I quite agree. I know there are other questions that can and probably should be added to the complicated mix, especially a very large one."

"Which one do you have in mind? Surely that's enough inexplicable problems for one small community!"

"Yes, I agree, but nevertheless there is another huge one. What do you make of mystery man Abe? You seem to know a fair amount about him, Charles. Like to fess up someday? When we speak of secretive topics, that one's near the top of my list. Understand, I don't know the man. He's never attended church once during my time here, but I often see him in the community. And I've been told that you were friends of sorts in bygone days."

"It's a deal. We'll talk someday. But to break the ice on this topic, I'll give you one truly intriguing aspect of mystery man Abe to think about in the meantime. I've never known what to make of his love of children. People say they've never seen anyone take to young kids as he does and in a completely wholesome way. It even gets the notice of some of those tough characters in the mine. I've heard them speak of the magic tricks Abe does around kids. Yes, we'll get together soon so I can give you a little background on Abe—at least some info you may not know."

"We need to talk, Charles. What about coffee someday soon?"

"Sounds great. Just name the day." Charles was looking at a picture of Jude with his grandma as they neared the end of their conversation. "And when we do, I wonder if we ought to explore another avenue I've never had the nerve to pursue."

"What's that?"

"Talking to Rosetta."

"She was just here in church."

"Yes, I saw her. Recall that all those years ago she wouldn't talk at all about the accident. Clammed up tighter than a Malayan box turtle. Do you think I ought to give her a ring and gently work my way to the forbidden subject?"

"Why not? Jeremiah loved you, and out of respect for that friendship, Rosetta might just disclose in a way she hasn't to this point. Having Jude with her this summer and knowing his love for Cory might leverage Rosetta just a bit."

"I'll call her right now. It's not that late. Good night, Gabe."

"Good evening, sir."

After hanging up the phone, the pastor came to the kitchen table to join his wife, Martha, and relate the details of his conversation with Charles. Martha listened intently, since she always had an interest in Jude, Cory, the two families, Abe Badoane, Old Mary, and many others. In her perceptive mind, they linked together in a complex drama. She had been especially saddened by Jeremiah's tragic death in the barn, the loss of his novel, and its impact on Jude. It was generally known that Jude's grandpa had uttered some words to little Jude before he died. According to hearsay, Jeremiah had even spoken, held up his arm, and said he had hurt it in the fall. But what did he say to Jude? Why couldn't Jude remember those important dying words that possibly contained the key to the novel's whereabouts? How the entire tragedy must have scarred that seven-year-old boy!

Sitting at the table and sipping their bedtime cup of tea, resourceful Martha hit on an idea. "Gabe, I just thought of something. We know that Jeremiah buried the novel before his death. We assume that he might have said something about its location to little Jude with his dying words. Why not preach a sermon about a Bible story that centers on something being hidden? Maybe this will enable Jude to dredge his subconscious mind and locate the words he has hidden." She looked at Gabriel to study his reaction and then continued. "The event was so traumatic that he probably repressed it completely."

"Excellent, Martha. Yes, and 'by indirections find directions out.'"

"I have no idea what that means."

"It's a line from *Hamlet*! I can do that. It's the one Shakespeare play I know pretty well by the way. I could preach on Achan's hiding the treasure in the book of Joshua or maybe Christ's parable of the hidden treasure. We could tell Charles to watch Jude's reaction, just as Hamlet and Horatio watch Claudius' reaction during the staging of *The Murder of Gonzago*. That's a short play Hamlet asks a traveling troupe to perform for the king and queen. At any rate, maybe the sermon will prompt him to dredge up Jeremiah's last agonizing utterances—that hidden treasure of words." He drained the last sip of tea in his cup. "It's worth a shot. Great idea, Martha—thanks! I'll tell Charles about this right away." He smiled warmly to his wife, who had faithfully stood by him through many years of ministry.

Gabriel was on the phone in minutes. "Charles, hello, this is Gabe." A pause. "Yes, I know we just spoke." Another brief pause. "Martha came through yet again. She thinks I ought to preach on a Bible story that centers on burying something or possibly a hidden treasure. I could easily work such a hiding motif into my current series." A pause as Charles responded. "Here's where you come in. During the sermon, you position yourself so that you can watch Jude, especially his reaction when I start to explore the hiding theme. Carefully note his body language. Such a parallel might force Jude to rummage through the treasure of words stored in his brain and locate the missing handful!" Another longer pause. "Thank you, Charles, but I take zero credit. This is Martha's brainstorm. I'll keep you posted on the details. 'There are more things in heaven and earth, Horatio, Than are dreamt of in your philosophy.' Good night."

"One more thing, Gabe, before we hang up. I just spoke with Rosetta. You wouldn't believe it. She was cross with me. Gentle Rosetta, ever the picture of calm, even raised her voice a little. She said I was never to bring up the 'forbidden subject' again. Imagine that. I was dumbfounded. So much for thinking time has healed that wound!"

"We have to respect her wishes and tackle the mystery from a different angle. Don't worry about Rosetta. She's a good soul and will settle down. The topic remains too tender for her to talk about. She's probably addled at seeing Jude's strife with Cory. Jude's daily presence has most likely awakened many memories of Jeremiah. Good try, Charles. Sleep well."

Chapter 21

The next morning at the mine, Jude, preparing for the workday, was in the locker room where the workers kept their personal belongings. As he made his way to his locker, he saw Abe Badoane bent over and unaware of his presence. Jude warmly said hello as he came near him, and Abe, taken aback that someone was nearby, nervously stuffed something into his locker and hastily locked the door. Jude paid no attention to this gesture even though Abe was embarrassed. It was none of Jude's business, so he chose not to notice it, but later when Jude reconstructed the events of that summer, he flashed back to that seemingly insignificant event and only then realized its importance.

That same morning, Abe returned from one of his runs to the packhouse, having delivered thousands of freshly picked mushrooms for packaging and shipping. Knowing that his crew wouldn't need him for a while, he detoured into a nearby corridor and sought out Bull Chestnut, one of Duke's friends in the mine. Duke was nobody's dummy. Abe recounted different instances when Duke's intellectual prowess was clearly evident. Abe, for instance, one day at lunch several months back spoke of the Revolutionary War and Benedict Arnold's betrayal of his country but couldn't come up with the name of the British officer with whom Arnold had planned to turn over West Point to the British. During the moment when Abe rummaged through his mental database, Duke spoke. "It was Andre."

"Excellent, Duke," the dumbfounded Abe had commented.

One of his cronies quipped, "How'd you know that, brains?"

Such instances of Abe sharing info on hundreds of topics were quite frequent, especially during lunches when he recounted the history of the county or the nation and offered tidbits of information. In another instance, Abe was speaking of Pickett's Charge at Gettysburg. During a lull, as Abe in an uncharacteristic moment had to grapple for names of Southern generals, Duke jumped in. "Pickett gets the credit for the heroic July 3rd charge, but many Southern officers, and not just Pickett, were involved. Let me see. You got your Pettigrew, Longstreet, Kemper, Garnett, Armistead, and others." Some of the men surrounding him looked in amazement. Duke, an intellectual? "How'd you come up with all those names?" "You're gettin' as bad as Abe knowing all this nonsense!"

Cory and a couple of Duke's close friends were not surprised by this exhibition of learning because they had come to know of his interest in knowledge generally and of history in particular. Duke had performed decently in high school and aspired to go either to college or at least a technical school, but the allurement of a good-paying job derailed him from his master plan, and so, years later, here he was— still in the mine and going nowhere fast.

Bull, on the other hand, was not, in Duke's sarcastic language, "the most gifted mind on the planet." Making fun of Bull's naiveté and lapses of common sense, Duke laughingly said to his face, "You, Bull, are the dumbest, most gullible guy in the mine. You might be well endowed physically, but you sure aren't mentally."

Bull and Duke along with a handful of others were good drinking buddies who enjoyed their hunting and fishing outings like mid-April's opening day of trout season in Western Pennsylvania. This annual ritual for area sportsmen was often the occasion of bawdy anecdotes, endless ribbing, and peals of laughter, especially for Duke and Bull. Their escapades to the mountains were even more notorious in the mine. Bull's hunting camp was near famous Benezett in Elk County, Duke's near Penfield in Clearfield County. Their antics became the source of conversation and bantering for weeks on end, especially the jokes that Duke managed to pull on Bull. After one of the outings, Bull was heard to say after the opening day of buck season, "I had such a good time I might even take a gun next year!"

Abe Badoane's name for Bull was Stooge, and while he didn't frequently call him that to his face, Abe had often manipulated him so subtly that Bull remained oblivious to Abe's conniving. Today's instance, another in a long series, was a key component in Abe's master plan. Driving his mule on a return trip from the packhouse past Bull's crew, Abe thought about Bull. Compared to many of the hardworking men in the mine, especially the muscular Duke, Bull was pudgy and out of shape—"endomorphic as compared to Duke's mesomorphic build"—as Abe commented to Bull one day in the lunchroom. His round face, bushy eyebrows, and slicked, greasy hair set him apart from the other men. Bull's slumped shoulders and shuffling walk were so distinguishable that people identified him a couple hundred feet away. Drawing near, Abe reflected more on his character than his appearance. How could a man be so sexually obsessed and so carnally minded that little else in life mattered? "They're jungle creatures," Abe reflected, "little more than naked apes, crops of hair about their napes."

As he approached Bull's crew, Abe drove quickly, acting as though he was in a hurry to get somewhere. He waved to Bull in typical fashion, shouted a hearty hello, and continued on his way as he passed him. Pretending an idea had just come to mind, he screeched to a halt and backed up to Bull, who was slightly separated from his crew. Abe pulled his mule to the side of the corridor and climbed down to speak to Bull.

"Hey, Bull. I only have a second. I have to get to an important meeting, but take a look at this." He peeked around to make sure they were alone. "Seeing you here gave me the idea that you might want to see this precious little gem." He reached in his wallet and pulled out a photo. "Have you ever seen anything as lovely as this?"

"What you got there, Smiley?"

Abe handed him an alluring photo of Cory, posing seductively. A man, only part of his body visible, stood behind her.

"Unbelievable!" Bull said. "Holy moly, she's gorgeous! Who would ever think Cory looked like that?"

"So you've been taken in all this while, Bull. Don't you get it, El Dumbo? Cory's pious, religious act is just that—an act. More than one man has told me from firsthand experience that she's hot as blazes. Can't you see? As I like to say, she's the mistress of the mine, the tigress of the tunnels, the cunning courtesan of the cool corridors."

"You gotta be kidding! Cory Mohney? The religion nut?" Bull looked at the photo in disbelief, guffawed, and said to Abe, "Get out of here! I can't believe this is Cory Mohney. This has to be phony."

"So you too have been sucked in by her Miss Goody-Goody routine! You can't be that dumb, Bull! Are you going to be the last one in the mine to see through her? Well, I wouldn't want to damage your reputation for stupidity. Just keep swallowing her Miss Righteous act. Okay, this photo is a lie. It's a figment of my imagination. It doesn't exist, and these aren't reality either."

"I can't believe it. Look at that body, and look how she holds her shoulders back. Who'd have guessed she had all that beauty hidden underneath those sweatshirts! Tina, move over. You've just been bumped to second place in the Miss Beautiful contest. Look at her. I can't believe it."

"If you want proof, check with Butch. He said he thought he was tangling with a tiger that last time he was with her. Wonder if Duke knows what he's dealing with or maybe what he's missing." Abe looked at his watch. "Hey, look at the time. I gotta run. Keep this under your hat, okay? No need to tell anyone. Promise? Good!"

With that, Abe shuffled the photo into place in his wallet, but as he did so, a couple other photos fell out and landed at Bull's feet. Younger than Abe by a few decades, Bull deftly bent over and picked them up before Abe had a chance to do so. "Hey, give those to me!" Abe screamed. Abe reached out to grab them, but Bull turned his back and darted away from him, thinking he might have the chance to see other girlie photos, maybe even additional pictures of Cory.

Bull looked at them, but what a disappointment. He was looking at two school pictures of a handsome, smiling boy, probably about ten, Bull figured. Who cares? On the other hand, what were school pictures of a young boy doing in Abe's wallet? Did he have family members whom people didn't know about? Nonplussed that Bull had seen them, Abe grabbed them out of his hand. He jumped back on the tractor, flashed Bull a look of disgust, and raced off. Bull didn't see the look of savagery on his face or hear the cursing as Abe sped off. "You stupid man!"

Except for Bull's seeing the photo of the young boy, the brief exchange had gone exactly as Abe had planned. After Abe pulled away, Bull bounced into his seat and raced off to the packhouse with his loaded trays of mushrooms.

Watching him depart, Abe thought of the proverb he had memorized in Sunday school class: "He who sends a message by the hand of a fool cuts off his own feet and drinks violence (26:6)." *Well, in this case I won't be cutting off my own feet. True, I send a message by the hand of a fool, but it will accomplish my purpose!*

At the packhouse, Bull inquired about Duke's whereabouts and learned that he had just finished his run there and had returned to his crew. "I just missed him!"

Moments later, Bull took a side route to Duke's crew.

Chapter 22

rriving there, he told Duke about the picture that Abe had shown him. "I don't believe it. It couldn't have been Cory, Mr. Einstein. Bull, you're dumber than I thought! You gotta be twins. One guy couldn't be such a moron."

"Duke, I'm telling you it was Cory. She has the most gorgeous body I've ever seen. I'm telling you, she was unbelievable. If you don't believe me, ask Abe to see the photo."

"I'm still not convinced. Cory's the most religious girl I know. She doesn't miss a day reading her Bible. She's even been trying to get me off the booze, and her plan's working. I've been sober for two weeks. Posing for a suggestive photo is completely impossible." Duke took his helmet off and ran his fingers through his hair. "Cory Mohney? Sorry, genius, no way. You've been taken in again. Brainless wonder, when are you going to learn?"

"Yeah? Think again. Abe's talked to different men who have been with her. He even gave me their names. And there was a dude standing behind her in this photo. Okay, brains, don't believe me if you don't want to. But she's one hot-to-trot babe, and you're blowing it, man. You have no idea what you're missing." With that, Bull drove off.

By himself, Duke looked back in Cory's direction. She was bent over, her jeans stretched tight as she picked one of the lower beds. The shapely figure was real. There had never been any denying that, but surely Bull wasn't right. Yet what was one to make of the photo?

How could that lie? He wanted proof. "Until I see that photo, I'm not going to believe anything."

After his next drop, Duke had a few leisure moments. In charge of his crew as all the drivers of the personnel carriers were, he made sure the women were picking as ordered and departed briefly. "I'll be gone only a few minutes to run an errand." He barked his order, "Keep picking and no clowning around. And I mean it!" Off he sped. He knew of Abe's location and went directly to him.

Moments later, he tracked down Abe. "Hey, Smiley, what's this I hear of a photo of Cory?"

"I see Bull found you already. I told him to keep his mouth shut. The guy's an idiot. Well, the picture's nothing. One of the guys thought I might be interested, so he gave it to me when he quit working at the mine. Do you remember Butch McCluskey?" Duke indicated that he didn't. "I didn't think so. He was one of the truck drivers for a short time. I wasn't even going to show this picture to you, but I came across it last evening when I was throwing out some old papers. On my way to work this morning, I picked it up out of my waste basket thinking you might be interested. It's no big deal."

"I want to see it. I told Bull I don't believe that it's Cory in the photo."

"You don't believe it's Cory? Now who's being Mr. Stupid? Well, I wasn't going to show it to you no matter what Bull said, but since you want proof, take a look for yourself, and you decide."

The trap was perfectly laid. Abe nonchalantly reached for his wallet, pulled out the photo, and handed it to Duke. He even had the audacity to feign disinterest. "Hey, Duke, hurry up. My darling pickers need my assistance."

Duke was visibly shaken. To him Cory was the very embodiment of the godly woman. Never missing church, she consistently arranged her Sunday and Wednesday evenings so she could attend worship services. She talked to him often if discreetly about God and the Bible and had been the repeated impetus for him to straighten out his life. "Well, the first thing you need to do is get off the bottle," she used to say to Duke. "You're killing yourself. You could be such a fine and decent man." He believed she could recite Bible verses by the hour. Yet she was, ironically, the embodiment of sexuality as much as spirituality. He fantasized being with her by the hour.

Spiritual or not, here she was in all her voluptuous, naked beauty and with that hauntingly alluring pose. She had a smile on her face as though she couldn't wait to get together with the lucky guy behind her. Speaking of which, who was he, and when had this picture been taken? The small part of his face that was showing reminded him of a guy who had worked in the mine a couple years back. Cory Mohney— as sexual as she was spiritual, as hot as she was holy, as wild as she was wonderful! Duke looked at the photo with shocked disbelief. Could it be true? What more proof could one want?

"Duke, I must run, but before I go, let me educate you a bit." Abe carefully looked at Duke's face. Would he fall for the ruse or not? Abe's task was not easy. Eradicating Duke's wholesome perception of Cory and replacing it with a deceitful one was, given Duke's savvy nature, risky business. Abe quickly planned his strategy and proceeded to work on Duke's mind. "Many women cultivate a righteous front to disguise a carnal nature. I wasn't going to show you this picture. As I said, I offhandedly lifted it out of the trash can on my way out the door. I don't want you to be the last guy to know. I'm sick and tired of men being played by crafty women. If you don't wise up soon, you'll be competing with Bull for the dumbest-guy-on-the-planet award."

He paused to check Duke's reaction to his purposely charged label. No negative reaction. He gave Duke a pat on the back and continued. "Don't be sucked in by a woman's cunning, Duke. A woman once pulled the wool over my eyes. I don't want it to happen to you. Wise up or you'll be the laughingstock of the mine. It's time to dine at her vine. Do you comprehend my metaphor, good sir?" Abe winked at Duke and was gone in a flash.

Duke was shell-shocked. The picture was definitely of Cory. No one would dispute that. Once back with his crew, he looked at her in a whole new way. *Cory, I know you,* he thought to himself. *I know* the beauty you're hiding under those faded jeans, flannel shirts, and old sweatshirts. So that's part of the act. Wear the tattered clothing as a decoy. Ah, ha, I see through you. You're the Pharisee who'd bare for me! Abe would be proud of my little rhyme. You sweet little kitty!

As Duke was returning to the crew and peering at Cory, she stood up from her lowered position at the bottom tray and, like most of the pickers, arched backward to straighten up again and allow the spine to uncoil from the torturous bending. Duke happened to look just as she bent backward in a full stretch, her arms pulled back behind her head in a deep, spine-curving stretch. Yes, he thought, the exact same pose as in the picture with the shoulders pulled back! Was that a smile on her lips, a slight hint of that maddeningly seductive look in the photo? Did Cory know Duke was looking at her, and had she put on this show just for him? Possibly so since Duke was looking directly at her as she stretched. They even made brief eye contact. Cory, you have no idea what I know about you. Sweetheart, I'm onto your game.

He went back a short while later to pick up her basket for deposit in the train, and as he did so, she was again leaning over and picking the mushrooms on the far side of the lowest tray, the most difficult part of the picker's job since they had to bend deeply and stay in that awkwardly crouched position until the tray was picked clean. Emboldened by what he had seen in the photo, he lustfully peered at Cory.

"Don't look at me that way!" She was in the back row and slightly away from the other women. Not wanting them to hear and attract their notice, she snapped in a hushed if angered tone.

Duke interpreted this gentle rebuttal as an affirmation that his new view of her was accurate and that, although surprised, she hadn't minded his gaze. After all, a truly pure woman would have stood up, shot back a fiery response, and slapped him hard. Cory didn't. Come to think of it, maybe her hushed statement was actually an invitation. She probably had admonished him gently so as not to scare him away. Kitty probably liked it.

"Nice, Cory. Yeah, very nice."

"Duke, what's come over you? Don't ever look at me that way again." This time she spoke with real anger but still kept her voice low so she didn't attract attention. No need to feed the mine rumor mill. It had taken months to silence the gossip about the photo of Jude making love to Meg, and even to this day, a few of the women fell for the doctored-photo ruse. That incident had faded from minds only as other juicier gossip replaced it.

That evening on her way home, she reflected again on the incident. What had happened to Duke? While he was nobody's saint, Cory had made real progress in his transformation. "You are made for better things, Duke—a higher calling, Pastor Gabe calls it. You can still save money for tuition, get out of here, and get to college. I'm the one stuck, not you."

Encouraged by her relentless theme song, he had quit smoking, drank less, and even promised to start going to church. Against that backdrop of recent progress, what was the meaning of this carnal gaze? Even when he had first started coming around the farm and his language elsewhere was vulgar, he respected her and never hinted at any immorality, never attempted to touch her, and never looked at her lustfully, knowing that Cory would rebuff him and that he'd ruin his chances for any sort of future relationship. What in the world was going on? What had happened to Duke?

Chapter 23

That evening, Jude picked Cory up to take her to a planning meeting at the church. The class officers for the Crusaders Sunday School class were meeting to plan the annual class-sponsored summer social, which featured games, a hayride, and a culminating campfire hotdog/corn roast.

On their way to the church, Jude spoke to Cory, who remained quiet, even sullen. He looked closely at her, but she stared straight ahead. "You're subdued this evening. I'm assuming everything is not wonderful?"

"I could never hide anything from you, Jude Hepler. Nor would I want to." She turned and looked squarely at him.

"All right, shoot. I'm all ears. I know something's eating at you. Your mind's an open book."

Cory thought anew of the incident in the mine—Duke's untoward gesture, his lustful look, and the mocking grin. "Duke looked at me sinfully today when I was alone at the back of room 8. He's never done that before. I can't figure it out."

Anger immediately seized Jude. "Unbelievable! What's the guy thinking? What did he do?"

"He looked at me in a really carnal way and gestured when I was picking a lower tray."

"I can't believe it. Based on what you've said about his conduct in recent weeks, he's been completely civil." Jude could see a tear in

Cory's eye as she clutched her hands tightly. Trying to suppress his own anger, he said nothing for a moment but then spoke. "Let's just hope it was an isolated event. Maybe you should stay close to the other women for the time being? Let me know if it happens again. Promise? I won't stand for it. I want nothing happening to my baby." He put his arm around her as he drove.

"Thanks. That's a good idea—staying close to the other pickers."

The planning meeting at the church proceeded well. The date was set and long-range planning details deliberated. The talk of summer parties and picnics, church socials, and outdoor fun soon brought Cory out of her funk. The meeting was also a welcome break for Jude who had been, in his words, "overexposed to a postmodern worldview that has politicized the study of literature in recent years." His time in Armstrong County afforded him a much-needed break from month after month of scholarship and research. Reading a couple books per week, writing endless papers and essays, studying for his candidacy and final comprehensive exams, squeezing in his reading mastery of French and German, preparing for conference presentations, staying on top of class preparation, composing his dissertation prospectus, and much more—this had been his daily grind for many long and weary months. The expenditure of psychic and mental energy had been relentless, and while Jude wasn't burnt out per se, the physical labor and the complete break in Armstrong County offered him valuable rest—a "sabbatical to rusticate like Thoreau," he had quipped to his professors in the Leonard Hall lounge prior to his departure from IUP.

His only difficult moment in the planning session for the festive summer event occurred during a brief but tense moment when a game was described to a newcomer on the planning committee. For this game, the church family assembled in the host's barn to watch the men compete in the annual "feedsack climb." To participate in this contest, each contestant began at a common starting point, sped in turn across the barn, flung a full sack of grain from the pile onto his back, climbed the wooden steps affixed to the upright beam, thrust the bag into the loft, and hustled back down the ladder. The person who returned to the starting point in the shortest amount of time won the race. The men, many of them farm boys or day laborers who were accustomed to throwing around full sacks of grain, cement blocks, or equivalent weights, were very competent in such a match and enjoyed the annual test of strength and agility.

Charles Claypoole sat in on the summer planning meeting since he was the advisor for the event. Seated across from Jude and Cory— intentionally so, he later revealed—the professor inconspicuously watched Jude when the feedsack climb was discussed. The professor noted what appeared to be "a slight quickening of Jude's breath, fidgeting in his seat, and a clutching of the paper that he held in his hand," as he later mentioned to Pastor Gabriel. Schooled in body language, Charles read volumes into those innocent gestures and couldn't stop his mind from racing. Jude's phobia about the barn and his grandpa's death must have something to do with that barn ladder, or possibly with climbing of some sort, or carrying an object on the back, or maybe all of these. Jude's subsequent emotional disconnect from the planning session confirmed the professor's gut feeling that he may well have stumbled onto a missing link. He never took an eye off Jude.

As noted earlier, Jude had mastered diversionary tactics. During this planning session, the talk of the feedsack climb occasioned his reliance on the well-honed strategy. As the details of the game were elaborated, Jude, disliking the sustained discussion, suddenly developed a marked interest in Cory's Bible that lay on the pew between them. When he picked it up, it fell open of its own accord to a laminated dried red rose. Jude had picked up the Bible simply to indulge a comforting diversion, but the rose prompted genuine interest.

"What's this?" Jude leaned over and whispered to Cory. Not taking note of the faded color of the rose and its age, he thought for one fleeting moment that maybe Duke had given Cory the rose. Had there been more of a relationship with Duke than Jude first imagined?

"It's the rose Old Mary gave me when I was a little girl. She says it relates to the vision she had years ago. I'll tell you during our walk this evening," she whispered. As she held Jude's hand, Jude relaxed again and then put his arm around her. He looked around him and thought how comfortably removed she was from her unpleasant incident with Duke just hours earlier.

In talking to Gabriel later about Jude's response to the feedsack game, Charles asked the obvious question, "Wonder why he reacted that way?"

"Because Jude would have remembered this game. Recall that this game, which was created here at Center Hill far as I know, has been around a long time. Jude would have participated in this competition as a high school boy when he lived here during the summers with his grandparents. Come to think of it, I remember his competing in this game once at the Younkins' farm. I stood by Bob and Marian that year and distinctly recall Bob's comment about Jude's speed."

Charles took his glasses off and rubbed his eyes. "You indicate knowledge of the game through participation. What I witnessed was some sort of discomfort or anxiety."

In Cory's barn later that evening, Jude and Cory brushed down the horses. Just as they were finishing, Jude brought up the topic of the rose. He was looking for a way to distract Cory from the incident with Duke and himself from the feedsack climb discussion. "Is this a good time to talk about the rose vision?"

"Yes, it is, but let's first go inside so I can show you the picture."

Moments later, Jude and Cory were seated in the kitchen, the place where the family often met, even though the cozy family room—they often referred to it as the den—adjoined the kitchen. Somehow sitting at the kitchen table invited conversation just as much as the comfortable couch and chairs. Cory went to her bedroom and returned with a photo that pictured a rose garden in the foreground and a large and impressive English manor house in the background. Under the picture of the rose garden, at the height of its summer glory, was a poetic excerpt:

Footfalls echo in the memory
Down the passage which we did not take
Towards the door we never opened
Into the rose garden.

Jude recognized the famous lines from T. S. Eliot's *Burnt Norton*. The photo, he learned from the caption, was of the manor house called Burnt Norton in the English Cotswolds. The rose garden in the foreground was the actual garden Eliot alluded to in his masterpiece poem. Jude was struck by the picture and the poetic caption.

"Cory, where in the world did you get this? This is amazing! Do you know how famous these lines are?"

"Old Mary gave it to me when I was quite a young girl. She said she had stumbled on this picture in a magazine article in *Cotswold Journal* on the architecture and gardens of English Cotswolds cottages. She saw it about the time she had the vision of the rose. In her mind, the garden and house had become part and parcel of the vision itself. When she thought of the vision, the roses and even Burnt Norton itself came to mind, or when she saw this picture, it brought to mind the rose vision. She never gave me all the details of the rose vision—I was still a child then—but she told me that I was connected with it. Imagine that! What in the world did I have to do with her vision? She then gave me this picture and the rose I showed you at church but no further details about the story or my relation to it. She said she'd tell me it when I was older! You don't remember the picture from our past when we spent hours together every day?"

"No, I don't. Sorry. Maybe you didn't always have it out in the open back then?"

"That's right. Come to think about it, I used to keep it in a desk drawer. I took it out after we split up! I was looking for anything to console me in those days. I guess I should say anything that might help me get my mind off you."

She stopped speaking and looked deeply at Jude. Tears immediately filled her eyes. What a marvel to have him sit beside her here in the Mohney kitchen! Placing her hand on his arm, she looked closely at the picture of Burnt Norton's rose garden. "I'm sure we can talk to Old Mary together some time and learn the details of the vision. Perhaps Mary will think I'm a big enough girl by now! What do you say?"

"Sounds great."

"Ready to ride the horses up on the ridge?"

"I'd love that but how about a cool glass of water first?" Watching her get a glass of water at the sink, Jude thought to himself, *Surely I'm the luckiest guy in the world.*

"I came across a verse in Isaiah during devotions this morning."

"What did it say?"

"It reminded me of your thirst."

"Fire away."

"Get my Bible there on the table and turn to my bookmark." Cory walked to the table, a glass of water in hand, and ran her finger down the page. "Here it is. It's from Isaiah 44:3. 'For I will pour water on him who is thirsty, and floods on the dry ground.' I call that appropriate!"

Jude laughed. "Here's hoping the water falls on me!"

Chapter 24

After riding the horses up to Vinlindeer for their evening walk on the ridge, Jude and Cory sat along on the fence. They watched the full moon, vast as the Temple of Apollo at Corinth, rest for a while on the horizon, temporarily pausing before its long and lonely trek across the lavender sky. They said nothing, content to drink in the splendor of the early summer evening.

"What poem comes to mind as you watch the moon?" Jude eventually asked.

"Let me see. How about Sir Philip Sidney's 'With how sad steps, O moon, thou climb'st the skies.' And you?"

"Nice. Good choice." Jude held his arm tightly around Cory, cuddled closely to her, and thought for a moment. "Edgar Lee Masters' 'Lucinda Matlock.'" He recited some of the lines.

> I went to the dances at Chandlerville,
> And played snap-out at Winchester.
> One time we changed partners,
> Driving home in the moonlight of middle June,
> And then I found Davis ...

"Remember the poem? And then I found Cory, I should say. Then I found Cory in the moonlight of middle June. O happy day! Except it's still May! Oh well, an insignificant difference."

She rested her head on his shoulder as she watched the moon. "And then I found Jude. Of course I remember the poem. It's always been a favorite. How fitting these lines of poetry! All right, I concede. You win the first poetry contest of the summer." She gave him a peck on the cheek. "But don't rest on your laurels!"

"I love you with all my heart. You have no idea how much I love you. I ache with love. I've waited for this moment for months and years."

The full moon collected its nerve, summoned its strength as if on the starting line, and then as by signal slowly eased its enormous bulk off the faraway horizon to begin its voyage across the nighttime sea. Jude put both of his arms around her.

"Cory, I've never loved you more. I don't want to leave your side for a minute. I love you now more than ever in my life."

"You know how much I love you? You've changed my whole life in one rapturous week. I had been sad for years and couldn't shake my depression. I was so lost in the labyrinth of my own mind that I frightened myself in those dark days."

She stood up and moved his legs to form a Y. "Let's sit the way we used to." He nodded with a large smile. When he spread his legs, she sat between them and wiggled more tightly into his body. He folded his arms across her stomach.

They quietly lay and marveled at the beauty of the moment. "Let's play a game," Jude said after a moment.

"Name it. I'm in."

"Let's name a quality in each other that makes our love so beautifully different."

"Great idea. Who goes first?"

"Go ahead."

Cory thought for a moment, turned sideways so she could look into his eyes, and softly spoke. "Acceptance. You have always accepted me for what I am. I never had to act around you or project my perfect, idealized self. I could always just be me."

"I know exactly what you mean because I feel the same way. Think about it. Dating today among people is an essentially fraudulent activity. People project these glamorized renditions of themselves out of fear, I suppose, that their beloved would reject them if they saw the dark underside of their true being."

"Some of the women at the mine do exactly that. They brag about how they lead on their men or fake them out."

"I'm sure guys do the same." He kissed her on the head. "But not us. I've only ever told you the truth. Remember when we used to confess our sins to each other? The ones that drive us bananas. I loved you more, not less, when you told me of those ongoing moral battles."

"As I loved you the more for letting me into your deepest heart."

"What happened when you were deprived of that intimate soul sharing?"

"I became very afraid, to the point that I actually frightened myself. Then I really started to hide! I've always had that tendency, but then I hit jet speed!"

"Same with me. The tragedy of our breakup contorted me into a terrible shape. I allowed the events to wrench me loose from my own psychic moorings." He paused and watched the moon, slipping behind a vaporous cloud, deepen its shade of creamy yellow. "It's hard to say what I mean." He tilted his head and rested his chin more fully on her head. "I lost my sense of self and purpose. My moral compass had been thrown overboard. Adrift at sea, I became someone I didn't like and no longer knew."

"I completely understand what you're talking about because I felt the same thing. Let me tell you how bad it got for me. This will sound like a confession, but I want to say this. I need to say it."

"Go ahead. These arms will gird you, this love protect you."

"After we separated and I knew I lost you forever, I went into a terrible depression. You know about that part since I spoke of it in the cemetery. But the difference between us is this. You lost your moral compass overboard, but in my case, it was I who went overboard. What made it really bad was that I was daily exposed to a handful of women who ran out on their men. Cheating is a way of life for

THE ROSE AND THE SERPENT

two of the women on my crew, and adultery their norm. It was my luck to pick beside them much of the time. Well, hearing constant talk about their escapades and feeling terribly lonely, I began to be attracted to other men." Cory paused for a moment to watch the moon. "In the really weak moments, I was attracted by the idea of such a relationship. I guess I was looking for something to anchor me."

She folded Jude's arms more tightly against her. "Here's the tough part. At my low point, I fantasized about other stuff too. I was ashamed of myself for having such thoughts. I think the fantasies correlated to my lack of contact with you. You can understand that, right? It's simple really even if embarrassing. The more I missed you, the more I fantasized about others filling the ever-deepening canyon in my heart."

"We are human, Cory. 'We are of the earth, earthy,' and earthy people think of natural, physical things. You think I didn't have the same exact thoughts? I fantasized in those months like a nineteen-year-old kid. I looked at women everywhere and imagined that they were you. I dreamed of us together constantly."

For a while, they said nothing. Cory resumed speaking. "Thanks for making this easier for me. Feeling so full of shame, I didn't want anything to contaminate the purity of our relationship. Well, I should say the memory of the relationship, since it had been dead for a long time. All I had was the memory of our love, which gradually became as holy, perfect, and beautiful as a shrine. I wanted that memory to stay pristinely pure."

"I know the next lines because I'm a character in the exact same play, and I have my lines down pat."

"Then you know I'm near the end. Living in that muck changed me. I was becoming a transformed person. Not outwardly but mentally. That frightened me. I kept thinking people could see my mind, see how impure I had become. I'm talking about the mental realm. I became obsessed with guilt, desire for you, and purity all at the same time. Yet I also knew at the very same time that you'd forgive me and love me. You always accepted me. Always. That acceptance

I came to miss so much. I know I'm contradicting myself, but that's how I was—my emotions exploding in every direction!"

"You haven't said a thing that surprises me, nor has my love for you been affected one little bit. Are you kidding? I love you more than ever. I'm amazed that you had the exact same feelings I did. I'm a male, Cory. Do you have any idea how many of my waking moments are fixated on you—I should say us—and our being together? You know what I'm talking about!"

"You're making it easier for me to keep going. I wanted you to remember the pure and good Cory. I began to be afraid of myself. I was afraid that if we'd get back together, I'd start seeing you as I was starting to see other men. I didn't want you to be reduced to a manipulated partner in my ongoing fantasy script." She breathed a sigh of relief. "There, I said it."

"Let me get this straight. You rebuffed me because you were afraid that in time our relationship would be reduced to something impure?"

"That's part of it but not all of it. Being with you in that way is what I want more than anything in the world. I'm talking about after marriage of course. But I was afraid that if we'd get back together that I'd be afraid that I might want to seduce you on purpose just to make you violate your own high morals. Then you'd wallow in the same mucky guilt that had become my daily struggle. It was a strategy to bring Mr. Perfect down to my fallen level. You see how sick this is?"

"Not sick at all. I follow you perfectly, and I love you all the more because of your honesty. You've described my inner thought life to a tee. The only difference is that I don't think I could describe it as honestly as you."

"I know this is crazy because we've always vowed we'd save ourselves for marriage. Well, that honesty was another complex variable in the whole sordid mix. We were only ever 100 percent honest with each other, but I wasn't being honest with you about my mental state. I was afraid that if we'd get back together, I'd need to confess my inner thought life to you. Just as I am right now. I was afraid you'd be disappointed in me if I told you all the dark inner stuff. If you knew what I had become—this is how I reasoned in those long and lonely winter nights—I was afraid you'd change your opinion of me, maybe even stop liking me. So I concluded that it was best to keep my fantasies and my longings to myself, thereby killing in one fell swoop the emotional honesty that had always been the centerpiece of our love." She turned her head and looked in Jude's eyes. "Good riddance to those awful days."

"They're gone forever. 'We will grieve not'—how does the poet say it?—'rather find Strength in what remains behind.'"

"I know that one." She thought for a moment. "Wordsworth. 'Ode: Intimations of Immortality,' right?"

"Bingo! That's the poem. We too will separate ourselves from the dark past. We will control it and not let it control us. We can make a life together. Soon we'll make yesterday's fantasy life a physical reality. Is there a more pleasant thought anywhere on the face of this green earth than that we'll soon be free of these constraints? 'History may be servitude, History may be freedom.'"

"You're quoting Eliot. *Little Gidding*. Amazing! The poetry just rolls out of you. As usual, I might add. Well, you're right. We will make that torturous history, all those years of pain and unbearable loss, the gateway to freedom. I have the faith to believe that will happen. 'The just shall live by faith.'"

"You're red-hot tonight, Cory."

"I'm red-hot? I think you're looking in a mirror! If I do get some quotes right, it's because I have a master teacher."

"If you say so."

She lifted her arms backward over her head and held and placed her hands at the sides of his face. His arms folded across her stomach, he pulled her tightly into his body.

They paused and watched the moon. Two cirrus clouds formed a large V at its side. "Look," Jude said. "Those clouds are the wake the moon makes on its nighttime voyage through the misty sea."

"You poet!"

Jude eventually resumed. "We'll have a bump in the road as Duke learns you're leaving him. I don't think he'll be that much of a problem. Do you?"

"I hope you're right. But one other thing concerns me, if I can turn a fast corner. Pastor's been talking off and on for a couple months about the gift of discernment, the capacity to sense evil when you're in its presence. I sense evil when I'm in the mine. I didn't used to, but anymore I feel it lurking. It's almost like a demonic presence. That may sound crazy, but I do. It's been so intense at times that I had even talked to Pastor Gabe about it."

"It's not crazy at all. You're a very discerning person, and something made you feel this way. If some sort of evil is present, then we have to believe that God will help us fight those battles when the time is ripe. 'Ripeness is all.'"

"*King Lear.* Act 5, right?"

"Right you are! What I know is that I'm the happiest and luckiest man in the world, I wouldn't want to be any other place, and I'm with the world's most beautiful woman. I intend no sacrilege in the comparison I'm about to make, but I feel like Peter on the Mount of Transfiguration when Christ laid aside His humanity and transformed Himself into the King of Kings and the Lord of Lords. Remember how Peter wanted to build booths almost as if he just wanted to stay there and delight in the glory and never let it end? Well, that's how I feel about this moment. I'm in paradise, and I never want it to end. I want to stay right here forever. The world is full of evil, but here is joy forever." He again squeezed her tightly. "Ah, my America, my new-found-land!"

"You wit, You Romeo!"

With that Jude kissed her passionately. Cory later confessed that this was the first time she had kissed with a total surrender of feeling. No emotional reservation held her back as it did in the past. Her entire body, her every nerve ending, gathered together in her lips as she kissed him passionately again and again. She clutched him desperately to her. "Jude, I'm madly in love with you. I could never live without you. You are my Lazarus come back from the dead."

Cory settled again between his legs and leaned back on his chest. As he bent forward and rested his head against her neck, he squeezed her even more tightly. As she slid down to lay more comfortably on his chest, the moonlight shimmering above her blouse, Jude was dazzled by her beauty.

"Cory, do you have any idea how beautiful you are?"

"Tsk, tsk!" She smiled. "I don't ever want this moment to end. Wouldn't it be something to get married and live together and be with each other constantly? I honestly can't imagine joy like that. In some ways, it seems so close and attainable, but in others so very far away. When you've spent years in a desert, it's hard to believe that an oasis even exists. I keep thinking I'm seeing a mirage."

The two lovers, cuddled together atop the moon-blanched ridge, looked at the domed and softly rolling knolls below. They had reunited after years of separation, mended the wounds, and loved with a love that, like Poe's Annabel Lee, was more than love.

They were little aware of the serpent in the rose bush!

Chapter 25

The next morning at work, Jude waited impatiently for the pickers to fill their baskets so he could make the first run to the packhouse. His plan was to pass by the room where Cory's crew was picking. Knowing the approximate time when he made the first run each day, Jude had asked Cory that morning when they separated to keep an eye out for him at that time.

The plan went without a hitch. Jude had made his drop within minutes of the designated time and took the alternate route to his crew via corridor 7. There, in the distance, was Cory's crew. At a bend in the corridor near where they worked, Jude parked the personnel carrier tightly against the wall and out of sight of the crew. He hugged the wall as he walked so as not to be seen. Cory was picking by herself on a tray near Jude. He peeked around the corner and flashed his miner's light on and off at the tray where she worked—their previously designated signal. Cory saw the flash, knew it was Jude, who ducked back out of sight, and discreetly slipped away from the other pickers. Around the corner from the crew, she ran to Jude and flung herself at his open arms. They embraced passionately.

"Cory, I loved last evening. I could have held you in my arms all night."

"I couldn't sleep for joy. I kept thinking of how joyful it was being with you."

He kissed her and held her to him tightly. They both knew they only had seconds before needing to return to work. The women would likely have seen Cory's departure. Just as she turned away from Jude, Duke came running in their direction. One of the women, surmising the reason, had tipped him off. Jude was climbing onto his tractor when Duke approached them.

"Cory, what are you doing walking away from your job? Do you want me to report you? Hey, college professor, get out of here. You better lay low, or you'll both pay a heavy price. We don't want you here!"

Duke stood with his legs spread, his arms hanging at his sides, and his hands clenched into fists. Even under his sweatshirt, Jude could see his massive chest. Duke's lips, tightly pursed together, matched his angry eyes—three jagged slits chiseled in granite.

By this time on his tractor, Jude was unable to see that Duke gave Cory a shove in the shoulder and cursed her. "You little kitty. You better watch yourself!" As Jude drove away, Cory couldn't keep from smiling. Duke was dangerous—she was well aware of that—but she basked in the glow of the memory of these last days. The women around her noted the difference in her demeanor—upbeat, enlivened, loved, and radiant.

"See the change in princess?" one of the women whispered to another as they huddled under a tray after Cory's return.

Blanche, one of Cory's good friends, answered the question. "That's the picture of a woman in love."

"I've never seen such a change in a woman. I've always heard that love's what makes the world go 'round, but I've never seen it with my own eyes."

"She reminds me of Belinda Carlisle's song 'Heaven Is a Place on Earth.' I love that song. I turn up the radio every time it plays in my car. Well, I'm guessing Cory's found her heaven on earth."

"How about George Michael's song 'One More Try'"? Blanche responded. "That could also be her theme song." When the women remained silent, Blanche sang a line from the song. "'I'm so cold inside. Maybe just one more try.' Well, I'd say Cory's got her one more try, and, Lord, I do hope this time it works." She started singing again: "Now I think it's time, That you let me know, So if you love me, Say you love me . . . ." She stopped singing and looked in Duke's direction. "Besides Cory's love for Jude, there's one other thing I know for sure. Someone is not happy about it."

"I know. Duke's fuming mad. They better watch themselves. We all know what he's like when he gets mad. He'd kill Jude in a second with one blow with his fist. Look at him standing there—still furious!"

Cory saw the clustered women whispering and surmised that she and Jude were the topic. She didn't care. They were far away, and he was front and center in her mind.

After departing from Cory, Jude drove back to his crew. On the way, he slowed to let another personnel carrier pass by. As he did so, he looked down and saw at the edge of the road a water hole. Water ran across the mine floor in many places, since many underground springs and rivulets snaked their way through this underground world. Jude plopped a stone into this pool of water and was surprised to see a high spurting plume. This was clearly a deeper pool and not a shallow puddle of condensation runoff along the mine wall. Where did it lead? Was it an underground spring or stream? Jude was curious to investigate and made a mental note to check with the mine geologist about the underground network of streams in the county. Where were they located, and did any of them intersect with the mine labyrinth of tunnels?

At the packhouse a short time later, Duke ran into Bull. This was a frequent meeting place for the drivers who had a brief time to chat while the trays were unloaded. Bull motioned for Duke to come to him behind his tractor away from other people.

"Duke, you won't believe it. Remember the picture of Cory I showed you? Abe said that since you were so interested in that sneak preview, he'd show you the real stuff."

"What are you talking about?" he bellowed. Having seen Jude and Cory's sneaky rendezvous a short while ago, Duke was in no mood for Bull's mindless antics.

"I'm talking about this, dimwit. I have in this envelope a bunch of pictures you won't believe."

"Let me see," Duke snapped.

With that, Bull pulled out an envelope that contained several eight-by-ten glossy prints of Cory with a couple different men. The pictures matched the best photos Duke had seen in his skin magazines. In several of them, she even smiled for the camera. He couldn't believe what a seductive animal she was.

"Can you believe it, Duke? She's absolutely beautiful. You are one lucky duck!"

Duke raised the pictures to his eyes to study the details. "She's beautiful all right, and I bet her professor knows it."

"Maybe not. Abe says she hangs around Jude just to make you jealous. She's trying to force your hand and get you to speed up the pace. Abe says she's done the same thing with each of these guys. You're taking forever, man." With that, he motioned to the men in the photos. "When they come on to her, she plays the pure little girl act. She's got her religious routine down to a science. Jake saw through it right away. Her resisting and kicking and screaming were the times she wanted him the most. Don't be put off by her thing for Jude. It's a smokescreen. She's dying to have you, man." He flashed the pictures under his nose again. "Proof, Mr. Scientist, you said you wanted proof." He kissed the photos, stuffed them into the envelope, and drove away, looking back at Duke with a big smile.

Duke was mystified. How could one person have two completely different personalities? Playing the psychologist didn't particularly interest him but getting together with Cory definitely did. Given what Bull had just said, it was his move, and he wasn't one to delay. Little did he know that he was looking at doctored photographs. Cory's face was the one in the photos but not the body.

Returning to his crew, Duke was inflamed with both lust and anger. He wanted Cory desperately and was enraged that Jude had intervened. The plan of getting together with Cory had proceeded well until the fish-out-of-water college professor showed up. Yet this new information excited him greatly and gave him renewed hope. He quickly mapped out his strategy. Pick up the pace, don't be fooled by the pious routine, and soon enjoy the fruits of his labor. How could his plan fail? He had seen the proof. What a wanton tigress she was! He would wait for the opportunity when she was more or less off by herself so he could make the first move.

The opportunity presented itself shortly afterward.

Chapter 26

*B*ecause Cory stayed around the other pickers as Jude had advised, Duke didn't have the chance to be with her alone after his return from the packhouse. This forced him to revise his plan. The driver, as head of the crew, performed the final inspection of the mushroom beds to see if they had been picked clean. If he didn't approve, the women who were responsible for the slovenly work were forced to go back to pick the mushrooms they had carelessly passed over.

The newer pickers were not so adept at determining which mushrooms were mature enough for picking. Too often they were fooled into harvesting just the larger mushrooms, assuming the smaller ones weren't fully ripened. But that was not always the case. Sometimes the smaller mushrooms, a different species, had attained full maturation. If not picked at the proper time, these smaller, often-more-tasty mushrooms were wasted. The experienced pickers had learned through months and even years of experience which of these smaller mushrooms were fully mature, which were not.

"Hey, Cory," Duke shouted. "Come and pick these trays clean." He was standing quite a distance from the pickers and was motioning at several trays. She suspected a trap but had no choice. Because her running off to see Jude for those few minutes had made her vulnerable, she was forced to comply. As she drew nearer to him, he said. "These new pickers can't pick for nothing!"

He was right. A couple of the beds had numerous smaller mushrooms that, though ripe for picking, had been missed by the newer pickers. As she neared the back trays, she was around a bend and some one hundred yards away from the other pickers. Cory knew that in such a setting she was in a precarious place, but owing to her dereliction of duty earlier, it was predictable that Duke would punish her in some way.

As she approached Duke, he was standing by one of the trays, looking at her with a cocky and smug grin. He had laid the perfect trap. When he gestured distastefully, Cory quickly deflected her gaze and went to the back of the tray on the opposite side. She hoped that the worst was over and that he would leave while she picked these few trays. He didn't. He watched her and was apparently waiting for her to get to the lower trays.

As minutes passed, she became more and more nervous. Concentrating on the task at hand—she wanted out of there as quickly as possible—she lost track of his whereabouts. When she stood up to move to another position, he was standing behind her, and she accidentally backed into him. She squirmed hard and tried to push away, but he held her tightly with his groping hands.

"Duke, what are you doing? Stop it!" She threw a hard elbow at him, intending to hit his shoulder, but just as she swung, he had lowered his head against her neck. As a result, her elbow delivered a vicious hit to his jaw, which knocked him backward into the wall. He retaliated in mad fury, flung her body at the wall, and pinned her forcefully.

"Please stop! You're hurting me!"

"Right! I'm really hurting you, you cagey kitty. I know you. I'm completely on to your game!"

"Duke, what's come over you? Why are you acting this way? Stop it. You're hurting me!" She tried to pry his strong hands away and turned sideways.

"Why am I acting? You're the one who's acting all pious and

self-righteous. I know what you're doing." He was looking directly at her, his face inches away.

"Please let me go. I'll scream." Letting her go, she escaped his wandering hands.

"So very nice, kitty."

It was a big decision for Cory, but she chose not to tell Jude of the incident. Her recourse was to stay beside other women at all times and never give Duke such an opportunity again. The incident, however, had shaken her greatly and tied her stomach in knots all afternoon. The women said nothing, but they observed Cory's trembling hands and winked at each other.

One of the women whispered to a friend on the other side of the tray, "Something happened between Duke and Cory when they were back there alone. Cory's a mess."

"I know. She dropped her knife three times!"

"Look at that! She just spilled her mushrooms! They're rolling everywhere!"

"I've never known Cory to have an accident like that before!"

For her part, Cory kept thinking of Jude on the hill the night before and Duke in the mine today. She had an angel and a monster in her life. And a serpent lurking in the rosebush.

Chapter 27

The next Sunday in church, Jude and Cory sat beside each other. Their reconciliation, fully out in the open by this time, caused the church folks to rejoice. They genuinely loved this young couple who had prevailed through "some pretty awful tempests," as Wes, one of the head elders, had opined.

When asked earlier in the spring by a colleague to describe "his rural friends" and his "season of rustication," Jude replied, "They're salt of the earth folks 'in whom there is no guile.' Do you recognize my allusion to Christ's assessment of Nathaniel, one of his disciples?" The professor had looked blankly at him. "I didn't think you would." Jude had explained to him: "When Christ chose Nathaniel to be a disciple, He saw him sitting under a fig tree, and Jesus said, 'This is a man in whom there is no guile.' I love these people, especially the church folks. They're real, they're authentic, and they're miles removed from the powder room politics, the conniving and backstabbing, and the catty pettiness that is the lot of many workplaces today. They're real folks. They're my Nathaniels. The more I'm around them, the more I love them." The professor, looking at Jude approvingly, admired him for his chance to get away from the pessimists, skeptics, and people like himself: ever yearning, ever floundering, ever haunted by anxieties.

The folks at Center Hill specifically and Armstrong County generally knew that Jude felt this way about them, and they loved him all the more because of it. Here he was, a highly educated man, but in their opinion he was down to earth—"one of us," as they often said. Seeing the two lovers seated together in church, Jude's arm around Cory, they felt genuine joy for both of them, especially Cory. They knew her cross had been heavy ever since her mother's death and father's injury, which resulted in a badly torn subscapularis muscle and severe pain caused by the injured acromion shoulder bone pushing against the rotator cuff. How had she managed to keep the family together through all these trials? The Mohney family and Cory particularly had been featured regularly on the prayer requests both at Sunday morning service and Wednesday evening Bible study.

Of this loving church family, no one cared more deeply for the Mohneys than Professor Claypoole. Chuck had befriended Cory's dad, Pete Mohney, and spent many lonely evenings at their home. Widely read in psychology and Christian counseling, he provided invaluable friendship to Pete during those long days after his wife's death. Ruby Mohney had been a saint and, in her day, as beautiful as Cory. Her early death due to cancer had badly rocked the Mohney household. Truth is, Pete had become borderline suicidal in those dark days. "I just can't take it. How much does a man have to endure?" Charles had been his right-hand man, and during the weeks and months when Charles spent so much time at their home, he had come to love both Cory and Joey.

So this Sunday morning, with Cory cuddled against Jude and both of them absorbed in Gabriel's sermon, the professor felt as much joy as anyone. While he had hoped that Cory and Jude would reconcile their differences, he didn't actually believe it would happen. Skeptical by nature, he believed that wounds that deep could never heal. The passage from Milton's *Paradise Lost*, which he taught a mere few weeks earlier at Grove City College, surged in his mind: "For never can true reconcilement grow Where wounds of deadly hate have pierc'd so deep." And how deep were Cory's wounds! Yet reconcilement had indeed occurred.

Charles startled himself to attention. His hand resting

characteristically on his breast, he had become so engrossed in watching Jude and Cory as a couple that he forgot to study Jude as an individual. His mission was to carefully note Jude's reaction when the pastor worked his way to the point of the buried treasure. Missing his Horatio-like assignment was something he didn't want to do. The plan was too perfect to botch.

Preaching on the account in Joshua chapter 7 of Achan and the buried treasure, Pastor Gabriel brought his sermon around to the point of application to his flock. Achan's sin of hiding the Babylonian garment along with the silver and the gold had caused God to withhold His blessing to the nation of Israel. Gabriel preached with conviction. "Sin had blocked the work of the spirit of God in their midst and interrupted the miraculous flow of blessings upon them. The objects that were hidden away thus had inflicted incalculable damage on these wayfaring people."

"By extension," Pastor Gabriel continued, "the same may well be said of us. The past things that we've hidden away from God or ourselves function like Achan's buried treasure. Completely healthy people have contact with and control of their entire being. They hide nothing, nor do they have the need to do so. They know that the hidden things block growth if not acknowledged and dealt with adequately. Thus, they confess them, deal with them, get them out in the open. These hidden things take many forms. They may be unpleasant truths about ourselves or disgusting past experiences we want to deny or escape. Whatever it is, that buried thing festers in our unconscious, as Achan's hidden treasure festered in the body of Israel.

"What's particularly deadly about this phenomenon is that people often hide away an unpleasant truth or reality so completely that they eventually deny its existence and remain oblivious to its damage and negative effect on their lives. What I'm saying here forces all of us to contemplate some overwhelming questions. Have you hidden away some unacknowledged, suppressed thing? Question two: to what extent does our denial of this hidden thing or our avoiding it altogether harm our continued growth and knowledge of self? It's high time to unearth this buried ghost, stop living in fear of it, and rid ourselves of its contamination forever. How can this be done, you ask? By bathing it once and for all in God's forgiving love. We need no longer be controlled by our pasts. What is hidden in our lives? What a wonderful privilege it is to be able to take it to the cross, confess it to our Lord, and be rid of this albatross once and forever. If the Lord sets you free from this burden, you will be free indeed. Amen."

On this particular Sunday, Charles Claypoole sat in the front row of the adjoining Sunday school rooms. In bygone days, the Sunday school classes had been held in this side annex, but after completion of the new church addition, when the partition doors had been removed, the annex had become part of the church sanctuary where overflow crowds or latecomers typically sat. In this L-shaped sanctuary, people in these raised pews—the small leg of the L—were perpendicular to the main sanctuary, affording them an excellent side view. This was the case with Charles. Jude and Cory were seated directly in front of him in the left section of the main sanctuary, giving him a perfect profile of the lovers.

The whole discourse on buried treasures and suppressed realities was clearly disturbing to Jude. Always conscious of his behavior and intensely self-monitoring, he was typically adept at masking his feelings, especially those feelings that betrayed the landscape of the inner heart. He sat in the pew and smiled, looked interested, nodded his head in agreement, and appeared engaged, but he was, on this occasion, unable to mask the boiling turmoil within from the perceptive Charles Claypoole. The account of buried phenomenon that unconsciously controlled one's life went directly to Jude's heart. Badly shaken, he fought to suppress a visceral reaction to the searing message. At one point, he squirmed so much that Cory whispered to Jude, "Are you all right? You're fidgeting like Joey when he was a kid!"

"Oh, I'm fine. Another excellent sermon," he whispered as he crossed his right leg over the left, angling away from Gabriel.

In his case, two things were hidden: his grandpa's novel and the dying words that were the key to its location. While Charles could not be certain, he believed Jeremiah's novel was most likely a masterpiece and thus its loss was dreadful. He had, at Jeremiah's request, read over several different sections of the manuscript many years before and was astounded by the powerful use of language, the gripping storyline, the incorporation of the founding fathers' ideology, the use of visions, the inclusion of angelology and demonology, and perhaps most of all the sheer mastery of figurative speech. This was a book Charles had waited to read for years. "It's a brilliant work—I just know it," he had said to Pastor Gabriel.

Little did Cory know that Jude, at the reference to the suppressed reality, had flashed back immediately to the barn. He was again a seven-year-old boy in the barn, looking up at his grandpa in the loft. Jude had just entered the barn in pursuit of one of the barn kitties. "Here kitty, kitty! Where are you? I'm coming to find you. I'm coming to get you!"

"Jude, can you bring that small stool up to me?" his grandpa had asked from atop the upper loft.

Watching it all, Charles noted the look of horror that formed on Jude's face as the adult in a church became a boy in a barn.

After the service was over and the last person had departed, Charles approached Gabriel in his church office. Seeing Charles at the door, Gabriel said, "Were you watching him? Did you learn anything?"

"I did very well note him," Charles replied. "But I won't be as evasive as Horatio when watching Claudius in Shakespeare's play. That's Horatio's line by the way. Yes, I witnessed obvious signs of discomfort. That's some progress but perhaps not as much as we'd like. Your reference to the buried secret obviously would have made Jude think of Jeremiah's novel as his hidden secret. That's a given. But it's probably the other hidden treasure—Jeremiah's dying words that are deeply buried in his mind—that made him squirm the most. How can we catch the conscience of the king? More to the point, how can we untether words and give them wing?"

"'This kind comes forth but by prayer and fasting,' Charles. We must pray as never before. And I'll be praying for you, my professor friend. As I've often said, this is your Gordian knot. Now be an Alexander!"

The next week at the mine flitted by quickly and gloriously. Duke had been apparently convicted in his spirit to the point that he lay low and made no further advances toward Cory. On vacation this week, Abe Badoane was also removed from the scene. Jude and Cory nevertheless saw each other infrequently at the mine since both realized the peril of forcing any type of rendezvous during work hours, but they saw each other every evening and continued their reading of *Hamlet* together. Jude shared with Cory some of his favorite books and articles on Shakespeare, particularly those centered on *Hamlet*.

An eager student, Cory received this material with passion. "I just can't believe that an author could construct such a brilliant play. Shakespeare started with a blank stack of paper that he transformed into sheer genius! I positively can't wait to see it performed at the Three Rivers Shakespeare Festival. It reminds me of how an artist starts with a blank canvas and creates a masterpiece. Think of Caravaggio's *Supper at Emmaus*, Rembrandt's *Self-Portrait*, or Tintoretto's *St. George and the Dragon*. In each case, the ingenious artist started with a mere blank and created an immortal work. That is the power of art!"

"And how Shakespeare mastered his!"

That upcoming theatre experience, both agreed subsequently, proved to be one of the defining events of the summer.

Chapter 28

The following Saturday, the annual church picnic was held at the home of the Younkins, one of the pillar families of the church. During the afternoon, the group met in the area near the barn for games and fellowship. People played horseshoes, volleyball, badminton, Jarts, and other lawn games and ate snacks on picnic tables that were positioned near the barn. Laughter filled the air, conviviality was palpably felt, and an old-world form of jubilation was evident everywhere. Because these people genuinely enjoyed each other's company, the fellowship was spontaneous and refreshingly free of the self-consciousness of modern relationships.

Looking down on the proceedings, Cory turned to Jude and said, "Look at all this life. Teeming people everywhere engaged in all sorts of activities. I feel I'm in a Peter Brueghel painting—masses of churning bodies living vibrantly, even uproariously, enjoying life to the brim."

"Educate me about Brueghel. I know nothing about him."

"I'm referring to Peter Brueghel the Elder. He lived in the first half of the sixteenth century. One of his big contributions to art history was his use of landscapes. Up to his time, landscapes were used as mere backdrop—not so very important—but he actually used them to create story. I guess you could say that landscapes take on thematic importance in his art."

"Very good. That helps a lot."

By late afternoon, the annual volleyball game was held, which always pitted the church youth against the older folks. The games were quite evenly matched, the youth winning some years owing to their energy and endurance, the older folks other years owing to finesse and experience. At Charles' suggestion, the older group called themselves Vox Usus, Latin for the voice of experience. He had even had red sports shirts made with the words Vox Usus embossed on the back. "I'm number 8," Charles joked. "Same as Willie Stargell of the Pittsburgh Pirates!"

Jude and Cory participated in this contest and the other activities with lightness of spirit and hearty laughter. It was Jude's belief that the postmodern worldview grated against his naturally robust optimism, which, though greatly lessened in the years of separation from Cory, never completely died. How strangely out of place he was in the modern world of academia where, in his opinion, too many students floundered in a wilderness of cynicism. In many ways, he felt that he was a lone voice crying in that campus wilderness. Returning again to the farm and spending the summer with these tradition-clad country folks was a balm to his battle-scarred spirit. "I love how relaxed and real I can be around them," he had often said to Cory. "My authenticity quota is higher here than on campus."

"Whatever does that mean, my verbal professor boyfriend?"

"That I'm more fully authentic around them. That I don't posture, role-play, and wear masks in their presence. Eliot's Prufrock says we prepare faces to meet the faces that we meet. I do that. I think we all do. But I do it much less here. I wonder if a certain red, red rose has played a role in that change." He kissed Cory on the cheek.

"Yes, I know what you mean. We talked about that the night we were up on Vinlindeer. Remember when I said that I loved you for the way you accepted me as I am, not as you wanted me to be? That was one of the things I missed the most when we were separated."

"What do you mean?"

"I missed the way you always assured me and made me feel good about myself. Without that, I sometimes just stewed in guilt and shame. How awful that period was!"

By early evening, it was time for the annual feedsack climb. As people finished their games and ended their frolicking in the barnyard, they made their way toward the barn. Cory and Jude were standing on an elevated view up and away from the procession. Jude spoke first. "These people are spontaneously happy and uncontaminated by what Thomas Hardy called the 'ache of modernity.' At least I think that was Hardy's phrase."

"'The ache of modernity.' That's some phrase. I know what it means because I lived it. Notice I used past tense!" And she laughed.

The entire church family, as if on cue, proceeded to the barn. Jude's emotional state instantly altered. In a matter of moments, he trudged along as though headed for the gallows. He began feeling sick in his stomach. "Cory, I'm getting nauseous and lightheaded. I wonder if I should go home!"

But something from deep within told him he had to beat this fear to which he had been held hostage long enough. This fear that was so manifest in his earlier visit to his grandpa's barn. This fear that never went away. This fear that ignited wound flashbacks in a heartbeat.

He continued his death march into the barn. The event proceeded exactly as he remembered from earlier years. The competing men who had gathered in the corner were instructed to pick up a feedsack of grain, diagonally positioned on a stack at the other end of the barn from the starting point, scamper up the ladder, drop the sack in the upper loft, descend, and return to the start. Pastor Gabriel was the official time-keeper. The men drew numbers to determine the order and formed a line based on the numbers drawn by lot. A large crowd of onlookers formed a circle, sometimes two to three deep, along the outer edge of the perimeter.

Joey Mohney, Cory's brother, was one of the first to compete. A magnificent specimen of physique and muscularity, he worked out daily and ran for miles. His diet was nearly perfect as well— vegetables, fruits, high-grain and fiber foods, and so on. Girlfriend Laura's statement, "You're bulging with muscles all over!" was shared by all who had seen him with his shirt off, especially in these days when he had just completed spring training for football. His buttocks were so defined that one of the guys on the football team joked one day in the locker room, "You've got the gluts of a girl. Guess we'll call you Sweet Cheeks!" Joey had wittily countered, "I don't care what you call me, but hands off the 'Joey Jazz!'" The name stuck. To this day, he was often called "Joey Jazz."

Joey enjoyed competitive sports but remained exasperated about the football team. To Joey's way of thinking, the coach played his favorites. Therefore, he had seen little action through his junior year. He held out high hopes for this coming senior year and was encouraged by some of his teammates who knew that his considerable talent had been overlooked.

When it came to his time to pick up the sack, Joey sped across the floor, threw it on his shoulder as though it were a down pillow, and bolted up the stairs like a rocket. His motion of throwing the sack was fluid, his descent lightning. When he was still some six feet above the barn floor, he jumped instead of stepping on each of the remaining seven boards. Some of the women in the crowd gasped at this show of athletic dexterity. But it worked. He had set a very high bar for the others and even beaten his impressive record from the previous year.

Laura Hileman, his beautiful girlfriend, beamed with joy. Laura and Joey had been dating for about a year, and by now she had become an important member of the Mohney family. Laura stood five two and had dark brown hair, short and curly. Her broad smile was set off by deep dimples. Her long eyelashes accented her hazel-brown eyes, and the end of her nose gave the slightest hint of an upward tilt. Cory had come to depend on Laura's frequent presence since she often assisted Joey with farm chores, and she ably carried her own weight in the kitchen too. Clutching him tightly to herself after his dash up the ladder, she was the lovely young woman sparkling with joy at the side of her lover. "I'm so proud of you!" They stood hand in hand as they watched the others compete.

As he waited for his turn in the line, Jude stood in gloomy depression. How had he gotten himself into this mess? Why hadn't he found some way to extricate himself earlier? *Well done, Mr. PhD bright guy!*

As the fatal moment arrived, he took the last steps of his macabre death march to the starting line. His flight across the barn floor at the signal was impressive and greeted with hearty cheers, as was his agile lifting of the grain sack to his shoulder. While he wasn't the athlete of former years, he nevertheless was in fairly good shape. He managed to run to the upright beam ladder with similar ease. So far so good. At this rate, he could easily be a finalist, but after he took two steps up the ladder, he felt sick in the stomach, suddenly stopped, and stepped back down.

He tried to crack a joke and offered a lame excuse. "This crazy back! It ain't what it used to be!" He dropped the grain sack and slunk back to his place behind the men where he slouched from disbelieving eyes. The whole event was deeply exasperating to Jude. People tried to laugh it off and ease his embarrassment, but whispered comments could be heard about the barn floor. "Why'd he do that?" "Why did he drop out of the competition?" "What's going on with Jude?" "Talk about a sheepish look on the face—look at him!"

It was an enigma for Charles as well. By design, he had stationed himself out of sight in a back corner where he could clearly see the competitors. Charles carefully watched every detail of Jude's botched effort, which corroborated his growing suspicion that the barn, the ladder, and the loft were integral to Jeremiah's death and Jude's dilemma. But in what way?

Leaning against the barn wall, Charles came face-to-face with an even more profound question. Could Jude have been so scarred by the childhood tragedy that it accounted for his mental block about writing? *Even with the good help of people like Pastor Gabriel, will I ever be able to answer these complicated questions?* At least in Charles' mind, the feedsack climb had determined that steps like these had somehow been involved in the boy's childhood trauma.

After the competition, Jude tried to regain the spirit of fun and merriment, but he was too dashed to maintain a convincing charade.

Cory cuddled next to him, held his hand, and leaned her head on his shoulder. Putting his arm around her and squeezing her tightly, he whispered, "I wish I had a glass of water."

"We'll be outside in just a minute. I'll get you one then."

His love for Cory quickly counterbalanced his temporary depression. "I love you so much. I just wish we could be together alone right now. I prefer cuddling on a hill to competing for the kill."

"I know, my rhyming poet lover!"

Chapter 29

The feedsack climb was the last event before the hayride across the fields and the culminating evening campfire. This much-awaited climax featured the corn and hotdog roast and "the sunset vespers above the vale," as Pastor Gabriel always called them.

Moving en masse with the others, Jude and Cory made their way out of the barn to commence this final and favorite part of the day. Guests gathered around the two wagons for the hayride up the long, winding lane through the woods and across the upper fields. Jude and Cory keenly anticipated the hayride and events to follow. Walking toward the wagons, Jude's mind oscillated between profound love for Cory and depression over the climbing event that had instantaneously stoked the memories of his grandpa's horrible death—that catastrophic event that, since he was now back on his grandpa's turf in Armstrong County, had become more intensely alive than ever.

At the moment when the memory of Jeremiah Wakefield's tragic fall was most vivid in Jude's mind, a beautiful dog walked into the center of the group. Though he had no collar or identification of any sort, he was nicely groomed and did not have the appearance of a stray. According to the dog experts in the crowd, he was apparently a black Lab and border collie mix, the latter historically used for shepherding flocks. He was all black except for white paws and a white diamond on his chest. The dog was very friendly and, as though on a mission, marched directly to Jude and Cory and befriended them instantly. He licked their hands and nuzzled his snout against their legs.

Seeing the dog's warm demeanor and the instant change in Jude's mood, someone quipped, "Well, Jude, the dog surely has given you new life."

"Yes," chimed in one of Jude's good friends with whom he shared lots of mutual ribbing, "he compensates for your botched climb! Ha!"

"New life," Pastor Gabriel reiterated as he stood near the others. "We need to give our late-arriving picnic mascot a name." Everybody laughed, as he continued. "Why not the Greek name for 'new life'? That word is Zoe. Wouldn't that make a great name? I understand that's typically a female name, but we're emphasizing etymology, not gender. Remember the verse in the Bible that says Christ came to give us abundant life? It's in John 10:10. Well, the Greek word there is 'Zoe.' You do recall this detail from last Sunday's sermon, don't you?" As Gabriel chuckled, his eye twinkled, and the people laughed. Gabriel held his hand on the dog's head. "Beloved creature of God, I christen you Zoe, even if you are male." Everybody laughed at the pastor's wit. By now the dog had mixed with the crowd and warmed his way into their hearts.

"Zoe it is!" Jude replied. "Why not?" Patting the dog to send him on his way, Jude and Cory walked with the others who were boarding the wagons for the ride through the forest lane toward the upper open fields.

During the jaunt up the hill, the people sang the songs they had sung as children on these same hayrides—old country ditties like "Do, Lord, O Do Lord," "This Little Light of Mine," "Down by the Riverside," "Kumbaya," and many others. As they wound their way through the tree-fringed lane, Jude and Cory entered into the spirit of singing, though from time to time they recited lines of poetry to each other. Forgetting his humiliation in the barn, Jude soon recovered his emotional poise.

Years later, he realized how magnified his dilemma had become during the beginning of that slow climb up the hill. How could he pursue his life's dream—writing—when he was blocked so completely from doing so? Happily, distracting himself from this ongoing inner turmoil was easy as they drove through the woods on this summer evening. Immersed in the sheer beauty of nature, Jude spoke softly to Cory. "'Nature never did forsake the heart that loved her.' What poet?"

"Wordsworth," Cory said. "I'm sure of that, but I don't know which poem—'The Great Ode' or 'Lines above Tintern Abbey.' Which is it?"

"The second one—'Lines.'"

Cory said nothing but looked admiringly at Jude. "I have a question. What's it like having your mind?"

"I'll handle that question the way Socrates would."

"How's that?"

"By asking a question in return. Here's mine: what kind of a dumb question is that?"

"Your mind is a concordance, encyclopedia, and unabridged dictionary all rolled into one."

"Will you stop being silly? You must be looking in a mirror again. 'The summer's flower is to the summer sweet; though to itself it only live and die.'"

"There. See? You did it again. More poetry. It just flows out of you. What's that one from? I don't even know what it means let alone who wrote it!"

"Shakespeare's 'Sonnet 94.' Think it through. It's not hard. Everybody gushes on and on about the glory and beauty of the summer flower—the lovely red rose is a good example—but from its perspective, it lives, endures the cycles of life, and dies like everything else. No big deal. It's just another little molecule in a vast universe."

Cory thought more deeply. "I'm referring to how rich and deep your mind is. You have a unique way of connecting random and seemingly isolated bits of information to that mass of stored data in your brain. You interweave it all like the beautiful Turkish carpet in Chuck's living room."

"I guess I'll take that as a compliment—nice use of metaphor by the way—but understand one thing. My mind is all I've ever known, as yours is all you've ever known. I don't see my mind as different from yours or anybody else's. If we could switch minds—I mean, take turns seeing and processing reality through each other's minds and temporarily filter life's events through those differing perception grids—then we'd be in a position to compare differences. We'd see how different minds receive and process sense stimuli, but as it is, we're shackled to our own eyes, restricted to our entrenched ways of looking at the world. Most good thinkers realize to what extent people are imprisoned within the walls of their own minds."

"Okay, Mr. Philosopher. We'll let it go at that. But I'd do anything to have a mind as retentive as yours. You just don't forget, and you're so incredibly verbal."

"I'll quote the verse you taught me years ago. 'My tongue is the pen of a ready writer.' I remember the verse but not the citation."

"Psalm 45:1."

"Yes, that's it. Well, don't sell yourself short, Cory. You're light years beyond most of the students with whom I take classes at the university."

Cory looked at him as they passed under the low-hanging boughs. "Thanks, Jude. You have no idea how that encourages me. You've always done that. You've never belittled me even though I spin my wheels in a limestone labyrinth by day and farm fields by night."

The remainder of the evening with the church folks was magical for both Jude and Cory. The vale below stretched some twenty to thirty miles to the horizon from this highest point in Armstrong County.

It reminded Jude of a poem. "Do you remember Matthew Arnold's 'Dover Beach'? In the poem, the speaker looks across at Calais in France from England's white cliffs of Dover and reflects:

For the world which seems
To lie before us like a land of dreams,

So various, so beautiful, so new,
Hath really neither joy, nor love, nor light,
Nor certitude, nor peace, nor help for pain.

"You see how Arnold likens the diminution of faith in nineteenth-century England to the shrinking sea at low tide. But you and I, Cory Mohney, merrily float upon the expansive sea of faith, not the shrunk sea of unfaith. We are going to pursue our sanctified way to the safe harbor beyond. Despite the problems that we both face—and they have been nearly unbearable at various times in the past—we will in time make it to that tranquil haven."

"That's beautiful, Jude. Your reference to the harbor reminds me of my favorite Emily Dickinson line: 'Futile—the winds—to a heart in port.' You used to say how much you liked that line. I think it's from 'Wild Nights! Wild Nights!' right?"

"Yes. Surely that's one of Dickinson's best lines. Tell me what it means to you."

"Well, life's billowing waves and raging winds can't touch the heart that's completed its journey across the tempestuous seas and made it safely to its port at last. Yes, I think that's it. The wind is futile to a heart that's made it safely to the harbor. That is such a powerful image!"

"Yes, it is." Jude looked directly at Cory. "I want that rest. I want the journey to be done. Remember when I compared myself to Dante's narrator—lost in the wood, the right road lost? I've found you, my guide, and you've gotten me on the right path. I'm walking again, though not out of the woods. I'm slowly regaining my faith, but my soul craves something better."

Cory was shocked to see, in the glow of the campfire, a tear forming in Jude's eye. "Jude, you have a tear in your eye!" She slid closer to him. "I told Pastor Gabe that your soul was craving the higher road or some such thing. You know what he said?"

"I have no idea, but I know it would be good."

"On the spot, he quoted a text from Isaiah 29."

"I'd love to hear it."

"It was so good I memorized it. Here it is. The text says a man eats 'but he awakes, and his soul is still empty ... [H]e drinks; But he awakes, and ... his soul still craves.'"

"'His soul still craves.' That's me, kid; my soul still craves. But now I have you. Cory, I worship you. You know that. I keep flashing back to the dark years when I was separated from you. I still feel that pain. That's how awful it was!"

"I know all about that, believe me!"

"Now you don't have tears. I see the shooting lights of thy wild eyes."

"Jude, what a line that is! The shooting lights ... Say it again."

"'The shooting lights of thy wild eyes.' That's what I'm looking at—radiant light shooting out of your joy-filled eyes."

"That is beautiful. What's it from?"

"The same poem—Wordsworth's 'Lines Composed a Few Miles above Tintern Abbey.'"

"All right. I enjoyed that digression, but tell me what caused the tear in your eye."

"I haven't commenced the work to which I'm called—writing. That's my other big anxiety in life. I'll be more precise. It's the disease in my soul. I want to write! I say with Job: 'Oh, that my words were written! Oh, that they were inscribed in a book!' Amen is all I can say to that."

"I know you do. And one day you will. Mark my words."

"You always did give me assurance. Thank you for that." He cupped his hand to her ear and whispered, "Wish I could kiss you right now!"

"That makes two of us! Keep going. There's something else on your mind."

"I've been thinking about what you talked about—the pervasiveness of evil. I'm blown away by it. It causes people to do such crazy things. I can't stop thinking about Duke, his crazy behavior and what it might lead to." Jude twirled a twig in his fingers and threw it in the fire. "How sad it is to watch people pursue the sick and crazy things that wreck their lives. Claudio says exactly that in Shakespeare's *Measure for Measure*:

> Our natures do pursue,
> Like rats that ravin down their proper bane,
> A thirsty evil, and when we drink we die.

"There's another one I don't understand. Please explain."

"Rats greedily crave the very poison—that's what ravin is, poison—which kills them. Isn't that a perfect description of mortals? We eagerly pursue the very things—the habits, the addictions, the vices—that destroy us. Why do we indulge in that which kills us? Unbelievable!"

During a brief pause in their conversation, neither said anything as they drank in the splendor of the summer evening. At last Cory broke the silence. "If I were going to paint this scene, I'd foreground this section here." She had rolled her hand into a circular tube and looked through it. She took her hand down. "Right there! I'd frame the painting with the barn at right and the grove of trees at left. Can you see the painting? I'm seeing it on my easel right now."

"You artist!"

"You poet! We need to continue this talk later," Cory leaned over and whispered. "People will think we're antisocial. But sometime you need to talk about your heavy-heartedness. I thought the happiness I gave you alleviated all that." She winked at him and gave Jude a peck on the cheek.

Later in the evening, the campfire vespers complete, the group boarded the wagons to go down the lane to their cars, which they had parked by the barn. When the first wagon, the one Jude and Cory rode, approached the cow path that led to the lane, there "big as day" (Jude wrote in his journal), sat Zoe. He was "like a sentinel, keeping watch, observing from afar. He sat at the brow of the hill as if he had been waiting there the whole time." When the wagon approached him, Zoe, as though on cue and without hesitation, came directly to the wagon, jumped up, and sat down directly beside Jude and Cory.

"Can you believe it?" Cory said in amazement. They were about to learn that Zoe's entrance into their lives was not a passing thing.

Chapter 30

Zoe's coming to Jude and Cory down at the barn earlier in the evening hadn't attracted that much attention. A number of nearby folks witnessed the event, but that was it. Pets typically choose one person to greet and lick before moving on to the others, as Zoe had done down at the barn. For that reason, no one paid particular attention to the dog's instantaneous and seemingly arbitrary attraction to Jude and Cory. This incident on the hill, on the other hand, was altogether different. It was as though the dog had waited for this moment and intentionally came in a straight line to them, jumped onto the wagon, and sat down between them—their long, lost friend.

People were amazed. "Jude, are you sure you don't know this dog?" someone shouted from the rear of the wagon. "You've got your buddy back, Jude and Cory," laughed another.

"No, never saw him before. Cory's never seen him either."

"Look how he came directly to us," Cory quietly said to Jude. "Others are petting him because he's so gentle and friendly, but he's adopted us, especially you, as his masters. How amazing!"

"Now that's the strangest thing I've ever seen," a nearby friend commented.

Zoe stayed by their side on their journey down the winding lane under a star-filled sky.

Down at the barn, as people were disembarking from the hay wagon, Jude and Cory noted one little detail about Zoe. Everybody had dismounted from the wagon, but Zoe did not jump off as most pets would. In fact, he seemed to fear the height and actually stayed away from the edge of the wagon. Jude lifted the dog to the ground. In the rush of good-byes, Jude and Cory paid no particular notice.

After farewells were said, people went to their cars. Jude and Cory were by this time genuinely interested in their new friend. When Jude opened the car door a moment later, Zoe jumped into the backseat and sat immediately in the middle, king of his domain.

"Can you beat that?" Cory said. The dog looked at her as she spoke. "It's as though he hears and understands. What an intelligent dog! What do we do with him?"

"We could drive up to the end of Dutch Hollow Road and see if he gets out of the car there. Or maybe we should stop at some of the houses along Dutch Hollow Road and even Freeport Road to see if anyone is looking for a lost dog."

They drove around awhile, but no one appeared to be searching for their lost canine friend, nor had Zoe expressed any sort of recognition excitement when passing the homes.

"Do you think we should take him to your house for the time being?" Jude at last broke the silence. "Your dad might enjoy him."

"Great idea! Dad always loved dogs."

They drove to Cory's house to spend some time with Pete and recap the church picnic social. Pete had expressed real interest in the event, but, like many depressed people, he had decided against participating. "I think I'll just park myself right here today." He opted for sitting on the couch and wallowing in the glamorous days of old.

When Jude opened the door to let Cory out, Zoe immediately jumped out, ran ahead to the kitchen door, and waited for them to open it. Once inside, Zoe went directly to the den, a small room off the kitchen where Pete Mohney spent much of his time. Zoe crawled up beside him on the couch, put his snout on Pete's thigh and gently licked his hand. Then he contentedly rested his head against Pete's thigh.

"What's this?" Pete exclaimed. "Where'd you get this dog? He's beautiful!" When he rubbed Zoe's back and head, the dog started licking him again.

"Dad, look at you. That's the biggest smile I've seen on your face in months!"

Again, Jude and Cory were mystified by the strangeness of it all. The dog had made a beeline for Pete Mohney as though with purpose.

"He acts with cognition," Jude commented.

"Where did you find him?" Pete asked.

They filled him in on the background, and every time they mentioned the dog, by name or not, Zoe looked at them, an intent listener and observer of all proceedings.

"It's as though he knows we're talking about him," Pete said.

"We said the same thing, and so did the church folks," Cory agreed.

A short while later, Jude got up to leave. "What do we do with our new friend?"

"I think he's found a home," Cory said. "Don't you agree, Dad? Do you mind if he stays here? At least until we find out if an owner turns up."

"Are you kidding?" Pete asked. "I've never seen anything like him." Zoe went over to Pete and extended his paw to shake his hand. "Well, I'll be! The human dog!"

"He's a canine with human properties," Cory laughed.

"I'd say he's a human with canine properties," Jude quipped. Everyone laughed as Jude and Cory went out to sit at the kitchen table.

The lovers peered directly into each other's eyes as they sat at the kitchen table moments later. "Do you have any idea how much I love you?" Cory leaned toward Jude and whispered.

"You know how I feel. I want to marry you right now. You with the wild, light-shooting eyes!"

They spoke quietly in the kitchen as Cory brewed a pot of tea. Occasionally they looked in toward the den to watch her father play with Zoe and tussle the fur on his back, laughing and smiling in a way she hadn't seen in years. "Zoe's giving dad new life in the same way you gave new life to me."

"Yes, I know all about the new life, and I understand you perfectly. I love you, Cory Mohney, with the same love. I was the one who was walking around with a giant hole in my heart." He paused and looked into her eyes and held her hand. The changes in their lives in a matter of days astounded them both. This is what he had prayed for. His prayers had been answered more fully than he could have imagined. "What's your biggest wish right now?"

"Marry you, go to college, have kids someday soon, and spend each day like this in total bliss." She paused for a moment. "Oh, yes, one more thing. To paint with the talent and beauty of Mirlarna Armstrong. I love her work. And you?"

"The same. Finish my degree, I suppose, though that comes to mean less and less. I know I'll need the degree if I'm to land a university teaching job. That whole master plan has come to mean so little in just a matter of days. I just want to be with you." He drew her close to him. "Did you ever think we'd reconcile so quickly and so completely?"

"I'm not sure. I think so. At least I knew it was possible. I knew that if love had its way, we'd end up right at this point. I prayed daily, Jude. You have no idea how I prayed. Without you, every day was awful. I had nothing to look forward to, nothing in my life." She went over to him, kissed him, and sat on his lap. A moment later, she said, "Hey, I just remembered something. Dad said he came across an old map of the mine when rooting through some papers today. He said he wanted to show it to us. Let's take a look."

"Yea, let's do."

She brought the map from the den and laid it out before them. After getting oriented, he pointed to a spot on the mine. "This is where I parked the train the day you came to see me and we stole the kiss forbidden. See that slight bend in the corridor? That's where I parked the train when we saw each other. Right here around the corner."

"Right." She again chose not to comment about the little episode that followed.

"For sure! And here's the new section that the roof bolters have started working on. They say it's had some cave-ins in the past but will be safe once bolted and secured. Let's check it out some evening."

Looking at the map, Cory soon noticed something. "I'm having trouble figuring out where this is. Can you identify it?"

She was looking at a long corridor, lined with large rooms, which ran tangentially to the main mine corridor. Jude too was puzzled.

"I'll ask my dad. Hang on."

Upon returning from the den a minute later, Cory said that this had been an active section of the mine, the control hub actually, but owing to a disease problem with the mushrooms several decades ago, they shut down the entire section. "Dad says it used to be the very center of mine life. In the early years, the management used these offices as their headquarters instead of the separate administrative building outside the mine. In fact, it was years later when they moved the offices to the new, above-ground location. Maybe we ought to check out this section. That's one of our last underground frontiers."

"It's a date. Let's see what else we can find." Jude enjoyed this chance to explore the mine map in such a leisurely fashion. He ran his eyes over it and then came on a distant section of the mine, a long corridor that extended away from the mine proper. It wormed its way for some distance, an isolated lone corridor that had been abandoned by the original miners because the quality and quantity of the limestone was poorer. Jude took a closer look. In small barely legible print, he finally made out two barely discernible words— "Deep 50!" He scratched his head and raised the map to his face to look more carefully. Jude thought to himself, *Deep 50. Why does that ring a bell?*

Neither spoke until Cory, a few moments later, broke the silence. "Jude, I have an idea. We're both on evening shift next week. During break time, let's ride back into the mine to that abandoned section where the offices used to be. We've never explored that part of the mine."

"Great idea. Let's do it."

On the porch, Jude held Cory tightly against him and kissed her again and again. "Do you know how hard it is to leave you?"

"I know exactly how you feel."

"And to be able to show you love the way God intended for married people."

"That too! Of course I know what you mean. Don't you know I feel the same way? I think of marriage constantly."

"Good-bye, my lovely rose." With sheer force of effort, he pulled himself away from her soft embrace, sighed deeply, and drove home to his grandma's house.

Chapter 31

The next week in the mine was a busy one. Because officials from the EPA were scheduled for their yearly inspection, upper-level management had given detailed instructions to crew bosses and plant officials to complete miscellaneous jobs and delayed maintenance projects. The plant had to be in tiptop shape for these annual inspections. Painting projects were slated for completion, as were minor construction jobs, some of which were scheduled for evening hours after the day-turn shift employees departed.

Assigned to the evening shift, Jude was instructed to help out with a variety of odd jobs—repair equipment in the shop, grease the bearings on the trains, help install new shelving in the packhouse, and paint a variety of small areas, including one of the lunchrooms. The place had to be "spiffy and sparkling," as one of the managers repeatedly preached.

Because the packhouse was in many ways the nerve center of the operation of the mine—the place where the mushrooms were sorted, cleaned, and packaged—a rigorous cleaning and repainting of certain areas had been predictably mandated in anticipation of the annual inspection. As in other years, employees were given the opportunity to bid for overtime and work evening shifts during these pre-inspection weeks. Few opted for the overtime, however, preferring the precious light of the long summer evenings for their own use. While not all of the employees experienced seasonal affective disorder, many did.

Working in the chill and dark day after day, month after month, year after year took its toll, and so the extended light of warm summer evenings beckoned to them like the Siren's song. Cory's bid to work the evening shift, as a result, was relatively uncontested.

At break time—8:00 p.m.—on their first day of evening shift, Jude picked Cory up at the packhouse, and they raced through the mine, map in hand, toward the management offices that had been abandoned decades ago. Venturing down a long and dark corridor, they were surprised to see, a hundred yards into the tunnel and around a bend, a line of barrels with a rope between them that cordoned off this corridor and from which hung a large No Trespassing sign. One of the barrels, slightly away from the wall, allowed for passage of their cart.

"Should we go?" Jude asked.

"Why not?" Cory's eyes twinkled. "Go for it, my trail-blazer."

"Okay, wild, shooting lights!"

The corridor had obviously not been used for a long time. Discarded tools had been deposited here years ago, and many small chunks of rock, fallen from the roof and scattered about the area, reminded them anew of the real danger of cave-ins. As far as they could tell, the roof looked safe, so they drove deeper and deeper into this corridor that had been hastily vacated.

Although this had been one of the central corridors for mushroom growth in those early years, the disease epidemic had spread, plague-like, through the entire corridor. As a result, many rooms of valuable mushrooms had been contaminated and the entire crop destroyed. The loss in those years had been very great and almost put the fledgling enterprise under. Not being able to completely rid this section of the mine of the deadly disease, despite repeated efforts, and losing profits in those crucial first years, mine officials eventually made the difficult decision of closing this central hub altogether and relocating the management offices to a new, above-ground complex.

Jude and Cory found themselves in the corridor that had been condemned years before. Once officials made the decision to close this section of the mine, they acted quickly. Much of the equipment had been abandoned and left in place, so great was the fear of contaminating the other sections of the mine with the dreaded disease. Officials were shaken by the despairing accounts of other mushroom growers who, though not in such a unique underground setting, had been completely wiped out from the ravages of similar disease epidemics. In an attempt to prevent a similar operation-wide disaster, they cut their losses, quickly abandoned this section, and developed whole new areas of the underground labyrinth. The calculated decision proved to be the right one. The disease had been stopped altogether, and the newly opened sections produced an even more abundant crop in time.

Examining this abandoned world, untouched from the day when people exited in a panic, Jude spoke of similar instances in history when people were forced to run for their lives and make a fast getaway. "This place reminds me of the vacated cabins in the *Titanic*," Jude commented. "Or the empty rooms at Pompeii. At Pompeii, I saw the corpse of a man who awkwardly held both hands above his head. When one of the people in our party asked the guide why the man was holding his hands this way at the time of the eruption, the guide theorized that he had probably held his tunic over his head to keep off spewing ash and lava. The guide wryly noted, 'His plan didn't work!'"

Jude and Cory were awestruck by this abandoned world that had also been vacated so hurriedly. They ventured along the main corridor, exploring room after empty room where the mushrooms had been grown. They eventually came to one section of the corridor, from which a spur branched from the main line. These were clearly the rooms for some of the office workers.

At the end of this small corridor, they came to a room adorned, to their great surprise, with a massive, solid oak door—so out of place in this underground world of cold gray limestone. They parked the cart, kept the headlights shining, and were astounded to see that the carved oak door, though shut, was not locked. What in the world could this be? Opening the door, they stepped into a suite of offices, in the center of which lay a large and impressive room. After walking toward this imposing center room, they flipped the light switch. Two of the four table lamps immediately illuminated the room.

Clearly this had been the office of the CEO and company president. Secretaries and other employees apparently worked in the adjoining offices, but surely the manager worked in this large and atypically ornate office. The president, obviously well-traveled, had embellished the room with travel mementoes. Couches and sitting chairs, inlaid tables, and lamps, and a large mahogany desk were accented by lovely decorative touches throughout the room—a Turkish silk carpet on the floor with its made-in-Istanbul label, intricately woven runners on coffee and end tables, Egyptian alabaster marble lamps, Chinese statuary and bric-a-brac on the shelves, and tasteful pictures and paintings on the walls. Maps of Europe and Asia were fastened to the walls. The room was especially beautiful in this deeply buried, faraway world of brooding, dark silence.

Astounded by it all, Jude thought of Thomas Hardy's poem, "The Convergence of the Twain," wherein Hardy described the sunken luxurious *Titanic* that was so out of place as it lay on the ocean bottom: "Jewels in joy designed To ravish the sensuous mind Lie lightless, all their sparkles bleared and black and blind ... What does this vaingloriousness down here?"

"I can't believe you remember those lines, Jude. But that is so perfect. That's what this is— vaingloriousness. What a word! Well, it's so deeply buried and far removed from life above ground. What's it doing here? Can you believe this tastefully decorated room exists amid this world of gray rock and pitch-black silence? It's not that it's ostentatious. It's just that someone had a real appreciation for artistic beauty."

"You're right. That speaks to the love of beauty and aesthetics back there in the 1940s and fifties."

"Chuck has similar travel mementoes in his library too. Upon seeing it for the first time, Gabe quoted one of the Proverbs to him."

"Which one?"

"I memorized it because it so applied to Chuck's collection. It's

Proverbs 24:4, 'By knowledge the rooms are filled with all precious and pleasant riches.'"

"Yes, that's true of Chuck's house and this place too. Today, cheap steel-framed structures, with no aesthetic appeal, dot the landscape like sores on a plague victim. Everything's been streamlined because of austerity budgeting. But those folks of yesteryear appreciated beauty, and that includes the forerunners of this underground farming enterprise. Look at this place! It is indeed a celebration of beauty and refinement. The room is filled with ... what did the verse say?"

"With all precious and pleasant riches."

"Whoever used this suite must have traveled a lot to foreign places to gather these riches. Look at these small pyramids, Egyptian perfume bottles, inlaid boxes from Damascus, and cloisonné Chinese vases. They look like keepsakes that someone could have been picked up from travel abroad." Cory picked up a wood shepherd. "Look at this—handmade in Jerusalem from olive wood!"

"I know one thing," Jude continued after an additional moment of looking around. "We found our secret hideaway."

"Do you think so?" Cory reflected for a moment. "Why not? Yes, and I think I know where someone will be reading and writing his poetry at long last."

"And the studio where someone will complete her superb paintings and become as famous as the English artist Mirlarna Armstrong, whose work you adore."

"Jude, it's beautiful. Can you imagine what it will look like with just a little bit of work?"

"Let's explore a bit." They looked around at the coffee table and end tables. "Look here." Jude was examining a rack containing magazines and newspapers from the mid-1950s. He picked up a copy of the *Daily Leader Times*, Kittanning's newspaper, which, on the front page, spoke of President Dwight Eisenhower. "Listen to this article by Corbin Wyant. 'President Eisenhower is still resting comfortably at his farm in Gettysburg, Pennsylvania, after his heart attack in the middle of the night on Saturday, September 24, 1955. He had just completed twenty-seven holes of golf in Denver, Colorado, the day before.' Can you believe that, Cory? Remember when we visited Gettysburg and saw the Eisenhower farm?"

"Yes. I loved that trip." Cory leafed through a couple of magazines and shouted, "How about this one? You won't believe it—an article on the new singing sensation Elvis Presley!" The article featured numerous pictures of the youthful legendary rock star from Memphis. His smash songs, "Hound Dog" and "Don't be Cruel," were still popular. She read aloud from this 1957 magazine.

> It all began when Elvis Presley recorded his first smash hit, "Heartbreak Hotel," on January 10, 1956. Elvis Presley went on to record two more smash hits, which took the world by storm on July 2, 1956—"Don't be Cruel" and "Hound Dog." Mr. Presley further caught the attention of the world when, as a young man of twenty-two, he made a famous purchase: he bought a mansion in Memphis on March 25, 1957, from Dr. Thomas D. Moore and wife, Ruth Marie, who was the granddaughter of the original mansion owner, Stephen C. Toof. Mr. Toof was the proprietor of the *Memphis Daily Appeal*, and his wife, Ruth, was a noted musical prodigy. Elvis Presley had attained similar media notoriety back on July 5, 1955, when he purchased a pink Cadillac Fleetwood.

Cory stopped reading the article and looked around.

"This is a museum of the 1950s!" Jude said. "I feel as though I'm in a time machine that docked in 1957. Look at all of this memorabilia!"

"We need a name. We have to have a name for our underground haven."

"How about Little Gidding?"

"Little Gidding. That's the name of one of Eliot's *Four Quartets*, isn't it?"

"Yes, the last one."

"Why that name? I remember liking the poem, but it's been a long time since I've read it. What's the connection with our haven?"

"Eliot talks about the Pentecostal fire in the dark time of the year. That's what my soul needs. That's what our love needs. He also says in the poem that 'history may be servitude; history may be freedom.' Well, for us the sordid past—I refer to its stupidly sad ending—will no longer imprison us. We will no longer be in bondage to it but use it as our gateway to freedom. Remember when I said that before? This place is the very quintessence of that freedom. Don't you agree?"

"Brilliant, Dr. Jude. I love that. Why not?"

The shelves were empty, as if someone had cleared out the books and other belongings. "See the empty spaces here and there?" Jude said a moment later. "I'm guessing that the president took some of the valuables and left the other things behind."

Looking a bit more at the riches of the rooms, they noted on the wall a transparent aerial topographical map of Butler and Armstrong Counties that had been superimposed on the network of limestone mine. This enabled Jude to take note of that which had always fascinated him—the correspondence of the upper topography on the earth's surface to the caverns and tunnels underground. He searched on the map for a while to locate Little Gidding, their new hideaway, and note the terrain that was directly overhead. "Do you see what's directly above us, Cory?" Jude said, pointing to the map. "That, my dear, is what we folks who teach figures of speech call situational irony!"

"I can't believe it! That truly is ironic!"

As time had gotten away from them, they walked a moment later to the door and turned out the light. "Ah, Little Gidding," Jude sighed. "I know we're going to love this place."

They shut the door and hopped on the cart to return to their jobs. At the entryway to the corridor, Jude stretched the barrels the entire way across the corridor and spread some gravel over their tire tracks that were visible along the wall. Total secrecy was essential since this would be their summer hiding place.

Chapter 32

The next morning, Jude, Cory, Joey, and Laura commenced a Saturday workday on the farm. The various maintenance projects at the mine reminded Jude and Cory of the work that had been neglected at the farm over the last couple years. Because Pete Mohney had, in his depression, done little to maintain the grounds, its beleaguered state was becoming more obvious with each passing month. Joey and Cory, along with Duke on occasion, kept the farm running, but delayed repairs gave the farm a worn and tattered look.

The first task was to make a list of the jobs that required immediate attention—painting the milk house, replacing its shingles, painting the house porch, planting the flowerbeds, cleaning the barn, replacing loose boards in the corn crib, putting the main sliding door to the barn back on the track, mowing the neglected lower meadow, filling the ruts and potholes in the lane, and so on. They prioritized this in order to tackle the important jobs first. As they worked best in groups, they decided on the buddy system to paint the porch, hang the porch swing, put up the awning around the porch, and other similar jobs. Early in the day, Joey had made a run to Worthington Hardware for materials—paint, shingles, nails, and various supplies—while the other three worked.

Their progress during the day was impressive. Joey and Jude's final job, by late afternoon, was to replace a few of the shingles on the milk house roof. During that time, both men were on the roof tacking the last of the new shingles. They had propped the ladder along the gabled end. Zoe, present with the work teams all morning, watched as they worked. As the men were about to come down from the milk house roof, Joey started to lower himself from the gabled peak to the eight-foot ladder, which, without the men realizing it, had shifted position and was leaning perilously.

As Joey dangled his feet over the edge of the roof toward the ladder, Zoe began to bark in a loud, panicky fashion. Both men instantly looked.

"What's that all about?" Joey asked midstep.

Jude looked down at Joey, who was about to lower his weight to the ladder, and then saw that the ladder was out of position. "Wait, the ladder moved!" Joey caught himself just in time.

Safely on the ground moments later, the men looked each other. "What do you make of that?" Joey asked.

"I don't know. It's as though the dog sensed danger and tried to get our attention."

"Exactly what I was thinking." Joey petted Zoe and spoke again. "What do you make of this dog?"

They looked at Zoe who, as usual, was looking at them—always watching intently. They shook their heads in disbelief.

Jude and Cory gave themselves a well-deserved break from the day's work that evening by going to the mine. On Saturday evenings, the mushroom mine was a completely quiet world. No employees work, and guards make infrequent security rounds. Officials had granted them permission to put final touches on a small job in the packhouse, which they completed more quickly than anticipated. Having some unexpected free moments, they decided on one of their favorite, though obviously frowned-upon, pastimes—racing the electric carts through the mine.

On this particular evening, Jude detached the electric cable on Cory's cart and was preparing to unplug his own when Cory, seeing that the cable on her cart was already detached, jumped on it and, on impulse, took off. "Catch me if you can!" Off she sped, her hair blowing wildly as she sped along, a novel phenomenon since all entrants to the mine were required to wear helmets.

Soon Jude was in fast pursuit. Several years later, when Jude was obsessed with unearthing every miniscule scrap about his beloved Cory and that golden summer of love, Morley Spencer presented Jude with a stack of security camera film that had been taken that summer. An outmoded security system had been replaced by a more efficient model shortly after Jude commenced his summer work. The film taken by the various cameras during those first weeks after installation had been saved to make sure that bugs were worked out and that the new system met their needs.

This stored stack of film, for whatever reason, had never been discarded. Jude's friend had accidentally happened upon it one day, retrieved it, and presented it to Jude. Back at the university, Jude labored by the hour with the technicians to locate various sequences that depicted the two of them, especially Cory. Eventually Bill, the skilled videographer, isolated many of the segments in which Cory and Jude were visible in the footage. After enhancing them digitally, he produced some fine sequences.

One of the best of these clips, Jude opined much later, was taken this particular evening in the mine when the two of them raced on separate carts. One of the sections of the limestone mine had been originally quarried in unique fashion. A thick wall had been left standing between two huge rooms. In time, archways had been chiseled at equidistant intervals through this lengthy partition, creating a series of Roman-looking arches that resembled an ancient aqueduct.

In one section of the security film, Jude and Cory wove their carts in and out through this obstacle course of arched openings. From the angle of the camera, they braided a perfectly symmetrical pattern as they raced along, Cory swerving to the right, Jude to the left in the arch behind. Back and forth they reticulated their way along this corridor, weaving a perfect pattern of interlocking eights.

Bill the technician had located a second batch of film from the security camera that was positioned at the opposite end of this same room with the Romanesque arches. This cavern had been placed under high surveillance owing to the threat of disease among the high-grade mushrooms that had been grown here. From the angle of this second camera, Jude and Cory were visible from the front. When coming across this favorite bit of film years later, Jude played it in slow motion over and over again. There was Cory laughing and giggling, hair blowing wildly behind her, as she raced and swerved ahead of Jude.

After he had become the established author and was on the national lecture circuit, he occasionally showed highlights of a film about the mine and their love. The film contained a brief clip of this "Weaving Room," as it was later dubbed by media personnel. It had become a favorite for Jude and numerous audiences alike.

One evening at one of these lectures, he commented, "This is one of the few good mine clips I have of us together in that enchanting summer. Cory's rapturous joy is so amply evident in this sequence. See how she throws her head back in laughter. Watch the look on her face as she takes this next turn. I'll end with this sequence of still shots that we culled from this film clip." He projected a series of photos on the screen. "Does anybody recognize this photo?"

A gentleman shouted from the audience. "That's the one on the dust jacket of your book!"

"Right you are!"

The next day was Sunday, and after morning church and lunch, Cory and Jude went up to the orchard to continue their reading and discussion of *Hamlet*. They were reading the part in act 2, scene 2, when Claudius lures Rosencrantz and Guildenstern into spying on Hamlet.

"What stooges they were," Cory commented.

"But don't you think that's a big theme in the play?" Jude asked. "I realize that the vast majority of people don't know Shakespeare's play. I readily admit that they care absolutely nothing for the great playwright. But his plays, *Hamlet* included, are intensely relevant in our day for the way they depict controlling personalities who try to manipulate those around them. In the play, the power-players try to control and manipulate everybody else. Polonius plants a spy on his son Laertes in France, Claudius and Polonius spy on Ophelia when she's alone with Hamlet, Polonius spies on Gertrude and Hamlet in Gertrude's bed chamber, Rosencrantz and Guildenstern spy on Hamlet, and so on. In each case, the manipulators reduce these underlings to mere stooges who willingly sell out to a superior intelligence. They don't even know they're being used!"

"So that's the consequence of not heeding the still, small voice in the heart," Cory responded.

"That's one fascinating way to read the play!"

Chapter 33

The next day in the mine, Abe Badoane—"acting all the world like Shakespeare's evil Claudius," Jude quipped to Cory—was walking along when he spotted an employee working in the room where the miners' hats were stored, cleaned, and recharged. "Hi, Bert Conley. What's going on?"

"Not much, Smiley. Just cleaning and recharging the helmets."

Nat King Cole's "L-O-V-E" was playing on the radio in the background. Abe walked up to Bert with his winning smile. "I got a joke for you, Bert. Are you up for one?"

"Always. Your jokes are a riot."

"An elderly man was stopped by the police around 2:00 a.m. and was asked where he was going at that time of night. The gentleman replied, 'I'm on my way to a lecture about alcohol abuse and the effects it has on the human body, as well as smoking and staying out late.' The officer then asked, 'Really? Who's giving such a lecture at this time of night?' The man replied, 'That would be my wife.'"

Bert laughed hard. "You tell more jokes than anyone I know."

Abe then turned his attention to the batteries. "Tell me how these work." He gestured to the mine batteries surrounding him. "This is one part of the mine operation that I know nothing about. What's that solution you're putting into the batteries?"

"Well, it's simple really. This solution of hydrochloric acid provides the current for the battery lamps."

"I see. How long does that solution keep the lamps burning?" Abe struck his normal pose—chin resting on his thumb, index finger pointed upward across his cheek, and his other three fingers curled under the lips.

"About an eight- or ten-hour shift. After that, the light dims quickly."

"What happens if you err and don't fill the batteries clear to the top with the acid solution?"

"Exactly what you'd guess. It's lights out for Missy. Half-full, half the light. Get it? It's simple."

Abe continued looking at the contents of the room. "How long have you been working here?"

"I've had this job for a few years. I love it. I'm away from the gossip and backbiting." Bert finished capping one of the lamps. "The work's simple, and I never have to meet bosses' deadlines." He grinned at Abe.

"I caught your little dig there," Abe smiled. "Thanks, Bert. You're on top of your game. You do nice work." Abe took a couple steps and then walked back toward Bert. "By the way, you're one of the few people I can talk to about politics, but I've missed doing so lately."

"I have too. We used to get into some good discussions at lunch."

"Well, here's a topic that's been in the news a lot. I'm referring to the Worker Adjustment and Retraining Notification Act."

"I'm embarrassed to say that I've heard of the name of the bill but don't even know what it's about."

"The bill recently passed both the Senate and the House. It means that big employers can't do massive layoffs or shutdowns without a two-month notification to employees. No wonder it's called the WARN act!"

"Nice name! And necessary too."

"You take care, my friend, and thanks again." As Abe walked away, he reflected on what Bert said about the helmets. *I'll tuck away this bit of information. Could be of use when I tighten the noose!*

What a good man, Bert reflected to himself as Abe walked away.

Chapter 34

On Monday morning of the next week, Jude and Cory were back on their respective daylight crews, but a couple changes had been made. Cory was pulled from Duke's crew and assigned to Abe's, a move that she at the outset relished. Although Duke had settled after the nasty incident when he assaulted her, she was still happy to be free of him, even if it meant working on mystery man's crew. One could never be too sure about a guy like Duke who was notorious for "shooting from the hip" in the parlance of the mine.

In a second change, Jude had been assigned as driver to a crew that handled the picking of specialty mushrooms. One of the experienced pickers had been given the job of making the final check of the mushroom trays to see if these exotic mushrooms had been picked properly, thereby freeing Jude of this very crucial responsibility. Apart from that detail, for which he lacked training, he quickly learned the other aspects of the crew driver's job.

Cory fared better with Abe than she thought she would. He was gentlemanly in his conduct toward her, and his jokey demeanor made him popular with the women. Yet she could not rid herself of an uneasy feeling around him. In the barn one evening, after stacking bales of hay, she broached the topic to Jude.

"He's sharp, Jude, very sharp. As I told you in the past, I often look at him and wonder what he's doing in a place like the mine. The other day, he started telling me the numbers on all the employees' helmets. He knew the numbers on the helmets for every worker in the mine—nearly 1,300 employees, including the brass. The pickers are convinced that he has a photographic memory."

"I don't have to tell you how much the guy interests me. Chuck knows him very well. Let's get the lowdown from him someday."

"Good idea. I hesitate to bring this up. I know we're not to judge or have critical attitudes since loving others is the hallmark of Christianity. But I feel the need to say this. Remember when I said I feel evil in the mine at times?"

"Yes, I recall."

"Well, I've tried to monitor my feelings of late to see what it is that upsets me. Are you ready for this? I get that uncomfortable feeling only when I'm around Abe Badoane. I didn't realize that before, but now that I'm around him most of the day, I know that's the case."

"Unbelievable. I've learned to sit up and pay attention to your gut instincts—what you call your Spirit-led intuition. I'd listen to that still, small inner voice if I were you. Remember your earlier counsel to me about heeding the inner compass?"

That Monday morning, Abe Badoane came into work early. Since no one was yet in the helmet storage room, Abe went in briefly and walked out before Bert Conley entered. The security camera picked this up, and when questioned later, Bert said he wasn't in the room at the time but could testify, based on the footage, that Abe had been in the room a minute or so. He wasn't able to ascertain the reason for Abe's entering, but as nothing was out of place, Bert surmised that Abe, who had been intrigued by his helmet operation, just wanted a second quick look as he passed by the room. Since the camera film ran on a continuously rolling loop, new footage was later filmed over it, so neither Jude nor mine officials were able to examine the film and were forced to rely on Bert's word. Only later, when Jude reconstructed the summer events, did he manage to figure out Abe's intent in visiting the helmet room.

As head foreman of all the crews, Abe carried some considerable weight in the mine operation. It was to Abe, therefore, that Jude and the head picker brought the discouraging word that afternoon that their crew, responsible for picking jumbo-sized specialty mushrooms, was running well behind and would not have their designated trays harvested by quitting time. They requested immediate assistance.

Upon making a quick phone call, Abe learned from the operations manager that the large mushrooms had to be picked this afternoon since they were scheduled for mandatory evening shipment to Kinosha, Wisconsin. The operations manager was pleased with Abe's suggestion that Abe pull his own crew to assist in the harvesting of the specialty mushrooms. With the help of the backup shift during the last two hours of the day—a not uncommon practice when deadlines loomed—Abe assured his boss that the combined crews would be able to pick the jumbo mushrooms in time to make the pressing deadline.

"Great job, Abe," the operations manager said. "Always reliable, always thinking ahead. This is a crucial deadline with a major supplier that we have to meet. We can't lose this contract."

Back with his crew, Abe gathered the pickers together. "Lovely lasses, the head kahunas have reassigned us. We have to hustle over to help Jude Hepler's crew 6 make their deadline. Those gorgeous jumbos have to go out in tonight's shipment. We only have two hours to finish all the trays. Let's go."

In this particular case, the women liked the reassignment. The mushrooms were easier to pick because of their large size, and, more importantly, the particular room to which they were headed was located nearer to the exit, giving these pickers a head start in the punch clock checkout line and a faster departure at the end of the long workday.

Abe went to Cory. "Since you're the low picker on the totem pole—you have just joined our crew—and since we don't need the entire crew to help out, you stay back here and pick all of these last trays. I'll send Jude by to pick you up a few minutes before quitting time and bring you back to your crew so you can punch out with the other pickers. I know you'd prefer to work with his crew, but this will be better. Set your watch. I gave him careful instructions to pick you up here at the back of this room and then take you to your crew. I figured you hot young lovers would actually prefer this arrangement. Just wait at the back of the room. I gave him very clear directions. Jude would never let down his true love, especially when he has a chance to be alone with her for a few minutes here in this lovely rear sanctum so far away from roving eyes and gossipy tongues. I know young lovers cherish private moments. And this time Duke won't be policing your little rendezvous. I'll make sure he's out of the picture." He gave Cory a wink and drove away.

Having given Cory her assignment, Abe tracked down Jude to explain the arrangement that the manager had dictated for the day. "The crew to which you've been assigned will be joined by Cory's momentarily. Cory, however, won't be part of this group. She's picking the trays at the very back of room 14 and will walk to the front when finished. I gave her careful instructions to meet you at the entrance of the room out in the main hallway. If she's gone when you pull up to the front of that room, you'll know she finished early and got a ride out of the mine on another personnel carrier. That's a common practice. Flash your headlights a couple times and then turn them off altogether so you can see her lamp return the signal in case she's not finished and is still at the back of the room. That's how we do it around here. I figured you'd like meeting and riding together. Wouldn't you like that?"

"It definitely has possibilities."

"Remember, signal from the front. That's the way I set it up with Cory. She'll be waiting for you in the main corridor, and if she's not there or doesn't return your signal, that means she's already left the area. Adios, amigo."

He smiled and was gone. Jude would have preferred having Cory here with him, but with the increased number of pickers, he wouldn't be able to talk to her or barely exchange glances any way. So maybe the arrangement Abe proposed was the best. At least it held the promise of a few welcome minutes together in a private place at the rear of the room.

Cory disliked being by herself in the mine. In learning that she had to pick by herself at the back of a very long and isolated room, her first thought was that it might be another trap. Was Duke lurking there in the vicinity and, a half mile from any other person, waiting to assault or rape her? His last words to her had been, "Paybacks are tough. Around here, they're hard, very hard," and he obscenely gestured. He and Abe, moreover, were very close and had spoken together recently on more than one occasion. With trepidation, she picked these beds by herself in the terrible dark, her little beam of light serving as the only speck of illumination in this monstrous cavern. The thought of seeing Jude in less than two hours, however, consoled her. *I can do this*, she steeled herself and picked alone in the dark.

After a lengthy time of picking, she was unnerved because the mushrooms, strangely, were getting harder to see. *Do I need glasses? What's going on here?*

She tried to stay calm. No Duke was lurking about, though she often looked around and listened for stray sounds, especially during the first half hour. Her miner's lamp soon cast a small beam in the area in front of her instead of the virtual floodlight that should brightly illuminate objects even a hundred yards away. She looked at her watch often. Despite her duress, she was bent on picking the trays clean as a way of maintaining her reputation as one of the top pickers in the mine. *I can finish the last trays. I'm almost done.* She tried to take heart, but fear crept over her. *Stop shaking, hands!*

She finished the tray just as the beam of light faded to a faint glow and then went out altogether. Cory was sitting in total darkness a half mile from the closest picking crew and hundreds of feet underground! *The two hours will soon be past, and Jude will soon be arriving. I just have to keep a cool head. Jude was told to pick me up back here at the rear of the room. He'll be here. Jude, I know I can count on you!*

A few minutes before the designated time, Jude made sure the women were picking industriously, boarded his mule, and drove to the front of room 14. He was preparing to flash his headlights a few times and turn off the mule lights to see Cory's return signal since she wasn't there as planned. At that very moment, Abe pulled up beside him. "I wanted to make sure Cory got picked up here," he yelled at Jude. "I came here just in case you were delayed. I wanted to be certain she wasn't left behind, but I see you made it right on time. Isn't she here? Did you signal yet?"

Abe was virtually screaming to Jude because the sound of the two mules side by side made speech extremely difficult. What dawned on Jude much later as he pieced together the events of that summer, especially the events of that sad day when they saw for the first time the nature of the evil they faced, was that the noise of the two shop mules kept them from hearing Cory's frantic screaming. More than that, the noise was exceptionally loud because Abe had been holding his foot on the accelerator to rev the engine. As if that in itself was not enough to diminish all other sound, he kept screaming the whole time in Jude's ear. Little wonder Jude didn't hear Cory's hysterical cries from the back of the room.

The two men carefully looked, but no return light signal had flashed. Total darkness. "Since she didn't return the signal, that means she left," Abe screamed. "You run ahead to the punch-out clock to make sure she got there all right. I don't want any mix-up about this. Check with Ben Dubart. I told him to inform you if Cory finished her picking ahead of schedule and went there early. I have you covered. I'll stay here for a couple minutes just to make certain she doesn't show up. I wouldn't want anything to happen to our Cory."

Jude felt uneasy with this plan, but knowing there was no good alternative, he drove away.

Cory was left alone in the dark!

Chapter 35

Ten minutes from the end of the workday, it was near time for Jude to pick up the women on his crew. If it was anything they hated, it was a delayed pickup at the end of the day. Knowing he had only minutes to spare, Jude raced to the punch-out clock where he saw Ben Dubart. "Did you see Cory Mohney?" Jude shouted from his mule.

"No, I didn't, but Clark Mauthe, one of the truck drivers, told me to tell you that he saw Cory on her way to the women's locker room. She finished early and was picked up by another driver."

The whole thing sounded crazy to Jude but was nevertheless plausible. On the other hand, why wouldn't Cory have waited those few extra minutes for him at the back of room 14? The two of them sought out these precious minutes of contact in the mine. *Now, for the sake of a few minutes, she departed from the designated pickup point? This makes no sense!* But she wasn't at room 14 or the mine entrance, so possibly she had gone ahead to the women's locker room. Jude had no option but to check it out.

He dashed to the locker room to look for Cory, even though in a few short minutes it would be time to pick up the women on his crew. Having just joined this crew as the driver, he knew that he would make an awful first impression if he was late on his first day as crew driver. But he had no choice. Cory came first. He braced himself for the wrath of the women.

Meanwhile, with Jude a mile away and headed for the locker room,

Abe had returned to his crew right before quitting time. Women from both crews had huddled together to board the personnel carriers to exit. Abe turned off his mule so he could be heard distinctly. "Best pickers in the world, I have good news and bad news."

"We'll take the good news," a woman shouted. "You can keep the bad news to yourself. Ha! Ha!"

"Very funny. You've completed your work, and the pickers on my crew can board the personnel carrier. Hop on. Your hard day's done, your race is won. And thanks to a bit of conniving on Mr. Badoane's part, you even get to knock off a bit early." The women nodded in hearty approval. "I knew that would make you happy."

"What of us?" the head picker from Jude's crew yelled. "We're done too!"

"This is information I'd just as soon you'd keep to yourself. When I was back at the place where Jude was to pick up Cory, I parked the mule some distance away and walked. Sneaked up on them, you might say. Yes, I was being cagey, but I figured in this case it was justified. I had heard how Cory occasionally sneaks away from her crew to be alone with Jude. You might say I wanted to confirm if these rumors are true. You can understand my motive." He gave the women a wink. "Girls, you won't believe it. While you were working your tails off here, Jude and Cory were—let me just say they were indisposed at the back of room 14. I kid you not. I heard the—well, you know the sounds I'm talking about!—a hundred feet away. Members of the other crew, I'm so sorry, but as your driver is, shall we say, engaged in a little extracurricular activity, you'll definitely have a late pickup time today."

"I don't believe it!" a furious woman shouted.

"Who does he think he is?" screamed another, her face red with anger as she threw down her basket in disgust.

"Abe, let us ride with you to the locker room. We can ride double since we're close to the exit. It's a short ride."

"Yeah, you know how we hate getting out of heel late," another joined in. "I gotta get my daughtel to the olthodontist." (Bonnie had trouble pronouncing her Rs and was, as a result, the butt of humor among some of the men, especially Bull Chestnut).

"And I have to get to the Pirates game. Mike Schmidt's in town. You know he moved into eighth place in all-time homeruns. I don't want to be late getting to the game."

"Sorry, women, you know I'd do that if I could, but ever since the accident when one of the women fell off and broke her arm while riding double, the practice is strictly forbidden. I could lose my job, sweethearts. Sorry. But as soon as I drop off my pickers, I'll be right back to get you. That's a promise. Sit tight. Abe Badoane won't let you down!" He reached his hand to the key as if to start the mule but hesitated. "By the way, if Don Juan is huffing and puffing the next time you see him, you'll know why!" Abe was gone in a flash, musing to himself, *They're dumber than clay, as at chess I play. They be the lout, whom I move about!*

"What a nice guy he is," said one of the pickers.

"A sight better than the college professor punk we have!"

"What a loser that guy is!"

"Who does he think he is? Causing us to be late his first day as crew driver!"

"Right. He put it to Cory and us at the same time."

"I call that a double whammy."

Jude, meanwhile, searched high and low for Cory—first in the women's locker room itself (a woman just exiting said it was empty and that Cory had not been there), the lounge by the punch-out clock, and even the lunchroom near the exit. He was genuinely panicked by now, mainly for Cory's sake but for incurring the inevitable wrath of his pickers as well. Yet getting them to the exit late paled in comparison to Cory's whereabouts. He sped back to his crew on the chance that Cory might somehow have ended up there. Moments later, he found the women of his crew huddled together in an angry mass. With frowns on their faces, they quickly boarded the train. Most were content just to flash an angry scowl and cold-shoulder him, but a few weren't willing to let it drop that easily.

"Wonder why you're pantin' like a dog."

"Or a monkey," another rejoined. "Ha! Ha!"

"A woman sure takes a lot from a man!"

If Abe Badoane's trap had been a disaster for Jude, it was even worse for Cory. When Jude had pulled up with his mule, she waited patiently at the back of the room, per Abe's instruction. She did not run to meet him in the corridor out front when the lights had flashed, since Abe made such a specific point of Jude's meeting her at the rear of the room. When Jude did not come toward her or respond to her repeated yells, however, she began a brisk walk to the corridor. Cory was not familiar with the layout of the trays in this particular room. Not positioned evenly, as trays typically are, these had been placed haphazardly about the room.

At first, she maintained a measured walk, thinking Jude would surely wait, but when it was obvious that the two mules were pulling away, she panicked, screamed loudly, and broke into a run. She caught her foot on one of the tiers, lost her balance, and fell headlong into another tier. In the darkness, she struck her shoulder and head violently and collapsed to the ground.

Knocked unconscious, Cory was lying, alone, on the cold stone floor!

Chapter 36

By this time, Abe had dropped his crew at the entrance, many of them thanking him for being such a gentleman. Duke was present as well and talking with a group of men. Several of the workers, wanting to take a look at the new additions Duke had made to his '57 Chevy, assembled near the punch clock to chat briefly before dispersing to their cars.

With great excitement and concern, Abe ran quickly to Duke, who was standing by the vending machine. "Duke, go and look for Cory at the back of room 14. Jude was supposed to pick her up there but never showed. Some of the guys saw him flirting with the women in the lounge instead of picking up Cory."

"You're kidding!"

"I am not, but why would he blow off his true love? The women are saying he's a rat. Is it true?" Duke sealed the lid on his cup of coffee. "Take a cart and see what's up. Please hurry. We don't want anything happening to the mine's star picker." Abe pulled Duke to the side of the vending machines so they were out of earshot and lowered his voice. "Duke, be gentle with her. This is your chance to score some points and get back in her good graces after the dumb stuff you pulled lately. Gently, gently."

Duke drove like a maniac back the winding corridors toward room 14. Whereas the mules were too big to drive into rooms and between the trays, the carts could easily fit even though they were strictly forbidden in an effort to reduce the risk of disease and contamination. The matter at hand constituted an emergency in Duke's book, so into the room he sped with no hesitation. If he was able to help Cory in some way, he just might be able to restore himself to her favor. He drove about the room and looked for Cory. Not finding her, he got off the cart and shouted loudly. Still, no response. *She must have departed*, he reasoned. He was walking back to the cart to leave when he heard a moaning sound. When he flashed his light, he saw nothing but nevertheless walked in that direction. Then he saw her—collapsed awkwardly against a tier and just coming to.

"Cory, are you all right? Cory! Cory!" Genuinely shaken, he dashed over to her and gently checked for injuries. Her sweatshirt was torn at the shoulder where she had crashed into the tier. "Cory, can you hear me?" She moaned in response. Having taken a mandatory first-aid course like the other drivers, Duke alertly went to the cart and retrieved smelling salts out of the first-aid kit. Administering that, he was relieved to see her slowly revive. He held her compassionately and laid his outer jacket across her. "You're shivering from lying on this cold floor! I bet you're chilled to the bone." He tucked his jacket around her shoulders to warm her and gently massaged her arms to get the blood flowing. "Cory, do you think you're badly injured? Can you move?"

"Is that you, Jude?"

"No! It's me—Duke!" Duke made no effort to suppress his anger but quickly calmed down as he remembered Abe's advice.

Cory stumbled for her words. "What happened ... to Jude?" She rubbed her hand on her shoulder to feel her injury. "He was"—a pause—"supposed to ... pick me up." She spoke weakly. Duke lowered his head to her mouth to make out the barely audible words.

"Don't worry about that now. We have to get you out of here. Can you move, or should I call for a gurney?"

After a pause, she said, "Let me try ... to sit up. I think ... I'm all right." With Duke's help, she sat up against the tier and slowly regained her senses. "I hit this ... I hit into this ... tier of trays." Her feeble words were little better than a mumble. "I was running ... for the ... corridor. Was alone ... in the dark. For ... so long. Light went ... out. It was ... awful!"

"Can you stand up and get to the cart? Or should I call the infirmary for help?"

"Let me"—a pause—"try to ... stand."

Duke put his arm around her and slowly helped her to her feet. He was as loving and caring with her now as he had been lustful and vulgar before. He steadied her as she rose to her feet and held her tightly for those first wobbly moments. Despite his real concern for Cory's injury, he delighted in feeling his body close to hers. As he held her, his mind flashed back to the nude pictures. *I'm pressing against her gorgeous body!*

"Can you stand here against the rick while I bring the cart closer?" Cory did not respond right away. Duke looked directly into her face. "I want to look at the pupils in your eyes. You might have a concussion. How's your shoulder? You should wait here until I get help if you're seriously injured."

She slowly tried to move her shoulder and was relieved that she could rotate it despite the pain. Again, she spoke weakly. "My, my ... shoulder hurts"—she garbled— "but I think ... it's okay." A moment later, she spoke again, this time with better enunciation. "I can swivel ... can move my ... shoulder. The layers of clothing protected me." She rubbed her shoulder and examined the tear in her sweatshirt. "I just feel a ... little nauseous. My head's spinning." She again struggled for words. "I better ... sit down. I might faint."

After checking her eyes again to see that they were focusing properly, he said, "Let's go to the infirmary to have you checked. You should have your shoulder x-rayed, and you might have a concussion too." Together they slowly walked the few steps to the cart. "Do you want to lie down in the back or sit up in the seat?"

"I think I ... can sit up." The smelling salts began to do their work. Gradually Cory's head started to clear. "Duke, thanks so much. You're such a help." Duke was encouraged to see that she was speaking more normally by now. After a moment's silence, Cory spoke again. "I can't imagine what happened … to Jude. He was supposed to pick me up."

Cory teetered a bit as she stepped onto the cart. "Are you sure you're okay to ride back? I can call for a gurney so you could lie down."

"I'm all right. Just avoid … the potholes." She attempted a faint smile. "Here. Sip some of this coffee. It will warm you up. You're still shivering."

Cory took a sip of the hot coffee. "That tastes so good. Thank you." She held it tightly with both hands to warm them. She took two big swallows of coffee, which also helped to revive her.

They rode slowly in silence a short distance, and then Duke started to speak. "Cory, there's something I have to say." He paused a moment, not knowing how much he should talk when she was obviously in such straits, but seeing the returning brightness to her eye, he began to talk.

"Go ahead. I'm starting … to feel okay."

"Cory, forgive me for what I did to you the other day. I'm sorry— it was wrong." He paused to see if this was the time to confess his wrongdoing or to let it go at that. Cory looked at him warmly and put her hand on his arm. "I was insanely jealous that you dropped me for Jude. You know that I never laid a hand on you before. That's how much I respect you."

"I know."

Duke clutched the steering wheel tightly with both hands. "But when you dropped me cold, I got mad. Real mad!" He paused to make sure his frank speech wasn't unnerving her. He was relieved to see that Cory continued to listen intently. "Plus, you turn me on. You know that. You're the sexiest woman I know, bar none. But that don't excuse my behavior. I'm really sorry." The confession, a completely new thing for Duke, felt good. "I accept full responsibility for my horrible conduct. I, Duke Manningham, am an idiot."

Cory didn't feel like conversing, but welcoming this change in Duke, she forced herself to talk. "Forgiveness granted." She took another sip of coffee. "This tastes so good! I'm glad you said that.

What you did ... was so unlike you. It bothered me ... a lot. You really scared me."

They continued their conversation while Duke slowly drove to the infirmary. Duke's intent, besides contritely confessing his wayward behavior, was to keep her talking to make sure she was all right.

After a short while, Cory spoke again, the coffee having animated her. "I'm thinking of what the apostle Paul wrote. I think it's in Ephesians. We read that back in the spring." She paused as he nodded. "You're being tested. Recall what Paul wrote. Something about no immorality ... there can be ... no immorality in one's ... reformed behavior."

She spoke in clipped sentences and tried to quote the verse directly, but memory failed her. She took another sip of coffee and held it against her cheek to savor the warmth. "There's more than that. But I can't think straight right now. Something about staying pure. About putting off our old selves. Paul is speaking about our former nature. It gets corrupted by deceit. By deceitful desire. I have such a headache that I can't think. But the idea's right."

She put the coffee in the cup holder and massaged her temples to ease the pain. She looked at Duke to make sure he was listening. "Duke, you agreed that you had to stop your immoral life. Please don't backslide. You were such a gentleman in the spring. You really disappointed me the other day. And hurt me." He saw a tear in her eye.

They drove along the corridors, which were already empty since the workday was done and the workers were checking out. Soon they arrived at the infirmary, where the nurse thoroughly examined Cory as Duke waited outside the office. She had taken a fairly hard hit to the shoulder when she slammed into the tray.

"Fortunately for you," the nurse stated, "the layers of clothing gave you good protection. Your head took a real hit when you fell to the ground, but your helmet softened the blow."

As the nurse proceeded, Cory continued to think about the whole ordeal, especially Jude. *What happened to Jude?*

Chapter 37

After sending Duke on his mission to check for Cory, Abe looked around for Jude. He spotted him in the lounge by the punch clock where a couple of the irate women were reaming him out. Most had cut Jude some slack, but a couple of the women were angry that he made them late and were giving him a piece of their minds.

Abe motioned for Jude to come to him away from the women. "You still haven't found Cory? I just heard that she's in the lunchroom back by room 14. She's been waiting back there the whole time for you to pick her up."

"No, she's not!" Jude drew closer to Abe. "I already checked the lunchroom." Jude was now in Abe's face. "She wasn't there!"

People in the area gasped. This was the first time they had ever seen anyone talk so aggressively to Abe Badoane. Feeling that he was being played, Jude wasn't backing down from anyone. His beloved was in danger. Still, with no recourse, he had to hear Abe out.

"She is there, Jude, and been waiting the whole time." Abe smiled warmly as he spoke. "She was apparently in the adjoining lavatory when you checked the lunchroom. Did you ever consider that possibility?" Jude was suspicious of Abe's explanation but, grabbing a fast drink at the water cooler, nevertheless took off for the lunchroom, happy to escape the women's tirade.

Abe smiled to himself. The whole scheme had gone exactly as planned. In many ways, he remained a mystery to himself. Never once during his entire life had he been able to satisfactorily explain to himself why he used his intelligence to manipulate people, especially since his game-playing achieved essentially negative ends. "What I'm doing in this case is not right, but it's definitely justified since I have such a good reason. Look at the disaster of my life. Game-playing affords me the manipulative control I find nowhere else. People are pawns in life's game of chess. I enjoy the rush of gaming them, I guess!" So went Abe's journal entry for this particular day, as Jude discovered many years later.

The part of it that remained the most inexplicable to Jude was Abe's repeated statements that he was justified for indulging in his evil trickery. Such behavior could never be justified, yet mystery man Abe remained unfazed that his tomfoolery harmed others.

One little detail remains, Abe reasoned. Jude would be gone for a minimum of ten minutes. He again looked at his watch to confirm that he had sufficient time to get some things out of his locker, so he drove toward the men's locker room. On the way, he passed the infirmary and was elated at the fortuitous timing. Cory and Duke were just coming out of the infirmary as he approached. The picture of concern and compassion, Abe ran to them to see how Cory was. "Cory what happened to you? Why are you holding your shoulder? Look at your helmet. How in the world did your miner's lamp get so bent?"

Not giving Cory time to answer, Duke hastily jumped on Abe's last question. "I found her out cold at the back of room 14. She was in a lot of trouble. She was collapsed in a heap and crumpled against a back tier. I put a coat on her and gave her some coffee. I drove her to the infirmary lickety-split."

As Duke spoke, Abe placed his hand gently on Cory's arm. "Oh, my goodness!"

Duke continued. "I was scared to death that she was hurt bad. The nurse says she's all right now, but she was unconscious, weren't you, Cory? Where was her loser of a boyfriend? Why didn't he pick her up if that was the plan? If he'd have done his job, this whole thing wouldn't have happened. That's how I see it."

Cory looked away in embarrassment but said nothing. Still, what

Duke said made sense. *Why didn't Jude pick me up?* The whole thing happened, apparently, because of his negligence.

"Well, we can't be judgmental about him," Abe rejoined. "He might have a good reason. On the other hand, he was in the lounge a long time shooting the breeze with the women. That's the one thing I am sure about. You should hear the women. 'That hottie sure likes the women!' 'You can tell he's a ladies' man!' That's what they're saying back there. I'm not one to jump to conclusions, but anyone would wonder why he was flirting with the women when his beloved was in such trouble. That's the only unexplained detail as I see it. But let's make no judgments until we hear Jude's story."

During this carefully crafted speech, Abe closely watched Cory's reaction. His reference to Jude's flirting with the women when she lay unconscious on the cold floor went right to her heart. Try as she might, she was unable to mask her visceral reaction. She turned away, folded her arms, and brushed a tear from her eye. *Good,* Abe thought, *a very direct hit. I hadn't counted on that little victory.*

Duke drove Cory to the exit where both punched out. The daily end-of-workday detail complete, Duke asked her, "Can I walk you to the car?" She looked around and still saw no Jude. Hurt that Jude wasn't there to offer assistance and still feeling wobbly on her feet, she reluctantly consented. She didn't want to fall in the parking lot and make a scene—a distinct possibility in the oppressive summer heat. Although she protested, Duke put his arm around her to steady her as they walked across the lot. She looked around as they walked. Where was Jude? She desperately wanted to talk to him so they could get to the bottom of the whole morass.

"Can I take you home? I'll be happy to drive you. The last thing you need is to stand around in this blinding sun when you have a headache. You're squinting like crazy."

Cory hesitated for a moment. What Duke was saying made sense. "No, I'm going to wait on Jude, but thank you anyway."

"He stood you up once today." Duke hesitated. *Just how far should I go to drive home my point?* "What makes you think he won't again?"

"Don't say that, Duke! You know Jude's a prince of a guy." Cory made no attempt to hide her anger.

"All right. Sorry, Cory. He may be a good man, but he made me mad today, and he definitely hurt you." He gestured toward her torn sweatshirt.

Though hot, the sunlight warmed her chilled bones and gave her strength. Duke saw her improvement but was still concerned about her well-being and didn't want to leave her alone. Sensing this compassion, Cory spoke. "Thanks for helping me out. You were there when I really needed you. I do appreciate what you did for me."

"You were in a bad way, Cory. A very bad way. It really scared me to see you lying unconscious on that cold concrete floor. It was the least I can do." He drew closer to her. "Sure you want me to leave you here alone? It's not a problem for me to run you to the house."

"Yes, I'm fine. Thank you. Good-bye." Duke walked over to his fancy car and drove away.

Standing by Jude's car, Cory rolled and massaged her shoulder to work out the tightness. She lifted her eyes to the fully leaved trees. *They seem especially lush and bright this year. How calming they are. What a lovely scene to paint,* she thought. *I can imagine what Monet would do with these trees! They look like the trees in one of his paintings. Maybe* Summer, 1874? *I'll have to check.*

She heard a yell, and there making a mad dash across the parking lot to his car was Jude. "Cory, are you all right?" Panic was in his voice as he sprinted toward her. She later said that she had never seen Jude so flustered. Even at a distance she could tell that his face was flushed, his eyes were red, and his hands were shaking.

"Yes, Jude, I'm fine," she weakly yelled in response. As he neared the car, she spoke again in a softer voice, not wanting other employees to hear. "Well, I think I'm fine." She again rolled her shoulder. "I have a sore shoulder and a headache—that's all."

When he arrived at the car, Cory could see that he was sweating profusely. The hair was caked to his forehead in ringlets, he was breathing very hard, and his flushed face was fire-engine red. As they stood by the car, he caressed her gently, making certain he didn't touch the injured shoulder. "Where do we start? I haven't been this rattled since my comprehensive exams," he blurted out as he gasped for breath. He gingerly helped her into the car, and they drove away.

Cory sat with her head tilted backward and resting on the seat, her eyes closed, but at last she spoke. "Let's talk it through this evening, Jude. I'm really tired, and I have a crusher of a headache from smacking my head and shoulder. Stop over later, all right? But don't worry. I promise I'm fine, and I'm not mad. I just need to have you explain a couple things."

They drove home without talking, one of very few times they were silent in each other's presence. The unnatural quiet in the car bothered Jude, so he reached over and held Cory's hand. He gave it a gentle squeeze. She responded with three hand squeezes: I - love - you. He responded, held her hand caressingly, and felt the calm come over him. Arriving at her farm, he walked her to the door and kissed her. "Cory, I love you. Please forgive me. I didn't mean to hurt you. It was just a huge misunderstanding."

"You don't have to say the obvious. We both know that. We'll talk it through later. I love you too. Stop by this evening, okay? I need to take a nap."

Jude drove over to his grandma's farm, parked the car, and went immediately to his bedroom. He immediately sought to reconstruct the tragic events of the afternoon—the misunderstanding, Abe's carefully laid trap, its marvelous intricacy, and his own gullibility. He kept coming back to Cory's point of sensing evil, especially when near Abe Badoane. He had apparently been badly hurt at some point in the past or possibly at various times. *Such hideous conduct,* Jude reasoned, *only emanates from a deeply disturbed heart. What series of experiences in life had contorted Abe Badoane into this awful shape? More than that, why had he chosen the path of hate? Why choose to inflict malice on those who cross your path?* He recalled Pastor Gabe's comment in a sermon years ago: "You can't give what you don't have." The cliché contained more than a nugget of truth. Pastor Gabe had opined, "Love never flows from a hate-drenched heart."

Standing by the window, Jude looked across the meadow, alive in its summer beauty. The hay in the fields swayed in the breeze and awaited the mower's cut. A small creek serpentined its way through the meadow. *What a lovely brook*, he thought, and Wordsworth's "Ode" came to mind. "I love the brooks which down their channels fret Even more than when I tripped lightly as they." *I'm glad I once tripped lightly*, he thought. *I'm not doing so now. The brooks have dried up, the sun has scorched the earth, and I have a perpetually dry throat.*

As he sat in a chair by the window, he began to reason more clearly. The whole ordeal had been caused by the conflicting directions and a malfunctioning miner's lamp. Those lamps were good for many hours. Why had it gone out when Cory was alone in a faraway place? That could not have been coincidental. But if Abe was behind it—and already he suspected Abe's fingerprints all over the events—how had he planned it? How did he know the light would go out when Cory was alone? How could he arrange such precision timing? Jude decided to check with the man in charge of the miners' lamps to see if he might offer some insight.

He looked at the cumulus clouds and thought of something the ancient prophet Jeremiah had said. "The heart is deceitful above all things, And desperately wicked. Who can know it?" If Abe's serpent bite had been purposely designed—and all details pointed in that direction—then Jeremiah's pronouncement aptly applied to Abe. A few days back in the mine, and already Jude was in a deadly combat with a monumental and sinister intelligence—desperately wicked and continually evil.

Chapter 38

After he had completed barn chores and eaten his dinner, Jude went over to see Cory. Having eaten and briefly napped, she looked much better than she had in the parking lot. Over a cup of tea in the kitchen, they commenced talking.

"You look so much better. How are you feeling now?"

"I feel pretty good. What a lovely nap I had. My neck's a little stiff, and my shoulder has tightened up a bit, but, thank goodness, I'm not seriously hurt. My head stopped aching. That's the real blessing." She looked at him warmly, smiled, and took his hand.

"That's good news. So where do we start?"

"How about with a horse ride? I'd like to go up on Vinlindeer but prefer to ride instead of walk. Can you saddle up the horses? We need to ride the horses a lot this summer to give them exercise."

"Good idea."

A short while later, they mounted the horses and rode up on the ridge. With Zoe walking along beside them, they discussed the whole mad affair and pieced together the misunderstandings and miscommunications—varied meeting places, wild goose chases, and the entire botched sequence of events.

"The central figure in the whole thing is obviously Abe," Cory continued as they dismounted, tied their horses to a fence post, and drank in the panorama below. "He clearly noted two varied meeting places. He specifically told me the back of the room was the pickup point, you the front. Then he deliberately sent you on two separate missions—one to check on me in the locker room and another to the furthest lunchroom clear back in the mine."

"Yes, and he got me in trouble with some of the women on my crew. Did you hear how badly that turned out? For a while I thought I was going to be torn apart by the Amazonians!"

"You referred to the Amazonians in the past. I remember because the allusion went right over my head."

"Guess I was reading Herodotus in those days."

"That explains it. At any rate, one of the girls on my crew called me to tell me what Abe had said about us making out at the back of room 14. Imagine that! A couple of those silly women fell for his story. Most are decent women—I like them a lot—and some of them are very good and even close friends. You'll come to like them as you get to know them. Did you know that Rochelle's daughter Katie was the KHS valedictorian last year? Don't kid yourself. A number of these women are bright. Only a couple of them fell for his lie."

"I bumped into Ben Dubart and asked him why he sent me on a wild goose chase to the women's locker room when you were out cold in room 14. He said Clark the driver emphatically told him that he had seen you leaving for the women's lounge and that you left careful instructions to have me meet you there. When I asked Ben where Clark was so that I could corroborate the details of this crazy story, he said I wouldn't be able to. Clark had just departed on a couple-day trip to Wisconsin and doesn't take calls on the road. How convenient! You see how Abe the snake thought through every single detail." Jude looked in exasperation at Cory. "What gives with him?"

"Remember when I said I sensed evil in his presence? Now see for yourself!"

"As we said before, he's as evil as King Claudius. The way this thing's going, we could end up in our own *Hamlet* and face-to-face with our own Danish king!"

Cory reflected on the incident as she marveled at the scenery below. "But maybe God's hand was at work in the whole thing.

THE ROSE AND THE SERPENT

Remember Shakespeare's line, 'There's a divinity that shapes our ends.' The Bard's saying in this line that there's a controlling sovereign hand at work that governs all. I have to believe that God's providence controlled even this mad little scene."

"How, Cory? Right now, I don't see it. I need to have your faith. You know I've been more than a little weak in that department in recent years."

"Well, not as much as our resident skeptic, Chuck Claypoole!" Cory laughed. "But do consider this. Duke picked me up and treated me in a humane and civil way. He gave me the help I desperately needed. The circumstance forced him to mend his conduct on the spot."

Noting that Jude remained unconvinced, she continued. "Think about it. He saw me as a human being and not the embodiment of his lustful fantasies! In those moments, I was a woman to be treated kindly, not a sex object to be used. Do you realize what a major step that is for him? You know what he's normally like. To him, a woman is a sexual conquest waiting to happen."

"Who doesn't know that about Duke?"

"Did I ever tell you what Pam told me? She said that Duke guesses women's bra sizes all the time, and, as if that isn't bad enough, he's even on a couple occasions had the nerve to ask them if he's right! Here's the kicker. Pam says that when he's with the guys and wants to refer to a woman, he does so by bra size instead of name: 'Look at 32-B over there, or tell 36-C to pick those trays clean.' I'm not kidding! He's never done it around me, but the guys told Pam that he does it all the time."

"But Duke's fixation over sex—if that's what it is, and it seems to be just that—interests me less than the pronounced evil in Abe. Know what I mean? It was Abe, not Duke, who was behind this awful episode."

"Yes, I agree with that, but let me say one more thing in Duke's defense. In the parking lot, Duke and I were reconciled even more. I know he regrets his conduct. Soon it will dawn on him that he was sucked in today, and he'll be mad as a hornet. You see my point? Yes, there's evil about, but through it all some good has surfaced too. That's one thing I can cling to on a dark day."

"I understand what you're saying, but that still doesn't avoid the inevitable question. What's going on with Abe Badoane? Why is he so vicious? You're the one who first sensed his evil. Any ideas about what we can do to avoid future traps?" Jude picked a flaking piece of bark from the fence post. "The guy's obviously hurting. He really needs help. That's what I was thinking about before I came over here."

"Yes, I know he's hurting." Zoe came and rested his snout on her knee. "What a dog," Cory began. Tussling Zoe's fur, she said, "I think we ought to talk to Chuck. He's the one with the most insight into Abe. He said he'd fill us in on Abe some time."

"How about right now? But maybe you need to take the evening off and recuperate a bit more."

"No, I'm fine, and I'd rather do this while the ordeal is fresh in mind. Besides, seeing this scene below has completely restored my sanity."

"It makes me thinks of Wordsworth's 'Lines.'"

"Quote it for me, please. You've been citing Wordsworth a lot lately."

"Somehow he comes to my mind in the spring. He says in 'Lines Composed above Tintern Abbey':

> Once again I see these hedge-rows, little lines
> Of sportive wood run wild: these pastoral farms,
> Green to the very door: and wreaths of smoke
> Sent up, in silence, from among the trees!

"Jude, that is so good. 'Little lines of sportive wood,' 'Green to the very door'—that is so accurate! That's exactly what we're seeing. Don't you just love it!"

Chapter 39

A short while later, Jude called Charles Claypoole. Finding that he was free for the evening, he and Cory drove over to his house, located adjacent to the church. Seated on his front porch across from Pastor Gabriel's parsonage, they narrated for Chuck the details of the afternoon fiasco and expressed their puzzlement over Abe's conduct.

"You're the one who said you had some insight into Abe's past," Jude continued. "Could we pursue that?"

"Yes, I promised to give you that information a long time ago. Even though it was years ago, I remember how we started into a certain conversation that we never finished. I recall it because of your deep interest. But then you always were fascinated with Abe."

"I admit it. The guy has always had a mystique about him."

It's a long story, but I'll cut to the chase." Chuck paused to formulate his thoughts. Because it was a difficult subject with many component vectors shooting off in a hundred directions, he had trouble selecting a good starting point. He stalled for time. "But before we get to that, how about one pleasant aside? How marvelous that Pennsylvania's former governor, Dick Thornburgh, was recently named US attorney general. I'm so happy for Governor Thornburgh. Many of my faculty colleagues think he was a superb governor." He paused for a moment. "Okay, I'm running from the matter at hand. Let's start at the beginning. Abe Badoane is a very brilliant man. Of course you realize that." Charles took a sip of iced tea. "Did you know that he finished everything for his PhD except his dissertation?"

"You're kidding!" Jude broke in.

"No, I'm not kidding, and at Carnegie Mellon no less."

"What happened?" Cory asked, also flabbergasted by this shocking pronouncement.

"Here's the story," Chuck continued. "Abe and I applied for the same job at Grove City College many years ago. I landed the job instead of Abe, even though—I'm being perfectly honest here— he was the more qualified candidate. His grasp of literature is phenomenal. He memorizes lengthy passages of literature in a way I've never managed."

"No matter what you say, Chuck, I can't think he was better prepared than you," Jude responded. "You're being modest. But even if he was the better candidate—I just know he wasn't—how did you get the job?"

"That's where the plot thickens. Both of us were candidates for the position and had been interviewed during the summer. A vacancy in the English Department had arisen unexpectedly due to a sudden death, so the search for a replacement was done post haste during the late spring. Only the two of us made the final interview stage. The difference was that I already had my PhD and Abe didn't, though he was slated to finish his dissertation by midsummer. He had made good progress and was nearing the end. If he would have produced a draft of the entire dissertation by the committee's midsummer deadline, I'm certain he would have landed the job, since the recruitment and selection committee thought Abe's areas of expertise were more suitable for their programmatic needs than mine. To say it simply, he made for a better fit."

"Yes, our Recruitment and Selection Committee speaks often of that very thing," Jude agreed.

"During that summer, tragedy struck. He had always been known for his temper tantrums, and his periodic fits of mental and verbal abuse of women were legendary in his early days when he was as green

THE ROSE AND THE SERPENT

in judgment as Shakespeare's Cleopatra. Nevertheless, he fell madly in love with a woman, wooed her, and after badgering her for months, she consented to marry the temporarily reformed Abe. A very frail woman, she loved him and wanted to be with him even though their relationship was rocky at times. There was no fooling anyone that she was on the loose side earlier in life. Understand that the details on all of this came out many months and even years later. From the first days of their marriage, which occurred just a few months before the college interview, there were isolated reports of his abusing her, even though she suffered from severe bouts of illness and depression. Even in the early years, we knew she had cancer, and of course that made Abe's behavior all the more inexplicable."

"Please continue," Jude said when Charles paused. "This is fascinating."

"Sit tight. You won't believe the next part. As I say, Abe had gotten married in the spring. It wasn't long until we learned that his wife was already several months pregnant. In fact, she was showing quite a bit at the wedding and didn't even wear a white dress—unheard of in our conservative community—but these good country folks were forgiving and loved them both. Folks didn't hold this shaky beginning against them. Not a bit. People were happy for the young couple and wanted the marriage to work. I remember being amazed at how forgiving everyone was. Of course, part of that owed to the respect people had for the Gehmans. People just loved that saintly couple.

"Abe worked frantically all that early summer on his PhD. He had made it to the final chapter or thereabouts, and then his wife gave birth—I think in July or maybe late June. It was a very difficult birth since his wife by that time was so weak. In fact, she almost died in childbirth. Abe's son, a strong and healthy little boy, was safely born despite her grave health. That in itself was a big praise item for these people who had prayed so fervently for a safe delivery. For those brief hours, everything was good. The child seemed completely normal—a "'beautiful child," as was said of Moses,' Abe repeatedly said. Then the tragedy struck as unlikely as a lightning bolt in a clear summer sky."

Charles was temporarily overcome with emotion and took a moment to regain his composure. "The infant died the very next day, the first example in the county of what later came to be known as sudden infant death syndrome—SIDS as the syndrome is now abbreviated. Abe was crushed. Wanting a son more than anything, he went into a black depression that manifested itself in ferocious rage.

"In his despair, he redirected his anger at his helpless wife. He just couldn't accept the idea that a seemingly healthy baby would die so suddenly. 'SIDS! What is that? Healthy babies just don't die! Something had to cause it. Something's going on here! There's someone behind this!' I can still hear him saying things like that to this day.

"Despite his anger, he tried to console his wife, but a broken man at his wit's end, he soon reverted to his old games of mental and verbal abuse. This all happened about the time he heard an account of a woman suffocating her infant child by falling asleep on him. He got it in his head that maybe that was what had happened to Little Jed, as he had named him at birth. Then his wife, completely heartbroken that her husband faulted her, took a turn for the worse in the early fall. She passed just a few months after giving birth. She had had cancer right along—as I say, we all knew that—but most of us thought she had lost the will to live and stopped fighting.

"So there was Abe Badoane, a brilliant and upcoming intellectual, with a dead son, a dead wife, and a dead dream. He's blamed himself ever since for his wife's death. His guilt was, and I think remains, very great." Charles coughed to clear his voice. "Well, back to the story about the teaching job. He gave up work on the dissertation immediately and from that day on became a deeply embittered man. Because of what happened, I ended up with the job, though I still maintain that he was the more promising candidate."

"This is why he looks so out of place in the mine. The guy is fit for the academy or even a judge's bench," Cory broke in. "I can just picture him in a dapper Jos. A. Banks suit."

Charles laughed. "Yes, indeed. Abe traveled a lot in those next years trying to run from his grief, but when he was home, he'd read endlessly on current events and politics. I think he knew most everything that was happening in the political world inside the Washington Beltway. Another thing we noticed was the way he'd visit his son and wife's graves so very often. They're over there in the back corner of the cemetery. He'd put fresh flowers on their graves just about every week. The caretaker of the cemetery used to see him sitting there by the hour."

Charles stopped speaking while a noisy truck on the highway finished its long climb up the hill. "He kept reading the great poetic elegies and had even memorized all of Milton's *Lycidas*, much of Shelley's *Adonais*, and even lengthy sections of Tennyson's *In Memoriam*. I was touched by the epitaph he wrote for his son."

"Really?" Cory said. "How touching that he wrote his own son's epitaph!"

"I have it lying on my desk in a stack of papers. Just a moment, please." He went into his house for a moment and soon returned. "Yes, here it is."

> The windy summer days and me,
> Together with you, Dear God, eternally.

"On the back of his son's heart-shaped grave marker, he inscribed these words, which memorialized his son as he imagined him to be in the future."

> The hills, the trees, the science of life,
> The fields, the breeze—all great delights
> Created by thee, explored by me,
> And joining us eternally.

After a pause, Jude commented, "That's a touching eulogy. I'm also struck with what you said about his reciting all that poetry. I guess the rumors of his great memory are true. Some of the employees at the mine think he has a photographic mind."

"I'm not certain about that, though I did hear rumors to that effect back when I was completing my PhD in Pittsburgh. I was in a coffee shop in Oakland one evening with some of my friends when a couple of the Carnegie Mellon professors with whom we were chatting recounted this story. Someone, probably for a joke they thought, told Abe on his way to his comps at Carnegie Mellon that, since he was a specialist in British literature of the sixteenth and seventeenth centuries, he ought to know all the names and dates of the Medieval and Renaissance-era popes. Someone else chipped in. 'And you better have all the English kings and queens down too, including their dates. I would have been killed on my comps if I hadn't memorized them.' Mind you, this conversation occurred just a short while before he entered Baker Hall to take his comps. It came out later that he had memorized both lengthy lists of names—every pope and their dates and every English monarch and the dates of their reigns. He had learned them virtually on his way to his comps! His intellectual gifts were the stuff of legend in those days. Maybe that's part of the reason why he won the prestigious Dietrich College Graduate Student Teaching Award at CMU. I think I have the name of the award right, but I'm not sure."

"That gives us real insight into the bitter man who fakes the smile day after day in the mine," Cory said.

"But it doesn't explain," Chuck replied, "the man who even as a kid was a walking volcano. He was fighting constantly in school. He had even been expelled a time or two in junior high and was notorious for his evil temper. He had a reputation for fighting kids bigger than he. His nickname was 'the Serpent.'"

"You're kidding! How could a young boy have such an evil nickname?" Jude was quick to ask.

"That part of the story I know well. Abe was in junior high, probably an eighth grader, when he got in trouble for fighting. He was in the principal's office, so the story goes, and the principal—his name was Mr. Miller, a good friend of mine—reprimanded him about the need to submit to authority. Leaving the office, young Abe turned and glared at him and said, 'To reign is worth ambition though in Hell: Better to reign in Hell, than serve in Heaven.' Then he said the second line again, 'Better to reign in Hell, than serve in Heaven.' He walked out and slammed the door. The principal was dumbfounded. It wasn't until later in the teachers' lounge that the principal learned from one of the English teachers that Abe had quoted verbatim Satan's speech from Book II of *Paradise Lost*. When the teacher checked the citation, he learned that the youthful Abe had quoted it perfectly! Imagine that—an eighth grader quoting Milton!"

"That's amazing," Cory said. "But how does an esoteric reference to Milton connect with the Serpent nickname?"

"Some of the school students had overheard a couple of the English teachers talk about this incident right before class one day. Of course the teachers marveled that a junior high student would even have heard of Milton's *Paradise Lost* let alone quote a famous passage from memory. Well, one of the teachers commented about Abe's quoting Satan the serpent instead of God. Other students passing just then heard about Abe's fascination with the serpent. For whatever reason, they called Abe the Serpent, and the name stuck. You know kids!"

Cory reflected on the origin of the name. "It does fit his temperament. My dad said he was the angriest boy anyone had ever seen."

"I don't have any insight on that per se," Chuck resumed, "though certainly I've heard people refer to it. I do know that once when we talked on this very subject a long time ago in the Fellowship Hall, Old Mary overheard the discussion and the reference to Abe as the Serpent. She broke in and said, 'Be kind to Abe. He's a good boy. You might be the same if you were in his shoes.' All of us felt duly chastised though we hadn't actually been gossiping or putting down Abe; nor did she, far as I know, intend any harshness."

"Sounds like Old Mary," Cory said.

"As Old Mary walked back into the kitchen after having made this comment, one of the women heard her say, almost to herself, 'He's a good man. It's too bad it happened. Father, forgive us, and especially forgive me.' When we subsequently heard this additional detail, we all looked at each other in disbelief, not knowing what in the world she meant. None of us ever had the courage to bring up the subject again, so the matter died right there, but of course it heightened the mystery surrounding the Serpent. What an awful name!"

"'Too bad it happened,'" Jude quoted Mary. "Was Old Mary referring to the deaths of his wife and son? It seems as though she might have been singling out some earlier event. Mystery man Abe— what a guy! And to think that his mysterious life even touches Old Mary."

Cory took a sip of tea as she waited for a car to pass on the highway. "So where do we go from here? Anyone who'd do what he did to us today just for fun has some real mental issues."

"The hate he carries is destroying him," Chuck responded. "Can you imagine a more lonely and forlorn place than the serpent-infested soul of Abe Badoane? Pastor Gabe is the one he should talk to about laying down that awful burden once and for all." Jude and Cory nodded in agreement.

"Love never allows failure to be final," Cory sighed. "Is the cliché true? Grandma Rosetta recently said that to Jude. Here's hoping we find out."

Chapter 40

Having resolved to treat Abe with kindness and to try to get past the awful incident of the day before, Cory and Jude entered the mine near the check-in room the following day. He was in the lounge and, not aware of their presence, was reading an article in *Time* magazine about Reaganomics and the positive effects of recent tax cuts. Arriving early in the morning and sipping coffee in the lounge was his normal routine. Jude tapped Cory on the shoulder and gestured to his own face. He made the face of an angry scowl and pointed to Abe, who wore the look of an angry and vengeful man. Jude and Cory tiptoed back to the clock, punched in, and turned toward Abe, as if for the first time.

"Good morning, Abe." Hearing the loud click of the time clock and knowing someone was in the vicinity, Abe had ample time to don the mask of "the smiling public man," as Jude whispered to Cory, adding, "That's a line from Yeats's 'Among School Children.'"

"Sorry about the confusion yesterday," Abe began. "I was given wrong information and irresponsibly passed it along to you. Mea culpa. I should have kept my mouth shut. Cory, you took a nasty tumble. I'd feel dreadful if you were hurt. Please tell me you're all right."

"I did take a nasty fall but nothing serious. Ca ne me fait rien [I don't mind.] Next time we'll repair the breaks in the communication lines so the messages get through with less static."

"Good job on the French!" Jude said to Cory.

With that they warmly smiled to Abe and departed for the mine. Abe looked after them in total bafflement. They had every right to hate him and to excoriate him for his conduct yesterday, and yet here they were treating him in friendly fashion. "*O, my offense is rank*," he said to himself. *It smells to heaven. My sin's like leaven. I am a walking curse who belongs in a hearse!*

As they walked to their respective crews, Jude said to Cory, "Well, there'll be the dickens to pay for my picking up the women late yesterday. Their tongues were wagging like crazy at quitting time. Imagine what I'll face today!"

"Good luck," she said. "But maybe it won't be as bad as you think." She gave him a peck on the cheek as they went their separate ways.

Fortunately for Jude, word had filtered through his crew about the misunderstandings of the day before. The women found out that Jude had not been inappropriately involved with Cory and was, in fact, desperately looking for her. Their attitude altered from the day before, the majority of the women were very civil with him. Some even apologized. *Good*, Jude thought to himself. *I'll get through this.*

And he did. The day in fact turned out to be a good one. As he had more opportunities than usual to cruise the mine corridors on packhouse runs, he found himself thinking a great deal about their imbroglio with Abe. On two separate occasions when he saw Abe from a distance, Jude noted the way Abe studied people and watched them intently, assessing them at some deep level and contemplating his next move.

Seeing Abe at the packhouse later in the day, Jude again witnessed this same phenomenon. Abe, out of sight, stood back some seventy feet from several of the men—Al, Smitty, Huddy, and Skeeter—and instead of entering into conversation with them, he was content to watch and study them. Then Jude, taken aback, realized that he was doing the exact same thing—watching Abe watch the others. *Guess I play the same game!* Jude thought to himself.

That evening in Little Gidding, their subterranean haven, Cory resumed work on her painting. She assembled her art materials and began painting a picture she intended to call *New Every Morning*. Meanwhile, Jude curled up on the couch with an evening cup of tea, which they brought in a thermos, and commenced browsing through essays and books on Shakespeare's *Hamlet*.

He read for a while and then spoke. "Cory, are you aware that *The Murder of Gonzago*, the play within the play in *Hamlet*, is probably the most brilliant and complicated scene in all of Shakespeare?"

"It's always been a favorite of mine too, but why do you say that? You're the scholar who's studied it so much. What makes it the apex of brilliance?"

"In part, it's the way everybody on stage watches everybody else during the enactment of *The Murder of Gonzago*. I know you remember that *Gonzago* is the play that the traveling actors enact for King Claudius and Queen Gertrude when they travel to Elsinore. Think about it. There are layers upon layers of perception during the enactment of this play within the play *Hamlet*, but that's something I'll talk about later."

"Why do you bring that up?"

"I've been thinking about Abe and how he just watches people so much of the time. Today I caught him doing it a couple times, but as I did so, I realized that I was doing the exact same thing. This business of watching and studying people is a pretty common human pastime."

"I can just picture you in the middle of *Hamlet*, interacting with the characters, watching them watch each other and studying their every move. And if that would happen, I'm sure Abe would be there beside you!"

"I can picture you too. Who knows? We're not out of this tragedy yet. I can handle it as long as our *Murder of Gonzago* scene has no real murder!" They laughed heartily.

"Keep going. I love it when you talk about Shakespeare."

"One thing about the character of Hamlet has always bothered me. He attended the university in Wittenberg, Germany, where he was exposed to the Reformation with its return to a Bible-based worldview. He would have imbibed the rarefied air of salvation solely by faith in Christ's grace, as manifest in love, forgiveness, and mercy to others. The emphasis in that heady culture would have been on self-determination. I'm referring to the cultivation of and reliance on the private enlightened inner conscience as the governing compass instead of the church hierarchy."

"That's some phrase, but from what Pastor Gabe has said, it's exactly right."

"Right. Well, this conscience, sharpened and tutored by Holy Writ, was the ever-important moral compass of one's life. Yet when he returns to Denmark, Hamlet throws his refined learning and his habit of relying on this emergent inner voice overboard and, instead, seeks Claudius' death like an old-world thug. Swayed by the ancestral voices of the past instead of his own exquisite, Wittenberg-based inner voice, which he had courageously cultivated in Germany, he reverts to retaliation, bloodshed, and aggression. That reversion to an underworld ruffian is insanely baffling to me."

"I agree. He even says something about wiping away all trivial fond records—'fond' meant foolish in Shakespeare's day, right?— 'All saws of books, all forms,' and so on. Why would he jettison that mountain of learning that he had acquired in Wittenberg in one fell swoop? How pathetic to watch the agonizing fall of the artistic and visionary prince!"

"Very good, Cory. You cite a very relevant passage, but keep going. You're coming to the main line in that famous speech."

"Let me see if I can recall it. I don't know the play nearly as well as you. Okay, here goes. Hamlet says the ghost's 'commandment all alone shall live Within the book and volume of my brain.' Or something close to that. Did I get it?"

"Yes, I think that's exactly right. So, what's he saying?"

"That he wants to replace the Ten Commandments and Christ's commandment of love with Claudius' commandment of death and destruction. He exchanges Wittenburg's grace, love, and mercy for

Denmark's age-old aggression, hate, and war mentality. Is that what you're driving at?"

"Exactly, Cory. That's certainly one obvious way to read the play. But during the horrible tumult at the Danish court, he reverts to a Neanderthal mentality—kill or be killed. In this undoing, he muffles his own precious inner conscience and chooses to follow the voice of the mob. That's it. He becomes a blood-thirsty Mafioso who reverts to tribal thinking." Jude took a sip of his Earl Grey tea. "Of course, this is the very antithesis of Reformation thinking."

Cory mulled over the profundity of these insights. "Here's a thought that comes to my mind. If we have a Claudius in our play in the form of Abe Badoane, then we have to do better than Hamlet and not revert to savagery as he sadly does."

"What do you propose? I detect a coming plan."

Cory thought for a moment before responding. "We need to be proactively good and kind and merciful."

"Great idea."

"How about inviting him to a church function? Old Mary told me that as a young boy he had been very active in church, but when an especially fierce period of anger came upon him, he drifted away, almost as though he had undergone a major personality change overnight. He was still just a young boy at that time. If you're ever around Mary when Abe's name comes up, watch her. She always takes his part and expresses real sympathy for him. You heard what Chuck said about that."

"Great idea," Jude said. "Maybe we could get in touch with the innocent, pristine, little boy inside Abe Badoane that existed before he was overwhelmed by embitterment and cynicism. The worst he can do is to decline our invitation."

"Let's hope that God convicts him of his evil chicanery. I'm going to pray that his heart melts like a scoop of homemade vanilla ice cream on one of Mamma's piping-hot apple dumplings."

"Nice image! We have to hope for the right opening to reach him."

Chapter 41

On the next day, Wednesday, Jude bumped into Abe in the lunchroom. *Do I or don't I?* he asked himself as he neared Abe. He steeled himself with a Bible verse that Pastor Gabe cited often: "Those who call upon God must believe that He is and that He rewards those who call upon Him." Mustering his confidence and breathing that prayer, Jude spoke. "Abe, Cory and I would like to talk to you. Got a few minutes some time?"

"Of course I do. Let me know where and when. Better yet, why not stop by the house? You're invited anytime, as I said before. If the door's unlatched and I'm not there when you come, walk right in and give a yell. I'll probably be out back or down in my basement workshop. When I'm downstairs or outside, I often don't hear when someone's at the front door. Please just walk in."

"Thanks, Abe. Much appreciated."

On the way home from work that afternoon, Jude shared with Cory the good news. "You won't believe it. Abe not only said he'd talk with us, but he also said to stop over to see him at his house. Any time, no less. Can you believe it? He actually seemed excited for us to come."

"That's great news."

That night at Bible study, Pastor Gabriel started an in-depth look at the book of Esther in the Old Testament. He provided fascinating background and situated the nation of Israel in that historical Babylonian context.

"The guy's even more amazing than I remembered," Jude whispered to Cory as Pastor Wyant continued. "Did you know all this history about ancient Babylon and Israel's exile there?"

"Some of it. Gabe is always giving us important historical background. Shhh—we don't want to miss this." She squeezed his hand and smiled.

"Above all else," Gabriel concluded, "we need to foreground the main point of our coming study. The book of Esther is about a very brave young woman who, when the time was ripe, acted bravely and decisively. 'Ripeness is all,'" and he flashed a wink at Jude. "Esther had a choice. Either say yes to God's carefully orchestrated and intricate sovereign plan—and indeed play an important part in it—or walk away from it. If she does the latter, she misses forever her important, one-chance role in God's eternal drama."

He paused for a moment as he built to his conclusion. "We too are given opportunities to participate in God's ever-unfolding drama. I pray that we might, like Esther, heed God's warning and fully obey when He prods us to action with that divine touch on the shoulder or that whisper in the ear. Amen."

During the time of prayer that ended the weekly Bible study, Pastor Gabriel called for "praise items and prayer requests." "What special concerns do you want lifted up?" Numerous hands were raised as people noted various prayer petitions, concerns, and praise items in their prayer journals. Near the end of these requests, Cory put up her hand.

"Yes, Cory?"

"Jude and I have a request. We've been around Abe Badoane quite a lot recently down at the mushroom mine—a number of you older folks will recall him—and we detect a slight softening of his heart. Please pray that we're right about this and that it continues. We're trying to get up the courage to invite him to the strawberry festival next Saturday. Thanks for praying."

Her request was met with a spirited response. "Good work, Cory," a man whispered from behind.

"Excellent, Cory and Jude," Pastor Gabriel said. "Any others?" A pause. "Let's pray."

When Jude and Cory returned to his grandma's house that evening, they discussed the matter of inviting Abe. The Center Hill Church was noted for its various festivals—strawberry, peach, and fall festivals, Saturday breakfasts, community fundraiser, and charitable outreach programs. These popular events generated much interest in the larger community and even in the nearby town of Kittanning, the county seat. Because the strawberry festival was an especially popular early-summer event, it was a happy occasion to which they were inviting him.

This invitation, however, included a twist. Frequently these festivals featured some entertainment—one of the singing couples in the church providing a few duets, the Bowser family quartet playing their musical instruments, the youth group Voltage enacting one of their skits, and so on. Cory told Jude that, because no such entertainment had been scheduled for the forthcoming festival, maybe the church should invite Abe to play his homemade violin. People in the community and even the mine knew of his violin-playing ability. "Maybe we should run this by the planning committee. Possibly they'd be interested in inviting him," Cory said.

"Right. Can you give a ring to one of the planners?"

"Why not?" Moments later Cory was talking to the chair of the kitchen committee. "Hi, this is Cory Mohney." A pause. "Thanks, and best to you as well, Bev." Another pause. "That's right. Jude is back in the mine. He and I have come up with an idea. Remember Abe Badoane?" A pause. "Good. Well, we thought we might invite him to the strawberry festival next Saturday. Here's where you and the committee come in. We heard that no entertainment has been planned for this festival. Is that correct?" A long pause, toward the end of which Cory cupped her hand over the phone and whispered to Jude, "They had asked Dan Schall from Butler to come and sing, but he declined at the last minute. They don't have anyone scheduled!"

A moment later, Cory spoke again. "Here's an idea, Bev. Jude and I wondered if we might ask Abe Badoane to play a selection or two on his violin sometime through the evening. He might jump at the chance, and it might get him back in church after all these years away. What do you think?" A long pause. "Yes, we'll take care of the invitation. Great! We'll be in touch with you real soon to give you his answer. Thanks so much. We really do appreciate it."

"So where do we go from here?" Jude asked as Cory hung up the phone.

"I think we pay a visit to Abe at his house. He told us to do just that. An invitation during a friendly visit is more personal than a handwritten note or even a phone call. Don't you agree? And he made a particular point of telling us to stop by to visit sometime."

"Right as always. This is great. Things are looking up!"

Chapter 42

C ory and Jude's visit to Abe started innocently enough. After completing dinner and chores the next evening, Thursday, they drove over to Abe's. They had kept a lookout for him in the mine that day to tell them of their intent to stop by his house, but they never saw him. Only later did they learn that, as head supervisor of the picking crews, he was in managerial meetings much of the day.

The door to his house was open—only the screen door was shut—when they arrived. Lights were on in a couple of the rooms, and enchanting violin music filled the air. Abe was clearly around; plus, his pickup truck was in the driveway. They yelled through the screen door. No answer. They peeked around the side of the house. No sign of Abe.

Upon finding Abe absent, Cory proposed that they depart right away and return another time, but Jude was intent on delivering the message, so excited was he at the prospect of Abe's attending the strawberry festival.

Jude cited a line from *King Lear* as an epigraph to his subsequent journal account of their failed mission: "We are not the first who with best meaning have incurred the worst." They too, with the best intention, stepped into the house to invite Abe.

While Jude went to peek in the adjoining room—the light was also on in this second room—Cory proceeded a couple feet down the hallway in search of Abe.

By now they both were genuinely concerned about Abe. Was he all right? He was clearly home, but where was he, and why wasn't he answering their repeated hellos? Emboldened by the thought that their errand to deliver an invitation had become a possible mission to help him in case he was in distress, Cory took a few more steps down the hallway toward another room where the door stood open and the lights were on. She mused to herself, *Might Abe, incapacitated, be lying helpless on the floor?*

Quickly looking inside this room, she was shocked to see the décor and contents. She did not enter the room, not wanting the invitation for a friendly visit to morph into an invasion of privacy, but she justified her look around through concern for Abe. Leaning in, she slowly swept her eye across the bedroom, carefully drawing a mental picture of its contents. A person with artistic talent even in her childhood, she was excellent at observing and recording detail for future use. "We artists have an eye for detail," she often said to Jude. "You stockpile words. We stockpile images, mental vignettes, and mountains of details."

When Cory rejoined Jude in the front room, he asked her if she could please get a scrap of paper out of the car so that they could dash a sorry-we-missed-you note. Jude loudly yelled again, per Abe's instruction, in case he was downstairs or out back. As Cory searched for paper in the car (which she never found), Jude proceeded into the second room, the library, which was "fit for a university professor," as he noted in his journal. Whole walls were lined with hundreds of books. The rapturous violin music that filled the air was the third movement of Max Christian Friedrich Bruch's *First Violin Concerto in G Minor op 26* as played by Sarah Chang. Jude wrote of the room in his journal:

> I looked around the room in utter amazement. There
> must be several thousand books in that library. In
> the center was positioned a beautiful mahogany desk
> with intricate inlaid woods, on top of which sat an

expensive Tiffany lamp. A large padded swivel chair was positioned at the desk, and other adornments of one who prides himself in his library study were tastefully positioned about the room. Alabaster bookends encased several antique books, one or two of which were rare first editions. An expensive German-made eighteen-carat gold-leaf Coventry pen lay on the desk. In the corner was a music stand and beside it Abe's violin case. On the music stand was the musical score of Mozart's *Symphony no. 40 in G Minor*. The strains of Bruch's *First Violin Concerto* were so beautiful I was nearly stopped in my tracks.

Jude yelled a couple more times but still no Abe. Certain that Abe would enter at any moment, Jude had his greeting comments prepared. He went to the desk to look for a scrap of paper, assuming that Cory's delay was caused by her inability to find note paper in the car.

That was my sole reason in going to the desk and looking at the contents on top of it. I was merely searching for something to write on. I was going to jot off a note and leave immediately. After all, it was a lovely evening, and the idea of being on Vinlindeer with my beloved appealed greatly. More than that, it was awkward to be in Abe's house when he wasn't around. I felt the need to get out of there right away.

On the desk he saw a huge and impressive Italian gazelle-leather book hand-tooled from Florence. It turned out to be Abe's journal—a thick volume written in meticulous calligraphy. It contained daily entries and detailed descriptions of major events. Turning a page or two, Jude was amazed at it. He thought to himself, *This is like reading*

Boswell's Life of Johnson *or Dickens' detailed notes of his tour through America.*

Seeing that there were three markers in this volume, Jude impulsively turned to the middle marker and, despite his best efforts, couldn't refrain himself from speed-reading for a few moments. "I was enthralled by the marvelous calligraphy and the exactness of detail. I had no intention of reading the content per se. Snooping into someone else's life didn't interest me, even if that content was about mystery man, the serpent!" Jude's face flushed and his hands trembled as he read the contents. *I couldn't believe that Abe Badoane keeps a journal like this!* Again, he looked for Abe as he nervously perused the pages. Still no Abe.

On impulse—this is the part Jude later regretted—he took the journal to the photocopier that was directly positioned beside the desk, intending to photocopy just a page or so. His intent, as he approached the photocopier, was to obtain a sample of the writing so that he could show Gabriel and Charles the masterful cursive and impressive detail. When he saw that the copier was a modern, high-speed model, he quickly copied several pages. Then he turned to another marker at the front of the journal and began reading.

> He told me he was in his 30s. He was a giant like
> Geliath. His arms was very big. He sed he was a
> wate-lifter and worked out daley. His tummy was
> like grandma's worshborde in the basment. That
> was a clew, but I missed it. He sed I could check
> out the other mounted raks in his caben. There was
> a caribew from his Alaska trip and a large grizley
> bear carpet from Koddiak Iland. A mule deer from
> Montanna. He had a big marlen from Mexico and
> others. 'Come on,' the man sed. 'You can see them all
> if you come with me.' I was a sucker and went with
> him to the caben.

Jude's heart was palpitating from nervousness, scared to death that Abe would walk in while he was holding his journal. Despite the danger, Jude skim-read several more paragraphs. He could not resist and again photocopied some of the pages from this earlier section in his journal. The third movement of Bruch's *First Violin Concerto* hit its dramatic climax as Jude photocopied the pages. He didn't know if his heart was racing because of the danger of his task or the power of the music. Breathlessly, he replaced the journal to its exact spot on the desk and hurriedly walked toward the door to leave, just as Cory entered.

"Jude, what have you been doing all this time? I couldn't find paper, so I decided to look around the back of the house. I still can't find Abe. Have you seen him? I'm really worried about him. What were you doing in there all that time?" She saw the papers Jude was clutching. "What's that bunch of papers in your hand?"

His pulse racing, Jude barely managed a clipped response. "I'll tell you outside. Just hang on." He was gasping for air. "Let me catch my breath." They ran to his jeep and drove away more recklessly than he realized.

"Will you please slow down? You're driving like maniac, Duke. It's as if you're running from something. Tell me what's going on. You're scaring me to death!" She looked at Jude. "Jude, look at you! Your face is flushed, and your hands are trembling." She looked at the steering wheel. "For goodness sake, Jude Hepler, your knuckles are white! Tell me what's going on!"

Chapter 43

"*L*et's walk up on the ridge to Vinlindeer. I need to clear my head. I promise I'll tell you everything in a short while."

"If you say so. But I must say you're acting strangely, sort of like mystery man Abe Badoane himself!" She paused to allow Jude to calm down and then decided that changing the subject would help settle him. "You'll be surprised at what I have to tell you. I can't believe what I saw in that bedroom down the hall."

"You won't believe what you have to tell me? Are you kidding? I have a few things to share that will distill you to jelly."

Jude sped along in silence as he thought about what he had read in Abe's journal. Cory was annoyed that he didn't share his findings, but, respecting his wish, she'd have to be patient for the time being.

Jude's head, meanwhile, was anything but silent, as he noted in his journal. "As I drove along that evening from Abe's house, I could barely keep my hands steady on the wheel. When I managed to distract Cory—'Is that an eagle flying there in the distance or a red-tailed hawk?'—I took my pulse. It was racing as though I had just run a hundred-yard dash."

On the Vinlindeer ridge that evening, Jude and Cory sat down by a fence post overlooking the valley, Zoe by their side. He was in their or Pete Mohney's presence most of the time, and this evening was no exception.

"So how much longer are you going to keep me waiting?" Cory began.

"Not a second. Let's read together."

"Read what? Jude, what's that? Are those the papers you were carrying when you left Abe's house? Did you pick up a magazine article or what? My guess is that you found some papers on the history of the mine. Is that it? That's all you talk about these days. Well, that and Shakespeare!"

"Not even close. Yes, I got this at Abe's house. Maybe I did a bad thing. When I was in Abe's library—" Stopping midsentence, Jude struggled for words. "I don't know where to begin. Well, you ought to see it. He has the library of a very learned man. When I went from the den, the front room we entered, to the adjoining room, I was in his library. Remember how I went for a quick look into this room while you took a few steps down the hall? The longer I was in the house, the more concerned I was about Abe. Well, during the few minutes when I waited for Abe to come, I started to skim-read his journal, a massive tome lying wide open at the center of his beautiful mahogany desk. I couldn't stop reading, and seeing the photocopier beside the desk, I impulsively, and in a weak moment, photocopied these pages."

"Jude, I can't believe you did that. Surely that was wrong. I consider that a pretty major invasion of privacy." She looked at him in disbelief. "What in the world possessed you?"

"I agree, but as I read a few pages that he had marked, I quickly saw that this information was about Abe—who he was, the trauma of his childhood that scarred him, and other amazing stuff. I couldn't help myself."

"Whatever are you talking about? You're saying you saw all that in the five minutes we were separated?"

"Hey, give me some credit. You know I'm a fast reader. Abe had bookmarked three passages, so I skim-read two of them, and when I saw how dynamite the content was, I photocopied some ten pages or so at each marker. I haven't read it closely yet. That's why we're here."

Jude held up the pages. "I welcome you to the world of mystery man Abe Badoane, the ever-smiling serpent."

"You can justify what you did?"

"Sort of. Probably not." Jude swept his hand through his hair in exasperation. "Cory, I don't know. But what if these pages contain the key to this man's heart and what if, because of this information, we get to the bottom of the mystique, the mystery, the malady, and mythology surrounding this man?"

"How you do love alliteration!"

"I intend no blasphemy here, Cory, I really don't, but what if— just what if—my seeing this is an answer to our prayers." At this point, Zoe, seemingly for no reason, barked. They looked around but saw no provocation for this unexpected bark. He was, as was so often the case, looking directly at them.

"What was that all about?" Cory asked. "Have you been watching Zoe? He's tracking our conversation again. He listens like a human! But I think you might be pushing it when you say that obtaining these pages of Abe's journal was somehow an answer to prayer." Again, Zoe barked. They looked at this strange pet, and then Cory said, "But maybe it is. Let's read. You may convince me yet."

Jude and Cory spent the next hour reading and talking about the most complex man they had ever met. They were staggered by his intelligence, manifest in the way he wrote, and the tragedies he had experienced. Two life-changing traumas had clearly wrecked his life, as the journal entries made clear. Jude had no time to check the third marker but wondered if it too described a third horrific incident.

The first trauma occurred to him when he was a bright, eight-year-old innocent boy. His life had been completely turned upside down when he was enticed by a man to visit his cabin in the woods. The second centered on the deaths of his son and wife.

Jude broke the silence. "If only we had access to more of the journal, especially those raw and naked passages when he subsequently tried to process, work through, and analyze these two horrific traumas.

Even in these fleeting pages, I see a highly intelligent man groping in the dark canyon of his mind. If only I could read his entire memoir!"

"So that's the mind we're up against!" Cory exclaimed. "I now know what we're pitted against, and I think we've met our match. Jude, he's brilliant. What a wordsmith! I've never read prose like this. Except yours of course, sweetheart. Don't be jealous." They both laughed. "Seriously, you're more like Abe than anyone I know— love of learning, bright head on your shoulders, always thinking, analyzing, retaining, and integrating—yeah, a chip off the old block."

"It kills me," Jude continued, "that I didn't photocopy more pages. Why didn't I copy just a couple more in each section? What a place to stop the first section. Jude read again. "'He sed he was hot and he kickt off his shoes. Then he took off his jeans. My face got red. I looked away. He told me I dint look comfterbel. It was hot. There was a big fire. He lifted wates. His mussels was very big. He rubbed himself a lot. I dint like that. That wasn't nice or gud. But I liked the animal picktures. They were nice. His hand brushed my thigh. He said scuse me it was an acident. It kept happning.' End of page. What a place to stop!"

"I can see why you're so upset."

"The second section is the same thing. I stopped photocopying right in the middle of something really important." Jude again read the last photocopied lines. 'I cradled the dead child in my arms, as pathetic and inconsolable Freda cried hysterically. The whole time I rubbed the head of this dead babe—my son, my son, my Absalom—I kept looking at the woman and child in the adjoining bed. She was stroking the head of the most beautiful infant I had ever seen. Her little boy turned his head toward me, and I looked into those large, bright eyes. Why couldn't her healthy, living boy ...' That's where that page ends. Why'd I get so nervous and quit photocopying at these two important places? You can bet I'm kicking myself!"

"Jude, I just thought of something terrible. What if Abe finds out we were in his study and photocopied his journal?"

"How could he? Relax. I left no trace of our intrusion. I replaced the journal to its exact spot and didn't disturb the bookmarks either. He's smart—I'll give you that—but he's not that smart."

"It's not wise to underestimate your formidable opponent. You've noted his extreme intelligence time and time again."

They paused and stared across the valley below. The evening was clear and the visibility very good. "A halcyon day befitting ancient Greece and 'the ringing plains of windy Troy,'" Jude said to Cory as they looked across the valley and spotted the generator plant smokestacks in Shelocta and Homer City under the carnation-pink-colored evening sky.

"What poem is that from?" Cory asked. "'The ringing plains of windy Troy.' I love that phrase."

"Tennyson's 'Ulysses.'"

"Of course. How could I forget?" She paused a while. "Look at these clouds. They remind me of Thomas Birch's 'View of the Delaware near Philadelphia' or maybe Canaletto's 'Venice: The Quay of the Piazzetta.' Okay, I'm doing what you have mastered so thoroughly. Using diversionary tactics to keep from telling you what I did in my weak moment. Now it's time that I come clean."

"Come clean? About what, pray tell?"

Chapter 44

"**W**hat does that mean? What do you mean that you have to come clean?"

"Remember when you went into Abe's library? Well, I took a few steps down the hall and looked into a room. You won't believe what I saw—a boy's bedroom! Jude, there's a young man, probably a teenager, living in that house. There were posters of athletes on the walls—Bill Mazeroski, Roberto Clemente, and Jack Lambert—and Steelers paraphernalia everywhere, a rumpled bed where someone had been sleeping, tennis shoes beside the bed, a couple athletic trophies on the chest of drawers, a sweatshirt thrown over his desk chair, some dirty clothes lying on the floor, notebook paper with writing on an open page, and—get this—even some milk in a glass, and beside it on a napkin, cookie crumbs and a partially eaten cookie."

Jude interrupted. "You're kidding!"

"I'm not. Not at all. Does Abe have a son? Or maybe a nephew who's living with him? On the desk was the sports page of the *Leader Times*. I could see the headline—something about the Edmonton Oilers sweeping Boston to win the Stanley Cup finals. Here's the strangest part. There was a picture on the dresser just inside the door of the youthful Abe in Kennywood Amusement Park. He was standing in front of the Racers roller coaster. A young boy is beside him in the picture, but because I was so close, I could tell that the picture of the boy had been cut and pasted. Mystery man just got a whole lot more mysterious in my book!"

"I can't believe it. You saw all of that in that short time when you wandered into the hallway?"

"Hey, give me some credit. We artists mentally record lots of detail so we can paint it later. You paint your scenes with words. I use oils and acrylics. And sometimes watercolor."

"Wonder if Chuck, Gabe, or Old Mary know anything about this," Jude said. "Let's ask them at church on Sunday. Abe Badoane—what a sad man! He obviously loved his wife whom he lost, and to think he lost the other love of his life, his dear little boy too. Reminds me of John Milton. Lost his wife, his children, the parliamentary-based government, and his dreams—everything."

"Yes, but remember what came out of those monumental losses. In the intensely heated forge of Milton's soul, those experiences were molded into the epic of the ages—*Paradise Lost*."

"Ah, yes, 'gold fears no fire.'"

"I know that one," Cory said. "Wait, hang on a second. Got it—that's from Shakespeare's *As You Like It*, right?"

"Well, he used it. But it could be biblical too."

"Jude, let me tell you about a sermon Gabe preached a couple months ago before you returned in early May. He was citing stories of violent murders and the criminals like Ted Bundy who commit such heinous acts. Well, in his sermon, he used an image that for me was extremely good and made me think of Abe. Reading these pages in Abe's journal reminds me of that sermon. Pastor Gabe said to think of your heart—your soul or your spirit—as a wineskin. Life's misfortunes and tribulations cut gashes into that wineskin, causing the wine to leak out. 'We need to take this seriously, good people,' Pastor Gabe said, 'for it happens to all of us. I would remind you that Ted Bundy was an honor student who was well liked by his professors.' He went on to say that if the cut is high up and if the Holy Spirit inhabits the heart, then the gash can be repaired, and love, grace, and mercy eventually will fill the soul again."

"That is a great image!"

"'But,' Gabe continued, 'if the gash is down low or, worst of all, at the very bottom, then all the wine of grace and love leaks out. Yes, the Holy Spirit can mend even such a lethal gash, but if the Holy Spirit is not resident in that person, then the gash remains and even widens as the heart continues to experience life's torments. Because the love and mercy and grace have drained away, the victim goes through life unable to love, bond, or emotionally attach to other people.' Pastor Gabe said that such an individual fears intimacy and even repels it in an effort to protect the heart from further hurt. I think that's what psychologists call attachment disorder. For me, that's a perfect description of Abe the serpent."

"It may well be. No wonder you liked Gabe's sermon. What a great image—the heart with an irreparable gash through which the person's finer qualities and character traits leak away—yes, very good! And this connects to Abe because ... Please connect the dots."

"Because Abe's former tragedies cut him at the very bottom of his heart. When all the love drained out, he slowly came to embody evil. He means to be good—I won't ever doubt the goodness of his intentions—but there's not enough love in his heart to counterbalance either the negative experiences of his life or the hate in the world."

Jude pondered Cory's profound insights into Abe and commented after a moment's thought. "Let me expand your image. If people possess a deep reservoir of theology and spiritual insight, then when life's tragedies strike, they can dip into that reserve to find the applicable truths that will sustain them in a dark hour. People are able to shore up damaged emotions and weak spots in their philosophies by drinking liberally from the reservoir of truth. But if the reservoir has dried up, then one can't combat or neutralize the slings and arrows of outrageous fortune. Sorry about all the mixed metaphors!" Jude paused to consider the weight of his words. "A mismatch between theological constructs and experiential phenomenon is most unfortunate. I know whereof I speak, Ophelia dear!"

They laid the photocopied journal pages aside and reflected on

Abe. What a tortured human being, what a twisted life! Cory said, "We need to pray that God will heal his psychic wounds and, if it's His will, work through one of us or our friends to reach this despairing man."

Their meditation complete, they reclined against a tree and gazed at the distant horizon. It was a lovely summer evening. The day had been very warm, but up on Vinlindeer, the evening air had cooled to a soothing balm. The lazy breeze, redolent with the aroma of the new-mowed hay, lazily wafted across the vale like a flower-soft zephyr. The sun, nearing the horizon, turned the sky a deep roseate hue. Soon a gray cloud, backlit with the flaming iridescent glow of the setting sun, settled over it. Pointing to it, Jude said, "That's exactly the natural phenomenon Eliot described in 'Burnt Norton,' one of the *Four Quartets*."

"I don't know it. Please quote the lines."

"'Time and the bell have buried the day, The black cloud carries the sun away.'"

"That is great. Eliot was so good. No wonder he's one of your favorites. I must read more of his poetry." They watched the slowly setting sun jab its spear-like rays through the overhanging curtain of cumulus cloud and speckle variegated patches of spangled gold along the valley floor.

Cory's journal entry indicated that their time on the ridge that evening was special:

> What a marvelous evening! I have never experienced such tranquility and serenity in my life. As the sun softly settled into its feathery bed, I reclined in Jude's arms for the longest time, neither of us saying anything. I couldn't get over the power of his male scent—deodorant, cologne, even the talcum powder—as I cuddled close to him. And one other scent I can't identify. Maybe something in his hair? But Jude doesn't use hair cream. At least he doesn't

normally. I'll have to ask him tomorrow. At any rate, time stood still, and we just held each other tightly. After all the dark years, I couldn't believe that I was in my lover's arms again! Our love has an it's-too-good-to-be-true feeling about it. Oh, how I do love this man! To think that just weeks ago I was in a pit as deep as Abe's!

That evening on the ridge, however, more or less closed the book on their rapture that summer. They could not have known what lay around the bend ahead.

Chapter 45

When Jude and Cory were in Abe Badoane's house, he was on the upper, back-lot strawberry patch weeding his prized June-bearing strawberry plants—the Lester, Redchief, Annapolis, and Seneca varieties. Completing his joyful task on the hill, he entered the house and instantly smelled the pungent aroma of the photocopier. He looked around, wondering if someone had been there or was possibly still present. He yelled to see if anyone, maybe a neighbor, had popped in. It was one thing to have a guest drop in unannounced and leave a few fresh tomatoes or a bag of freshly picked lettuce on the porch, a frequent occurrence, even in these mad times, in many rural Pennsylvania homes. But to have intruded into the room, snooped around, and possibly made use of the photocopier was another story altogether.

The longer he thought of it, the more suspicious Abe became. Soon these emotions gave way to a kind of panic, and he sprang into action. He hurriedly put on a pair of latex gloves that he kept in his desk drawer and went first to the photocopier. He lifted the lid and placed his cheek against the surface. As he suspected, it was quite warm. Somebody had copied enough pages to heat it to this extent! He dashed to his desk and opened his journal to the bookmarked sections and again placed the side of his face on these treasured pages. They were warm! His precious and intensely private reflections had been copied! He took fingerprints everywhere—the photocopier, the journal, the desk, the door handle, and other conspicuous places.

Who could have been here? The feminine scent of perfume or possibly hand lotion—he couldn't tell which—lingered in the air. What female would have come to his house? Who would have stopped by to see him? More importantly, who would want to read and be insane enough to photocopy his coveted journal? Overwhelmed by the shock that someone had peered into his deepest secrets, he was instantly overcome by depression and rage. He slumped into his chair and ferociously stared at the ceiling. Moaning to himself, he pounded the desk when another horrible thought crossed his mind. Might the intruders have walked around and found Martin's room down the hallway? Still wearing his latex gloves, he dusted the doorknob, doorframe, and the furniture in the room. While he couldn't be certain, he was fairly sure that the doorknob emitted the faint smell of hand lotion.

Abe took a walk up to the garden to collect his thoughts and plan his course of action. *Who would have done this? Who and why?* He paced back and forth, not even seeing the lush plants whose tendril vines were starting to droop with a multitude of variously shaded berries. Back and forth he paced, and then it dawned on him. *It must have been Jude and Cory! They had expressed interest in stopping by and no doubt did. Why didn't I think of them right away?* The shock, he surmised, had impeded rational thought.

The next day at work, Friday, Abe resorted to the sneaky subterfuge of a trained spymaster. When Jude's tractor was untended, Abe dusted the steering wheel for fingerprints, as he did Jude and Cory's time cards at the punch clock near the mine entrance. At lunch, he carefully noted that no one used the salt shaker after Cory had. Once the workers had cleared out of the lunchroom, he dusted it, as he did both Cory and Jude's hard helmets. Surely, he had enough samples. That evening he compared the prints and corroborated his worst suspicion. The prints matched perfectly. Jude Hepler and Cory Mohney had intruded into his home and, much worse, photocopied pages of his private journal!

Slouched in his chair and drumming his pen on his journal, he tried to think clearly. *What's my best course of action? Why would they want this information, and what will they do with it? Might they use it against me? How? What's their motive?* He could answer none of these questions, at least not yet, but one thing was certain. They had delivered the opening salvo, and it would definitely be reciprocated. "If war is what you want, war is what you'll get. The battle will be fierce. To death you'll owe a debt!"

The first thing the next Monday morning, Jude fortuitously bumped into Abe in the locker room.

"Abe, we stopped by to see you last Thursday evening. We yelled and yelled but couldn't find you, nor did we see you last Friday."

"Sorry I missed you. I probably was up in the strawberry patch checking out my beauties. What a crop I'm going to have this year. The Annapolis June-bearers promise to be especially exquisite. My goodness, but that is one sweet berry!"

"Interesting you refer to strawberries. Cory and I had stopped over to your place to invite you to the Center Hill Church strawberry festival on Saturday evening. I was going to leave a note, but we didn't have any paper in my car."

"Well, thanks for the invitation, but it won't work this time. All the history, especially the recent developments, gets in the way. I'm sure you know what I'm talking about."

"Not sure what you mean by that, Abe."

Abe's laser-beam eyes bore into Jude. "I think you do. You're very much like me, a bright enough fellow, and you'll figure it out."

Abe walked away, the conversation ending as quickly as it began. At the start of this short exchange, Jude felt that Abe likely didn't realize they had been in his house and photocopied the journal. After all, how could he know? In their initial exchange, he had been warm and friendly, again inviting Jude to his place. But through the day, Jude reflected often on Abe's parting comment. "All the history, especially the recent developments, gets in the way. I'm sure you know what I'm talking about."

What an enigmatic statement! Did Abe indeed know about the

photocopied journal? If so, how in the world would he have found out? Then too, how could any person have the presence of mind to respond so instantaneously and cunningly as Abe had and do so with tonal modulation that perfectly matched the richly nuanced language?

Apart from his fear of Abe and the consequences of his rash photocopying, Jude's respect for his intelligence and his verbal skills increased exponentially. "All the history, especially the recent developments, gets in the way. I'm sure you know what I'm talking about." Abe had even accentuated "you" as if to underscore his point. Jude thought, *He told me that I'd be able to figure it out, almost as if he knew that in time I'd connect the dots.*

Jude was unnerved the entire day and thought of Cory's comment, "We are pitted against an awesome intelligence." *How true that's turning out to be!*

Chapter 46

The Stephen Foster Memorial Theatre, adjoining the Cathedral of Learning on the University of Pittsburgh campus, was the site for many years of the Three Rivers Shakespeare Festival. Professor Charles Claypoole was seated in this auditorium two days later on Wednesday with the director, wrapping up the day's rehearsal for the upcoming production of *Hamlet*. The actors, still on stage, had just finished rehearsing the scene when Claudius, king of Denmark, speaks to Laertes, son of Polonius, his court counselor, in act 4, scene 5. The scene occurs after Laertes returns from France. Upon learning of his father's death, Laertes in this scene is so inflamed that he wants to instantly retaliate by killing Claudius. Director Winston Armrose—Winnie to friends—and Charles directed the scene from their seats in the auditorium and spoke to each other at the conclusion of the rehearsal.

"What do you think, Charles?" Winnie began. "What's your reaction to this scene? I'm especially interested in what you think of our casting and overall progress."

"I like it. I think we'll have a good production even if we don't achieve the same fame as the archeologists who found the original Globe Theatre in London this year. What a coup! To think they've unearthed the old Globe Theatre where Shakespeare and company produced all those immortal plays! All right. You want me to comment on our production. I've been giving some thought to our

Laertes. Jason has a powerful voice. His voice lessons since last season have obviously paid off."

"I agree. What of Claudius and the delivery of his lines?"

"He's a strong actor, a natural for this part. This is casting at its best." Charles looked at Rick, the actor playing Claudius who was currently engaged in conversation with fellow actors, and reflected on his performance. "Do you think Claudius ought to register so much fear of Laertes in this scene? It might be all right, but on the other hand, would a powerful Machiavellian tyrant cower so fearfully in the presence of a youthful, wet-behind-the-ears university wit? I doubt it. Claudius actually looked afraid there for a moment."

"I see your point—nicely articulated. Please keep going."

"I'm not the drama critic you are, Winnie. It's your reputation for fine directing that enabled us to acquire so many equity actors for one production. You talk. I listen."

"You humble me, Chuck, but don't underestimate the excellence of your insights. Didn't you once tell me that God specializes in using His consecrated vessels to confound the wise? Though somewhat of a skeptic, you're still much closer the Deity than I. In this case, that matters since *Hamlet* grapples so intensely with evil and ultimate spiritual realities. So back to Claudius, please. I really do want your opinion."

"If you insist. Claudius knows that Laertes seeks revenge for his father's death. He realizes that a man at the white heat of anger can be dangerous, but I'd still play that down a bit. This poised Danish king is a rock even during duress. Laertes is a mouse in the presence of a lion. The king of the jungle might turn his giant lazy head in the direction of the little annoying squeak, but he'd never show a trace of genuine fear. A mouse is a mouse is a mouse."

"Excellent point. So what do we do?"

"Make Laertes more youthful, less self-assured. He looks like he won the most-likely-to-achieve award. He's really sharp and confident in their exchanges. All of these men—Rosencrantz, Guildenstern, and Laertes—are putty in Claudius' hands. Never unnerved, never caught off guard, he bends their wills without even trying. Jason's Laertes is too formidable an opponent against Claudius. I'd make Claudius—I temporarily forget his name."

"Rick Olzewski."

"Yes. Well, I'd make Rick a more awesome, even feared character. People should grovel in the king's presence, as everybody does to Vito Corleone in *The Godfather*. The all-powerful monarch barely notices a groveling courtier."

"Very valuable as always, Professor. Much appreciated."

At the back of the theatre, Gabriel Wyant was seated and watching the proceedings. He had ridden down to Pittsburgh with Professor Claypoole earlier in the morning to visit one of the church members who had undergone recent surgery at Allegheny General Hospital. The visit complete, he quietly slipped into the theatre, sat down in a back row, and caught the final act of the rehearsal. While he couldn't catch every word of Charles and the director's wrap-up conversation, he followed the general drift.

The rehearsal ended, and Charles and Gabriel stood on Forbes Avenue across from Carnegie Museum. "I have a yearly pass that admits guests free to the museum," Charles began. "Want to take a quick peek at some of the museum gems? We have a bit of time since you said you were taking the afternoon off. Goodness knows there's much we need to talk about."

"Yes, it's been too long since I've seen these Pittsburgh marvels." Pastor Gabriel looked across the street at the museum. "What an ingenious philanthropist Carnegie was!"

As they crossed Forbes Avenue and turned left, they strolled in front of the statue of Stephen Foster. "This man surely wrote a lot of famous songs back there in the nineteenth century," Charles commented as they looked up at the statue.

"His *Beautiful Dreamer* has always been a favorite of mine. Old Mary said that song entered into her rose vision somehow. She had seen a Charles Connick stained-glass window of Stephen Foster's *Beautiful Dreamer* and had the rose vision that very night. She's always associated the vision with the lovers in the Foster window. You should try to locate the window in the Stephen Foster Memorial Library-Museum someday. I've never seen it."

"We've been in the theatre for weeks, but I've never checked out that window in the Foster Museum on the lower level. I'll have a look tomorrow."

Entering the Hall of Antiquities of the Carnegie Museum, they walked by the statue of Sophocles where Charles and Gabriel resumed their discussion of *Hamlet*.

"I realize you saw only the last part of the rehearsal," Charles began, "but were you able to form an impression?"

"I like it. I'm really keen to see the entire production. I caught part of your comment to the director about Laertes and Claudius. I think you were right on target since I see Claudius the same way. Except for Hamlet, nobody's a match for him."

"Have you ever seen the real doors in Florence?" Charles asked Gabe. They had walked to the front corner of the large Hall of Architecture, turned right at the bust of Homer, and were soon face-to-face with the replica of the doors that adorn the Baptistery in Florence. Like myriads of viewers through the ages, they were awed by Ghiberti's masterpiece.

"No, I haven't seen the original doors. Have you?"

"Yes, and I see why Michelangelo said they were suitable for the doors on heaven's gate. Imagine that compliment from a master like Michelangelo!"

"What's on your mind, Charles? I sense a preoccupation."

"You're a perceptive man, Gabe. Yes, my concern is very real. Did you hear about Jude and Cory's recent run-in with Abe Badoane?"

"Yes, I've heard."

"And the business of the photocopied journal?"

"That's the incident I heard about. Jude gave me a fast ring to talk about it. I think it's very serious. My spirit tells me that Abe is looking for a fight. He's the angriest man I know. When he gets like this, he's a walking volcano waiting to erupt. The least little provocation causes him to emit an indescribable stream of red-hot verbal lava. Jude and Cory could be incinerated!"

"The pattern's been there for a long time. His angry outbursts are the stuff of legend."

"His scalding lava could vaporize their love. What's scary is that Abe—we all collectively deduced this many months after the fact—was responsible for their breakup five years ago. I couldn't help but see Abe in Claudius tonight during rehearsal. Same cunning, same intelligence, same serpentine smoothness, same oily charm. Abe manfully manipulates the men in the mine as surely as Claudius controls the castle courtiers."

Now he's been given a kind of justification to plot against them again. I feel we're in the middle of our own Shakespearean tragedy right in Armstrong County."

"You're surely right, Charles. What do we do about it?"

"I can only offer the counsel you would—pray. And, of course, give Cory and Jude all the support we can. How can one know what Abe's up to? I confess to having an uneasy feeling."

The men continued to enjoy the exhibits in the Carnegie Museum and the reprieve it offered them from their exhausting schedules, but soon Pastor Gabriel looked at his watch. "Well, we have to go. We need to get up the road to Bible study, and I don't want Martha worrying. She'll also want to know how Hazel's recovering from her surgery."

They walked out the front entrance of the museum by the colossal statues that adorn the front of the Carnegie Music Hall. Gabriel Wyant looked up at the large statue of Shakespeare. "What a genius! Can you imagine anyone writing so many brilliant plays?"

"For me, it's his use of poetic language that remains unrivaled."

"I completely agree. What was that quotation you mentioned last Sunday, the one about awakening faith?"

"That was from *The Winter's Tale*. Paulina says, 'It is required You do awake your faith.'"

"That's it. So epigrammatic and profound too!" Gabriel looked again at his watch. "What can I say but that such a Shakespeare text will preach! What a wonderful Christian insight!"

Later that evening, the Bible study was, again, well attended. The discussion centered on Esther—the exquisite timing of her involvement, her boldness in standing up to Haman to save Israel, and her awful loneliness as she faced powerful forces by herself. Cory was riveted to the discussion of the brave young woman who, placed in a position of peril, accepted the challenge and acted wisely at this most defining moment of her life.

After Bible study, a small group clustered near the parking lot at the back of the church to continue the dialogue. Cory started the discussion. "Do you think most people accept the challenge when they're at the crossroads of their lives as Esther does?" The assembled folks looked at each other.

"It's a great question. Jude, what do you think?" Pastor Gabriel asked.

"I prefer to hear your and Chuck's response."

"I think Cory asks a pertinent question," Charles said after a moment of silence. "Few people accept life's ultimate challenges. They hold back through fear. Cory, you've obviously been thinking of this. What do you think?"

"I have *Hamlet* on my mind and keep tracing parallels between him and Esther. My thoughts aren't fully formed, but I do see intriguing parallels. I'll get back to you later on that one, but I will say this. It would take an immense amount of courage to face that sort of evil alone."

Chapter 47

The next day at work, Cory and Jude had lunch together. There were three separate lunchrooms in the mine, and rarely did their crews share the same one. Today, joyfully, they did.

Jude began. "I've been thinking about your comment last evening after Bible study about Esther. You're right about her bravery in the face of the king and the diabolical Haman. Haman is a shameless rat. He schemes to get rid of Mordecai, Esther's guardian cousin, as surely as Claudius schemes to get rid of Hamlet. No wonder you picked up on the similarities. That was such a good insight. Bravo, my star pupil!"

The dialogue that continued for a short while centered on the uncanny parallels between the two men, Haman and Claudius—their shrewdness, cynicism, and heartlessness. "They don't care who they hurt or how they do it," Cory opined. She was gently touching a small bouquet of summer flowers that someone had brought in and placed in the center of this particular table. Most of the flowers were healthy looking and vibrant in color, but a few, like the single red rose, had shorter stems that were above the evaporated water level. "Look at this. All the flowers in the water are beautiful, but the ones out of it are shriveled and dying." Marveling at the exquisite beauty of the rose, she ran her fingers softly across the red petals. Immediately, they fell to the table.

Seated alone and out of sight around the corner, the eavesdropping Abe Badoane heard every word of their lunchroom conversation and spoke to himself. *Your insights are very fine, my children. I see your point about the similarity between Haman and Claudius. But perhaps we should triangulate the characters in your drama and introduce a third one. Yes, I refer to myself. Your description is consummately accurate. But possibly you didn't know that Lady Macbeth's counsel to Macbeth has become my credo: 'Look like th' innocent flower But be the serpent under it.' You declared war when you ransacked my library, my journal, my dream. Now it's my turn to ransack your lives. Matters not to me if you call me Haman, Claudius, Serpent Man, or smiling Abe Badoane. What's in a name? It's all the same!*

Seeking revenge for Cory and Jude's invasion of his privacy, Abe decided to resume his strategy with the nude photos of Cory that had worked so successfully in the past. Over the months, he had mastered his newly acquired editing machine and was pleased with the enhanced images it produced. Looking at a professionally doctored photo, he smugly thought, *I'm ready for round two!*

The day after overhearing Jude and Cory, Abe found Bull Chestnut with his crew. He waited until Bull was some distance from his crew. "Bull, you genius, come here. I want your opinion. Look at these photos. When I looked carefully at the eight-by-ten blowups instead of the mini wallet ones I showed you earlier, I saw some interesting details you might want to check out. Look at the pictures carefully. See anything that would enable you to identify for certain that this is Cory? Look more closely."

Simpleton that he was, Bull saw nothing other than the gorgeous body of the most beautifully shaped woman he had ever laid eyes on. "I'm referring to her watch and jewelry, you simpleton," Abe snapped. "Here's a blowup of the same wrist." The ring, bracelet, and watch were very conspicuous on the blowup. "I'm wondering if these are Cory's. I have no way of being certain. If these match hers, then we'll know beyond a shadow of a doubt that the photos are of Cory no matter how hard she denies it."

Bull lifted the photos to his eyes to look more closely. "That might be Cory's watch, but I ain't sure. It shouldn't be too hard to find out."

"One more thing that I missed before. Look at the watch on the guy standing behind her. Here's a blowup of his wrist. I haven't had a chance to check on this either, but I wonder if this is Jude's watch. Surely that would be easy to find out. Check out the dabs of paint on the face and strap and take note of this little scar on his wrist. If you get a close-up look at Jude's wrist, you'll be able to tell if it's his hand." Abe handed the blowups to Bull. "Here, they're yours. I don't care what you do with them, but I thought you might want to do a little investigating as a way of making Duke stop calling you Mine Dumb Guy. If you can trace the owners of the watches, you'll be a smart detective and prove that Miss Holiness is nobody's angel. You must admit—that would impress even Duke."

Abe left the pictures with Bull and drove away, chuckling to himself as he ventured down the dark corridor. Bull feasted his eyes on the photos and, eventually, remembered to look at the jewelry.

In this rare instance, mental inspiration struck Bull. Instead of sleuthing to see if Cory and Jude's jewelry matched that in the photo, why not have Duke do it? *Yes*, he thought to himself. *Good job, Bull, you genius!*

Seeing Duke later in the afternoon, Bull said to him, "Airhead, I thought you might want to do a little detective work. I refer to these, my friend." He pompously whipped out the eight-by-ten photos.

"Not those again. We've been down that road before, and I won't be suckered in again. Take a hike." Duke started to walk away.

"That's what I thought too, but catch this, Duke. Look at the jewelry on their arms. None of us caught that before. Seems as though we were too interested in the photo's other jewelry. Get my point?"

Duke scowled and then looked carefully at the photos. "I see what you mean. The blowups bring in the details a lot."

"That's not all. Look at the clothing on the bed and the chair. I'd swear that's Jude's IUP sweatshirt. Any way you can check out the bedspread or the painting on the wall? Maybe this was taken in Cory's bedroom. Want to do some checking, Sherlock? You used to be in the farmhouse all the time. It shouldn't be too hard for you to figure out if this is Cory's room."

Duke looked at the photos again. The details on the jewelry were unmistakable, and he knew of only one person who wore an IUP Crimson Hawk sweatshirt.

Alone by himself back in the mine a short while later, he concocted a plan to get to the bottom of the pictures. Caution was the name of the game since he wasn't about to be duped again. He knew it would be no problem to unobtrusively steal a glimpse at their watches. That by itself would be damning evidence.

Later that afternoon, he bumped into Jude. After changing his watch to the wrong time, he walked up to him outside the pasteurization room. "Hey, Hep." He lifted his watch, tapped it, and then held it to his ear. "This stupid watch is on the blink again. What time is it?" Jude lifted his arm to look at his watch. Duke had crept closely to have a good look and easily noted the paint spots on the face and strap. He was so close that he even saw the faint scar on Jude's wrist.

"Two twenty," Jude said.

"I hate this watch!" Duke reset it. "Thanks, man! Gotta run. Catch you later."

Well, well, it was time to reconsider the photos after all. The hand and arm in the photos were definitely Jude's. Earlier, when he looked at the picture, Duke had been hasty and suspended rational judgment, allowing his anger to get in the way. Now he looked with coldly logical eyes at the arm in the picture. Denial was no longer an option. But what of Cory's watch? Was the watch in the photo hers?

Later that Friday afternoon, Duke was driving his train past Cory's crew. Cory had walked to the lowboy trailer, which fastened to the end of the personnel carrier, to dump the mushrooms as the women often did through the workday. Normally this was not a problem for her, but raising the mushroom baskets had become difficult since her shoulder injury. Duke anticipated this difficulty, having seen her struggle earlier. He dismounted the tractor and walked toward her, timing his pace so that he arrived there precisely when she was extending her arms to dump the basket. "Chivalry lives!" he said as he took the basket from Cory's extended hand, making certain that his miner's lamp shined directly on Cory's wrist. Both the watch on her wrist and the ring on her finger matched those in the photo! Duke almost spilled the mushrooms, so intent was his gaze on her wrist.

"Hey, watch what you're doing. You're going to spill them!"

"Oh, sorry. See how I get flustered around you!" He put a big smile on his face and started to walk back to the tractor.

"Thanks, Duke. That was kind of you, especially when I'm not lifting quite so well these days."

The finding shocked Duke as much as the first time he saw the photos. Clearly these were Jude and Cory's bodies. The jewelry confirmed this beyond a shadow of a doubt. Despite the certainty of the findings, Duke still felt the need to proceed with caution. If he could only get a peek at Cory's bedroom, he thought to himself. The bed, the bedspread, the painting on the wall, the dresser in the background, though a bit out of focus—such details would offer conclusive proof.

He tried to come up with a plan all afternoon and finally, just before quitting time, conceived one. Sipping his afternoon coffee by the punch-out clock, Duke waited on Cory and Jude. After they clocked out, he walked with them to their car in the parking lot.

"Hey, guys. I heard you're doing a lot of work on the farm lately."

"We've made some good progress," Cory responded.

"Any big projects coming up that require an extra set of hands? I'm here to help if I can, and I miss seeing Pete. We developed quite a friendship for a time. I thought I might stop by tomorrow if you have any Saturday projects brewing. I have a free day."

"That's sweet of you, Duke. What do you think, Jude? You and Joey have been staying on top of the outdoor projects."

"For one thing, we plan to tackle the corn crib. We need to replace some of the boards and re-shingle part of the roof. Are you game for that?"

"I sure am. Just let me know the time."

RON SHAFER

"We like to start bright and early before the heat builds. We'll begin around 8:00, maybe earlier, but swing by when you want. Thanks a ton, Duke. It's kind of you to offer."

"Yes, we really appreciate it," Cory joined in.

"No problem." They went to their cars.

Once in the car, Cory said, "Wasn't that sweet of Duke?"

"I think so" was Jude's only evasive comment.

Chapter 48

*B*right and early the next morning, another workday commenced at the Mohney farm. In the last few weeks, many miscellaneous repair jobs had been completed. The porch had been painted, the swing varnished and hung for the summer season, flowerbeds planted, milk shed sanitized, the barn cleaned, broken windows replaced, the house shutters rehung and painted, and so on. Their feeling of accomplishment was considerable, especially for Pete. Slowly but steadily, he was sloughing off the accumulated layers of depression.

The Saturday work session progressed well, and Duke, true to his word, came and offered good help. The corn crib project went faster than they anticipated, and as a result of the extra hand, they even painted a section of the fence around the barnyard. Around midmorning when Pete had come out to note the progress, Duke said he had to go to the bathroom. Cory told him to feel free to go in the house and use the downstairs powder room.

Standing by Pete, Zoe watched Duke walk toward the house. He growled softly. "Easy, boy. What's the matter?" Pete said to Zoe as he smoothed the raised fur on his back.

Once inside, Duke looked out the window to make sure everybody was engaged in work and had not followed him into the house. Nobody had. He darted upstairs, pulled out a photocopy of the picture he had kept folded in his pocket, and found Cory's bedroom. He couldn't believe it. The bed, bedspread, picture on the wall, dresser, jewelry box on the dresser, the chair on which Jude's sweatshirt had been thrown, and other details were those in the picture. The photographs—there was no denying it—had been taken in this very room! And that innocent-looking woman was hiding a whole lot of voluptuous beauty and a boatload of forbidden desire underneath her work clothes. He rubbed his hand across the spot on the bed where the photo had been taken. Sweeping his eye around the room for a final fast look, he hustled back outside to resume work. Feelings of anger and lust welled up in him.

Because Cory had washed clothes that morning, the old and tattered work shorts she normally wore for painting and outside work were in the dryer. Since she didn't want to keep the men waiting, she donned another pair of older, discarded shorts that were tighter than she remembered. Duke discreetly stole a glance in her direction every chance he could. *What a gorgeous body!* The longer he worked, the more his hatred of Jude grew. *I hate him! I positively hate him! In time Cory would have been my prize. Everything had been proceeding nicely until Jude came back to the mine.* Anger and lust—the twin passions— bubbled in him like a boiling mineral spring.

As they worked on projects at the Mohney farm that morning, Abe Badoane was seated at his desk, reading and writing in his journal. He had just finished his morning journal entry. "I continue to feel exposed. I can't get beyond the feeling of being naked and used. My most precious possession was stolen from me. I was violated." He burned with anger toward Jude and Cory. "They are now privy to the most carefully guarded secrets of my life. How many people have they told? Has this information, by now, become common knowledge among the church people? To how many people in the mine have they blabbed this? How angry they make me!" He slammed his fist on the desk.

Even their love for each other infuriated Abe. He too had been in love, every bit as deeply as they. True, he never treated Freda as he should have, but he did love her, madly so in fact. Why had he ruined the thing he loved? He noted in his journal, "I'll say it again. I've mangled everything I've ever touched." He hated God for not giving him time to set things right with her before she died. "Why didn't God answer the cries of my heart, all those hours of prayer, and save her? Why did she have to die? I remember a passage from Job a former pastor at Center Hill quoted years ago: 'My spirit is broken, my days are extinguished, the grave is ready for me' (17:1). That is such a perfect description of me."

Abe had written at length in his journal of the "betrayal barrier." "Ever since God took her, I hit a barrier and can't get over it. God betrayed me and turned His back on me. What do I want with a God who refuses to answer heartfelt prayer, this God Who stomps you when you're down? I've had it. The Duke of Gloucester in *King Lear* had it exactly right: the gods 'kill us for their sport.' And Abe Badoane the Serpent is in God's crosshairs."

At this point, Abe turned to an earlier section of his journal and read again of those agonizing days after his wife's and son's deaths. The details surrounding his wife's passing had been shrouded in secrecy. He carefully guarded these secrets since they had come to embody his sole surviving claim to decency—the last "whimper of my paltry remaining dignity," as he had once written in his journal. Reflecting on the tragedy of his wasted life, he thought to himself, *Why keep the secret to myself? It was Freda's family that did it. They were the ones responsible for my losses. Maybe it's time to bring this out in the open. It's high time that you, Cory Mohney, got off your high horse and faced an ugly reality: it was your family who wrecked my life!*

Abe leaned back in his chair and folded his hands together. *Ready, my dear, for a reality check? I'll be the pain in your sweet neck.*

Abe's journal entries about Cory's family bearing responsibility for the deaths were enormously enigmatic. What was the secret Abe had so zealously kept all those years, and why did he choose to recall it at the very time he burned with such vitriol against Jude and Cory? An even more difficult question was of paramount importance. How in the world had Cory's family derailed Abe's life? These were the complicated underpinnings of the entanglements between Jude, Cory, Abe, and the others.

One morning early the next week, Charles stopped by the Center Hill Church Fellowship Hall to look at a malfunctioning freezer in the kitchen. Various village and church women had assembled for quilting day to quilt blankets that they sold to raise funds for a number of charitable causes in the West Penn District of the Church of the Brethren. The women were giving Charles some information on their recent contributions to various civic causes when Old Mary surprisingly appeared on the scene. She had been quilting rarely in recent months, so it was a pleasure for the other quilters to have her join them.

"Bless my soul, if I don't see her coming across the parking lot," a woman near the door exclaimed. "Hello, hello," the women shouted as Old Mary, a moment later, paused in the door to catch her breath from the brisk walk up the hill. She lived in the intersection below the church and always walked to worship services and social functions.

Ruth was standing near to Charles and spoke to him as Old Mary walked toward the Fellowship Hall. "If you'd get into a conversation with Old Mary about some of the things you've been talking about lately, you'd be taking notes for weeks." When one of the women added, "She knows more of the history of this place than anyone," all the women laughed and heartily agreed.

Catching the tail end of this conversation as she entered the hall, Old Mary turned to Charles and said, "I know a little about the history of this place but maybe no more than you. After all, you're the professor." She paused to catch her breath. "I guess I should know a little bit. You do realize that I'm as old as the lost stone marker at the top of Center Hill!" Again, all these good-natured women laughed.

Seating herself at the quilt a moment later, Old Mary turned to Charles. "I'm not doing a thing later this afternoon. Come on over. We can sit on the porch swing and talk. It's been too long since we've had a heart-to-heart, and you've told me a couple times lately that you want to chat."

In Old Mary's quaint apartment that afternoon, Charles plummeted to the depths of the entire mystery. As Old Mary's recall was excellent, she was the proverbial treasure trove of information. In a very short time, Charles was convinced that her rich mind stored all the missing links in the narrative chain.

Soon she asked one of the most important of questions. "You seem especially interested in Abe Badoane. That's something I've always noticed about you. Am I right?"

"Yes, since he plays such an important part in the narrative about Jude and Cory."

"I'll make this easier for you and broach the subject myself. What's really on your mind is the tension between Abe and Jude and Cory—you might say why Abe has it in for them. Am I also right about that?"

"A direct hit." Charles marveled at the sagacity of this simple but very sharp country woman. "Certainly that's one of the big things I've had trouble figuring out. Most of us in the village have wondered about that over the years."

"The answer's very simple. It gets back to genealogy. You're aware of that generally, but maybe I can let you in on a few important details you may not know."

"Sounds great. Fire away."

"Abe's wife, Freda, was the very good childhood friend of Cory's mother, Ruby. I realize you know that. Abe felt the two big losses in his life, his wife and little boy, resulted from a conspiracy on the part of Freda's family."

"You don't say!"

"Well, there were two other tragedies in that poor man's life." Old Mary stopped to fasten a stray strand of her hair with a bobby pin. Charles saw it as a diversion so she had time to think. "But I won't speak of them right now."

She spoke slowly. *Where do I start this story?* "Did you know that Cory's mother, Ruby, and Freda are not blood sisters?"

"No, I wasn't aware of that."

"They weren't. Freda had been orphaned as a very small child and came to live with Virginia and Erastus Gehman when a little girl. The Gehmans' little daughter Ruby liked her so much that she talked her parents into adopting Freda, which they did. The Gehmans changed her last name—I can't remember her original name; maybe Schultz?—to Gehman. To this day, most people think Ruby and Freda were blood sisters. They weren't."

She paused for a moment and rubbed her temple, as if to clear her mind. "Here's how it went. None of us ever knew what to make of Freda. She was a troubled girl from the start but smart as a whip. My goodness but that little thing was intelligent! She was older than Ruby but not much." Temporarily overwhelmed with poignant recollections, Old Mary paused and looked out the window. "Even though the Gehmans gave her a wonderful home, she was always getting in trouble while growing up. Especially as she matured into her teen years." Old Mary looked directly at Charles. "Surely you recall some of the low moments. I tell you that girl broke her mom and dad's hearts when she started running around. You know that didn't go over well in our community. Sex before marriage is a real taboo around here. Well, her sister, Ruby, married Pete Mohney later in life. What a prince he always was! The joy that marriage gave the Gehmans offset Freda's craziness, as did their two children, Cory and Joey.

"So that's Pete, Ruby, and the children, but let's get back to Freda. Her life worsened as she got older. She was a sickly woman, even had been that way as a girl—frail-like, if you know what I mean. Later we learned it was lung cancer that at the end of her life metata ... I can't say that word! Well, it went to her brain. But that part of the story comes later. Abe Badoane fell crazy in love with Freda when she was about twenty or twenty-one. You'll remember that part. You used to socialize with them, didn't you?"

"Indeed. we did. We saw many movies at the State and Columbia Theatres in downtown Kittanning."

"Yes, I thought so. Well, we all felt that their love was doomed from the start. Although, I must say, when Abe was not in a temper tantrum, he could be a nice enough man. And sharp as a whip. My

THE ROSE AND THE SERPENT

goodness, but that man's brainy. Well, he loved Freda madly. As I think back on it, I guess you could say she cured him of his awful temper, and he cured her of her wildness. We began to think they might make it work after all.

"As the months went by, Freda became a fine woman and more or less got that sordid past behind her, but then she got pregnant. All of us thought that was a mistake and not just because they weren't yet married. How could such a frail, sickly woman birth a healthy baby and nurture it properly? By then we knew of her cancer. It seemed to us she was going downhill fast. She looked terrible in the final months of pregnancy, and we feared she didn't have long to live. Surely you remember how sickly Freda was in those weeks."

"Yes. About that time, four of us went on a double date one evening to see a movie. We went out to the Cadet to eat Poor Boy hamburgers after it was over. The dear woman was so sick that Abe had to take her home. The sandwich sat on her plate never touched. I recall that like yesterday."

"I figured you'd remember that part well. As it turned out in the end, we didn't have to worry about the problem of their raising the child. Word went around that the baby boy died of SIDS in the hospital. Abe had already given him his name by then. Funny I should remember it. I guess because it was an unusual name—Jedidiah, little Jed. Freda was dealing in those days with post-partum depression and the tragic death of her son. But that wasn't all. She also had to deal with Abe. He kept saying that the SIDS explanation was a mere excuse. 'It's a lie! I tell you it's a despicable lie!' I can still hear him saying that. You can imagine how that nearly drove Freda crazy. I guess that was his way of ventilating his horrible anger. Pretty much from the start he blamed Freda for the death of the baby. Said that she had fallen asleep while breastfeeding him. Abe believed she rolled over on the baby and suffocated it. Can you imagine anything so awful? He got that idea from reading the account of the two women who approached King Solomon's throne. Remember that story? Each said she was the mother. Well, the one mother's baby died because she fell asleep on top of it and smothered it. Flat killed it! Well, I think that's what gave Abe the idea. I believe that story's in 1 Kings. But I'm not sure."

When Old Mary again stopped, Charles could see a tear in her eye. She paused for a time before she resumed speaking. *How hard that must have been on Old Mary!* Charles thought.

"The horrors of what he dreamed up in that brainy head of his don't stop at that. Abe actually got it in his head that Ruby's mom, Virginia—she never had much time for Abe because of the way he abused her daughter—that Virginia was the one behind it. He said it was all a plan and that Virginia put Freda up to it! I get sick to my stomach thinking about it! Abe said it was the mother's idea to suffocate the baby on purpose. And to make it look like an accident. Why? Because Freda's death was coming fast. The doctors had already given her only months to live. Abe believed that Virginia didn't want him to raise the baby. Once it was clear that Freda had only a short time to live, Virginia talked a lot to Ruby about how the child faced an endless life of heartache. That part is true, and Freda took it to heart. I know it's a crazy story, but this is what Abe has believed his whole life. Everyone knew the little boy died of SIDS, though Abe thought he was suffocated. Either intentionally or unintentionally." Old Mary again paused, took off her glasses, and rubbed her tired eyes. "Neither of these accounts is accurate."

Charles looked at Mary in dismay. "You don't say!"

Old Mary took a small embroidered hanky from her pocket and dabbed a tear and then continued. "Why do I know so much about this?" She paused as if she wanted Charles to answer.

"I have no idea."

"I was the nurse on duty in the obstetrics unit when the whole thing took place."

Chapter 49

"**Y**ou're kidding!" Charles interjected in disbelief. "That's incredible!"

"No, I'm not kidding. I wish I wasn't, but I was there. I witnessed the whole thing—the birth and 'death' of the child. I witnessed the parents' awful sorrow and Abe's anger. Here's the one detail—the really big one, the main one—I've never shared with anyone else, Professor Charles Claypoole." Old Mary proceeded slowly and again fidgeted with her hair. "You are the first to know the secret I've carried with me my whole life." Charles sat so near the edge of his chair that he almost slipped to the floor.

"A woman in the bed beside Freda had a son the same day Freda birthed little Jedidiah. Well, when Ruby's ..." Old Mary started to talk, uttered a word or two, and stopped immediately. She leaned her head back, thought deeply for a moment, and then spoke with a trembling voice—"that hauntingly vibrato sound," as Charles wrote in his journal—"I guess I won't talk about that part, not just yet." Old Mary's fingers drummed nervously on the porch swing. "Except to say this. It was very hard for Abe to see the other woman's baby healthy and alive and his own dead as a doorknob."

"This is all fascinating," Charles said to cover the awkward silence and Old Mary's mounting emotions. He looked intently at her. *What did she almost say, and why did she stop?* Charles sat with bated breath, but she said nothing. *What other information does she have about that day in the obstetrics unit at Armstrong County Memorial Hospital? What else happened? The woman knows much more than she's saying!*

"Well, I'm almost done, but let me answer the big thing on your mind. Why Abe has it in for Cory? Because of what I said. To this day, Abe believes Cory's Aunt Freda suffocated his beloved son on purpose. He thinks that the Gehmans were behind the awful deed. Everybody is dead by now—Erastus and Virginia Gehman, Freda, and the baby. Who in the family line is left to bear the brunt of his anger? Only two people, Pete and Cory. Because Pete married into this 'sick' family and is not a blood member, Abe never blamed him. He gets a pass. But just lately Abe has been directing at Cory all his fury. It's a wrath that's built up in his sick soul across the years. Of course, he does a pretty good job of masking it behind smiles and sweet talk. Are you with me so far? I know this is a long story, but I'm just answering your question."

"Yes, I'm following you. I can't believe your good memory. You're like an oral historian. Am I right in assuming that you don't have much compassion for Mr. Abe Badoane?"

"No need to draw assumptions, Professor." While there was not a hint of admonition in her voice, she was firm and direct and looked firmly at Charles. "He's just misunderstood. Love for all. That's my creed, Professor, especially for those we don't fully know or understand. He's the most misunderstood man I've ever seen. Truth is he always treated Cory kindly enough despite the burden of his past and the hate in his heart."

Old Mary reached over to pick a dead impatiens blossom from the plant nearest to her. "Later on, things changed, and it was as though he couldn't stop seeking vengeance. You've seen that with your own eyes. I know you have."

Charles was again seeing Old Mary's legendary love. No one had ever heard her say a single unkind word about any human being. To a few perceptive people, Abe was a Claudius, a rat whose Machiavellian machinations were despicable, yet to the majority of people he was, if mysterious, a kind and sweet, smiling man. Only Old Mary saw him as a misunderstood wayfarer on life's path who deserved love and grace.

Charles was glad that the recorder in his pocket was running surreptitiously. He had forgotten to ask Old Mary if he could record her, and now, as he neared the end of their conversation, it was far too late to ask for her permission, so he nervously remained silent. Old Mary was showing signs of weariness. She yawned and slouched forward more than she had earlier in their conversation. Charles somehow thought the yawn was intentional. On the other hand, she wasn't getting out much in recent weeks, and he was conscious that she had had a couple very busy back-to-back days, including a walk up the hill to the Fellowship Hall earlier in the day. "Maybe we ought to call it a day," he tactfully but reluctantly said as he noted her conspicuous signs of weariness.

"Perhaps. But there's more. A lot more."

"How involved is this story? Well, I trust we'll get to the next chapter soon." Charles disliked cutting the narrative off at this critical juncture. She obviously was the key to the whole mystery and had been on the verge of sharing additional information. *What other riches are buried in the treasure chest of her mind?* Charles was sure there were some gems if he could keep digging deeply enough to find them.

"Thanks so much for your time, Mary. I've really enjoyed this. And the iced tea was great too! I love the hummingbirds. Do they always fly around like this and visit your feeders?"

"Always. And something I've noticed about them is really different. They can fly as fast backward as forward."

"Amazing! They seem fearless and feed just a few inches above your head. They are marvelous creatures. Jude says his grandma has a lot of hummingbirds on her porch too." He emptied his glass of tea and set it down on the tray. "I really appreciate your good help. You've given valuable information to me and filled in some important missing links." With that, Charles smiled, bade good-bye, and drove away.

In his car, he slammed his fist on the console. "What did she start to say? What happened at the time when Freda's baby was born? She was so close to telling me!"

Chapter 50

A short while later, Charles stopped for lunch at the Little Tokyo Restaurant in Mt. Lebanon below Pittsburgh. He was keen to process the wealth of information Old Mary had given him.

The facts were these. From Abe's point of view, Cory's family was directly responsible for the death of his son, and that son was the one thing above all others that he craved in life. Out of kindness to Cory, Abe had shielded her from the truth of her family's alleged culpability in causing the son's death. Abe had always felt that it was his moral obligation to protect her since, as a former pastor at Center Hill used to say, "The sins of the elders should not be visited upon the children." Cory, after all, was totally innocent of the family conspiracy. But how did she return the favor of his compassionate magnanimity, this stunning display of character nobility? By reading his prized journal, prying into his past secrets, and trumpeting his private sorrows to a cruel world! What a way to say thanks for his charitable humanity!

This part of the story was clear to Charles, but what was not clear was the part Old Mary left unsaid, the part she had started into and then backpedaled. *She obviously carries other important information that bears directly on the narrative*, Charles reflected to himself as he sipped his Asian tea. Old Mary had said, "I guess I won't talk about that part, not just yet." *What part?* Lying his glasses on the table, he rubbed his weary eyes.

Jude had earlier told Charles that Abe's journal described in graphic detail another trauma of his life, one that had occurred in his childhood when a man took him to his cabin. Charles could well imagine how Abe must have longed to know how many journal pages Cory and Jude had photocopied, longed to know how much of the story they knew and to how many itching ears their flapping tongues had blabbed it. Might they have copied those pages when, years after this childhood tragedy, he continued to rant and rave in gushing torrents of prose? How very private were the ruminations of those tortured days when he worked his way through the dark night of his anguished soul! With no shoulder to cry on, he resorted to the one recourse he had—writing gushing page after page of tear-drenched prose in his journal, every word an emanation from his cyanide-saturated heart.

Because the pages in that journal section were warm on the day of Jude and Cory's visit, Abe surmised that they had been photocopied. Yet other nearby pages were room temperature and not heated by the hot lamp of the photocopier. Did that mean they had not been copied like the others? On the other hand, maybe they had been copied first before the photocopier had been heated enough to warm the pages. *How can I be certain?* Abe agonized about these details incessantly, as revenge, his constant companion, intensified daily.

When Abe reread his journal later, it fell open to another frequently read passage, also bookmarked and photocopied by Jude and Cory. This one dealt with another of Abe's zealously guarded secrets—the death of his baby boy, little Jedidiah. Like those describing the event in the cabin, these pages were warm when he opened his journal. There could be no denying that they had been copied, an especially exasperating fact since this most zealously guarded of all secrets had always been concealed from a gawking public.

For most people in the mine, the details of these events were completely unknown. That's how Abe had always wanted it. Some of the older employees may have heard a few incidental rumors—especially those touching the marriage—but these were consigned to the trash bin of mine history as these employees retired or died off.

The younger workers knew next to nothing about mystery man, nor did they care to learn. To them he was a decent and intelligent man from whose mind poured an endless Niagara of amazing facts and fascinating life insights of the sort that therapists, psychologists, or even philosophers typically offer.

Nevertheless, the very idea that his work associates had learned of his past stirred Abe to great wrath. That they would have known about Little Jed nearly gave him a heart attack. "Just you wait, Cory Mohney and Jude Hepler! You haven't experienced my deadly serpent bite!"

Abe, Charles continued to reason, was apparently satisfied that his plan for retaliation had moved ahead to some degree, though to this point it had not achieved the ultimate goal—getting rid of them once and for all. It was now time to nudge the plan along. On the same Saturday morning when Jude, Cory, and the others completed their morning jobs at the Mohney farm, Abe had sat at his desk reading and thinking.

Frustrated that he couldn't come up with the perfect plan of revenge, he walked up to his strawberry patch, leaned over to pick some of the fresh strawberries, and the thought hit him like a flash. If he could get Duke to bed Cory or at least try to do so, Jude would strike back with explosive vengeance. Jude's fiery retaliation would spark in Duke the revenge Abe sought. Duke's hormones were bubbling wildly for Cory. There wasn't an idiot in the mine who didn't know that. Only his conscience had to this point restrained him. Biting into a large plump strawberry, Abe reflected, *That's it. A plan like that couldn't fail! Duke, first be the flirt, then take your dessert. Cory will soon be dirt, like ole floozy Mert!*

As Charles finished his lunch at Little Tokyo, he reflected on the difference between Old Mary and Abe, both of whom were key players in the Jude/Cory saga. To Old Mary, the lovers embodied the lovely rose of her enchanted vision. She had said to Martha Wyant on Saturday morning, "Their love is just like a beautiful red crimson rose. Same innocence, vulnerability, and divine beauty!"

As he descended the slope from the upper strawberry patch, Abe Badoane had a decidedly different perspective: *"Look like the innocent flower but be the serpent under it." If serpent I am, serpent I'll be. To my viper's den, I welcome thee!*

That evening, Jude and Cory rode the horses up to Vinlindeer, Cory gingerly carrying the long-stemmed red rose that Jude had given her earlier that day.

"It's lovely, Jude. I've never seen a more beautiful rose."

"I'm glad you like it."

"You said you were going to tell me the Shakespeare quotation about the red rose from one of the sonnets. I'm all ears."

"So I did." Jude reached in his pocket and pulled out a scrap of paper. "I copied these lines from 'Sonnet 54.' 'The rose looks fair, but fairer we it deem For that sweet odor which doth in it live.'"

"Okay, I think I follow so far. Shakespeare is saying that while we appreciate the visual beauty of the rose, we like its aromatic splendor even more. Correct interpretation, Professor? There's a lot on the line here; I must maintain my A grade for interpretation!"

"Exactly," Jude laughed.

"What else?"

"Later in the sonnet, the Bard says, 'Of their sweet deaths are sweetest odors made. And so of you, beauteous and lovely youth ...'"

"I get that too. Shakespeare refers to how rose petals were commonly made into potpourri. Is that what he means when he says their sweet deaths make sweet fragrances?"

"Yes, I think so."

"That's a lovely thought."

"Yes, it is, but there's a foreboding element there too."

"How?"

"Shakespeare says, 'Of their sweet deaths are sweetest odors made. And so of you.' See that? He refers to the death of the person to whom he speaks—'and so of *you.*'"

"I see. Then the poem does take a solemn turn. What do you make of this foreboding element?"

"I don't know. I guess that if the rose is truly to be appreciated, then it has to make the ultimate sacrifice—lay down its exquisite life and die."

"As Queen Esther did."

"Yes, and Hamlet too. Think about it. To rid the Danish court of evil, Hamlet has to be sacrificed." Jude touched the petal of the rose he had given Cory. "Here's the main point. For a rose to be appreciated, it must be sacrificed. Similarly, for a person to be appreciated or to hit her or his optimum potential in life, he or she must make a costly sacrifice."

"That's a marvelous insight, Jude."

"Let's say it metaphorically. If the rose is to defeat the serpent, it will require a terrible sacrifice."

"When we watch the production of *Hamlet* in Pittsburgh, I'm going to keep this discussion in mind."

"Angelically beautiful youth, it's there we'll find the truth."

"Well, I can rhyme too, Hamlet. How about this one? It's time to turn the page to that telling Pittsburgh stage!"

The End

CPSIA information can be obtained
at www.ICGtesting.com
Printed in the USA
LVHW041502241121
704363LV00011B/1749